# NO EXIT

BY THE SAME AUTHOR

FICTION

*Within the Centre*
*The Lonely River*
*Text for Murder* (Peter Fielding)
*Operation 10*

POETRY

*Adam & Eve and Us*
*When the Words are Gone*

GENERAL

*Secret Sussex*
*How Shall I Vote?*

# No Exit

HARDIMAN SCOTT

'The great tragedy of our situation is
that we have no way out of it. No exit.'

—Attributed to an old Russian intellectual, quoted
by Robert G. Kaiser in his book
*Russia—the People and the Power* (1976)

NEW YORK
THE VANGUARD PRESS

Copyright © 1984 by Hardiman Scott
First American Edition 1985
Published by Vanguard Press, Inc.
424 Madison Avenue, New York, N.Y. 10017.

All rights reserved.
No part of this publication may be reproduced or transmitted in any form or by any means, electronic or mechanical, including photocopy, recording, or any information or retrieval system, or otherwise, without the written permission of the publisher, except by a reviewer who may wish to quote brief passages in connection with a review for a newspaper, magazine, radio, or television.

Library of Congress Cataloging-in-Publication Data

Scott, Hardiman.
No exit.
I. Title.
PR6037.C925N6 1985 823′.914 85-13484
ISBN 0-8149-0907-8

Manufactured in the United States of America

## Acknowledgements

For invaluable help, information and advice, the author wishes especially to thank Mr John Osman, Mr Conrad Voss Bark, Squadron-Leader John Bloomfield, the ever-obliging staff of Sudbury Public Library, Suffolk, and his wife.

DEDICATION

For Conrad

# NO EXIT

# 1

The voice was disguised. It said only, 'Sokolniki Park, three o'clock.'

Michael North, BBC Moscow correspondent, replied slowly and deliberately, 'I understand. I shall be there.'

The call had come through to his office—No. 9 on the third floor of the huge apartment block on Sadovaya Samotechnaya Street, part of Moscow's Sadovoye Ring. It was known among the foreign community as Sad-Sam. He still held the telephone in his hand, waiting to hear the little click as Oleg, the translator in the outer office, replaced the receiver of the extension. North took it for granted that, as soon as he had left the office, Oleg would report the call. Not that it was necessary; it would probably have been tapped in any event.

When he had arrived more than two years ago, Michael thought it surprising that the Russians should go to so much trouble. Gradually he realised that suspicion was natural to them. It was a legacy of their history and was deeply rooted in fear and insecurity. It no longer bothered him. He had learned to take precautions.

Without a sense of humour, life in Moscow would become intolerable. As he leant back in his office chair, he was amused at the thought of the Russians taking the telephone message literally which, of course, was exactly what they would do. Sokolniki was vast—about fifteen hundred acres, much of it still birch forest. The vision of grey-coated KGB men playing hide-and-seek among the trees made him smile—especially as the rendezvous was not Sokolniki Park at all.

On any other occasion, after a message like that, Michael would have telephoned one of his Western journalist colleagues and said, 'Feel like a walk?' It was the rule that you never followed up such invitations alone. But this was different. He knew the voice beneath the disguise. It belonged to a friend, Alexei Mikhailovich Pachenko, and they had long ago devised elaborate arrangements for meeting. Sokolniki was the code for a different park altogether—the Exhibition of Economic Achievement, and the time was two o'clock, not three.

They would have met there in a couple of days anyway. Why had Pachenko advanced the meeting? Michael's journalistic instincts told him that something was wrong, perhaps seriously so. Pachenko wouldn't risk telephoning otherwise.

Even after eighteen months of friendship—the closest he was ever likely to achieve with a Russian—Michael was not completely certain what Alexei Pachenko did for a living. He was important. That was obvious from the luxurious apartment he had on Kutuzovski Prospekt. He was what ordinary Muscovites, with characteristic drab resignation, would call one of the *nachalstvo*—the big noises, the VIPs, the authorities. But who or what precisely, Michael had never discovered, and on the one occasion when he had asked directly, Pachenko had smiled wearily, and replied in an old-world philosophical tone, 'It matters not, comrade, what you do, but only what you are.' Michael had teased him to no avail. The bright, almost black eyes set deeply in that chubby face had twinkled, and the Russian had broken into a gravelly chuckle.

He was not a member of the Politburo, nor of the Central Committee of the Communist Party. All their names were known. The Russians didn't publish reference books about their departments of government, but Pachenko's name did not appear even in the lists so thoughtfully provided by the CIA. Michael guessed that he was probably a member of the *apparat* of the Central Committee's secretariat—a body of powerful officials working in the different departments of state and with direct access to the Party secretaries, who were members of the Politburo. Sometimes, however, he suspected that Pachenko was even more important than that—an official perhaps intimate with the leadership itself. In his own interests, Michael had settled for discretion rather than curiosity, and gave up trying to find out more.

They had first met standing up to their thighs in a fast-flowing stream out at Zavidovo, each casting with the skill of an experienced fly-fisherman. Afterwards, they had settled on the bank together and discussed the merits of individual flies and nymphs.

Fishing with the fly for trout or salmon was Michael's main leisure interest. Perhaps that was the reason he had reached thirty-five and never married. Not many women enjoyed standing in a trout stream. When he admitted that he tied his own flies, the Russian was delighted. So did he.

'You call me Alexei,' he had said. 'I call you Michael. We are friends, comrades.'

Within minutes they had gone higher up the bank, and Michael had met Pachenko's wife, Varinka, his young son, Andrei, and younger daughter, Novia. Pachenko had introduced them all proudly, his wide mouth grinning with pleasure. 'And this,' he had said, clutching Michael's arm warmly, 'is our new friend, our English friend—Michael North. He works for the BBC. The BBC, Varinka.'

Michael remembered suppressing his surprise. He had not mentioned the BBC in any of their conversation. Pachenko had noticed the momentary shock, and had burst into laughter, a warm all-embracing laugh in which Varinka and the children joined as though it was all part of a family celebration. The three of them had thrown back small glasses of vodka and nibbled salted fish.

Alexei Pachenko was no more than average height, shorter than Michael, and although he was by no means thickset, he had a homely, chunky appearance. The squarish face with a wide forehead, and those deeply set dark eyes, could look solemn and grave, but just as quickly would crease with laughter. Varinka was taller, dark, slim, serious, and rather beautiful in a sad way.

At first they had met openly as friends. Michael had gone to the apartment on Kutuzovski Prospekt, and sometimes the three of them had gone to the Bolshoi or the Tchaikovsky Conservatoire, while *babushka* was left at home looking after the children. This in itself suggested that either Pachenko was so powerful that he didn't have to worry about their meetings being known or, alternatively, that the contact had been officially approved. But after a few months, Pachenko had advised that they should arrange their meetings more circumspectly. He gave no reason, but each understood that even friendship—especially friendship between a Russian and an Englishman—could be a matter for suspicion in Moscow. If it was to flourish it needed guarding. So they devised a half-dozen regular meeting places on certain days, and if they communicated, the named meeting would always be the one after the next arranged. It had worked, provided Michael made sure that he was not followed. Usually the authorities didn't bother. Although the meetings were arranged surreptitiously they were mostly only friendly occasions.

As the months passed Michael developed a genuine affection for the man. Occasionally, and without ever passing any information that was not readily available, Pachenko would give Michael a Soviet interpretation of events. During the last two years of Britain's Labour administration the two nations had moved much closer together. This had clearly given Pachenko a great deal of pleasure, and when Michael had ventured to suggest that, for Britain, it might be a misguided policy, Pachenko had responded with a sad tolerance.

'We are friends,' he had said, 'why not all of us?'

'Because,' Michael had replied, 'we don't trust each other.'

'But now we do. Britain is leaving the Community, you're getting rid of your nuclear deterrent, the Americans are being sent home, you're getting out of NATO—now we *can* trust each other. Now we can be friends.'

The original cause of Pachenko's satisfaction was the election, in a Britain totally exhausted by incurable unemployment, of a left-wing Labour administration. That had happened five years ago, and the last two years that Michael had been in Moscow had seen the kind of developments that Pachenko welcomed as drawing the two nations closer. But all this had been changed, the whole atmosphere altered, by the recent general election which had returned a Conservative government with a good working majority. In the weeks immediately before the polls, Pachenko had become subdued. Some of his buoyancy had left him, and he had looked tired and worried.

The voice on the telephone had been worried, too—and urgent.

Michael looked at his watch, got up from his desk and went into the adjoining office. Oleg, although he wasn't typing, was crouched over his typewriter.

'I'll want the car in ten minutes,' Michael said.

'Sokolniki?'

'No. I've got some calls to make. He can drop me in Revolution Square. Afterwards, I'll get the Metro.'

Oleg grunted, and Michael went down the corridor to the little room where two wire machines—one for Tass and the other for Reuters—were chattering intermittently. He tore off the paper. There was nothing of significance. There seldom was much at this time of day. For reasons best known to themselves the Russians began spilling out their news around midnight. When things were busy, it made a damn long day. There had been a few of them in the past month as the USSR adjusted to the unwelcome return of the new government in Britain.

Michael thought of Pachenko and his wife, of Moscow slowly warming to spring, the trees in the boulevards just beginning to unclench their green leaves, the first flowers struggling out of winter. Muscovites loved flowers and Varinka's solemn eyes always glowed with pleasure whenever he took her some. At last the greyness seemed to be going even from Moscow's jostling crowds. Well, the next winter would be his last. Then home for good. A few weeks in Devon with his parents, and then—? It might be anywhere. He could envisage the parental conversation. After five years with the BBC, wasn't it now really time that he settled down?

His father, a conscientious general practitioner, had never really come to terms with Michael's career or his way of life. It seemed altogether too casual. There'd been that business at Cambridge—joining the Conservative, Labour and Liberal

Clubs all at the same time. 'It makes sense to me,' Michael had declared with a twinkle in his eye.

'It doesn't to me,' his father had said. 'You must make up your mind about things in life, my boy. What are you—a Tory, a Socialist, a Liberal?'

The father had stared into the soft brown, humorous eyes of his son, and was puzzled.

'I'm reading English, languages and politics,' Michael had said. 'I wonder if I ought to join the Communists as well?'

Back in his office, Michael now reflected that, had he joined the Communists, it might well have made his task in Moscow easier. But then he probably wouldn't have been in Moscow; he would never have got through the BBC appointments procedure. Joining the BBC had been disillusioning for the old man, although not as much as Michael's first job on a provincial newspaper. That, his father thought, really was a waste of his degree. Michael's subsequent elevation to the *Sunday Times* was accorded resigned approval, and then the BBC—well, it was a pity he hadn't followed the family tradition and become a doctor.

His mother had been more concerned that the years passed and he failed to get married. It was true, she had said, he might have had more success if he were a little taller, but he wasn't unattractive with his slightly angular, rather amused features. Why didn't he get his hair cut, though? It was always falling over his forehead, very untidy. His mother was essentially a tidy woman.

'Aren't there *any* girls?' she had said.

'Ah, that would be telling!'

And once Michael had reached thirty, his father had even ventured to say, 'You can talk to me, old man, you know—any fundamental problems.'

Michael had burst into laughter. 'I'm not a poufter, Father.'

And his father had laughed as well, with unrestrained relief.

Now that he was thirty-five, his parents had reluctantly become accustomed to his single state. That wouldn't, however, stop his mother declaring, 'You really can't expect to meet your future wife in a place like Moscow.' And his father was still just as likely to conclude, 'You don't take things seriously enough, my boy.' Nevertheless, after a busy day in the surgery, he might finally concede that Michael appeared to be highly thought of by the BBC, and as long as he was happy that was all that really mattered.

And was he happy? he asked himself. He supposed so. It wasn't something he thought very much about. He was interested. He was the observer, diverted, entertained, detached, and sometimes concerned. He wasn't dissatisfied.

Down in the courtyard, the driver, like the translator provided by the UPDK—the Department for Service of the Diplomatic Corps—was waiting in the Volvo which the Soviet government had allowed the BBC to import from Sweden on the understanding that, when they wanted another, the old one was to be re-exported. As Michael remarked to Pachenko at the time, 'Don't let some poor bloody Muscovite have a car cheap!' And Pachenko had smiled sadly and said only, 'It's a pity.'

'You can drop me in Revolution Square,' Michael told the driver casually. 'Then you can come back. I've got a number of calls to make.'

The driver nodded. The car moved smoothly beneath the archway of the huge apartment block and out into the wide Sadovoye Ring. The time was logged by the militiaman in his sentry-box outside. In a few minutes the car had swept down Tsvetnoy Boulevard, and then directly south to Revolution Square.

Michael watched the Volvo drive away and out of sight before he put his five-kopeck piece in the slot at the entry gate and went down the steep escalators of the Metro. Revolution Square was less extravagant in marble and mosaic than many of the stations and contented itself with monumental arches sheltering bronze sculptures representing the builders of the Soviet state. He took the orange line direct to the VDNKh—the huge parkland dotted with pavilions to commemorate the various achievements of the USSR. It was a popular place with Muscovites seeking relaxation, and was almost a compulsory stop for Soviet and foreign tourists alike.

It was nearly two o'clock when Michael came out of the Metro and hurried past the obelisk of brilliant titanium that curved and soared three hundred feet upwards. It commemorated the Soviet conquest of outer space. He walked briskly towards the central pavilion. Alexei Pachenko was already there. He stood on the lowest step, dwarfed by the square, columned wedding-cake of a building, with its topping of gold spire and star. He looked swiftly in both directions as Michael approached, and then embraced him quickly but warmly. The Russian's eyes seemed to retract more deeply and darkly with anxiety.

'What is it?' the BBC man asked, as they moved away to walk with studied idleness along the many paths that threaded between parkland and pavilions.

'I'm afraid,' said Pachenko, speaking in English.

'For yourself? What has happened?'

'No, not for me. For you.'

Pachenko paused in the middle of the path, and turned as though he were assessing his friend, weighing the youthful, almost athletic appearance against his own knowledge of Michael's experience.

'I mean,' Pachenko continued, 'for your people.'

'Oh, come—a Conservative government can't be that dangerous.'

From the Russian's expression, Michael saw immediately that his light-hearted attempt at unconcern had been a mistake.

'It has still taken us by surprise.'

'But why?'

'I suppose we'd assumed too much—too ready to see the British like ourselves. There were many reasons, eh?'

'Yes—unemployment was one of them. There'd been no fall in spite of the promises. In fact it had continued to increase. Then Britain had borrowed itself into enormous debt.'

Pachenko nodded. 'And leaving the EEC lost you important markets.'

'And that threw more men out of work,' Michael interrupted. 'And inflation rushed up again. But Britain had also lost its traditional friends. It was becoming more and more isolated. Frankly, the people were sick of it. They'd had enough.'

'I know, I know.' Pachenko sounded weary more than impatient. 'But it is hard to understand—hard for us.'

'But you've been to the West—you must know?'

Pachenko hunched his shoulders. 'We have different histories,' he said. 'Freedom for us is not the same as it is for you. For us it is to be secure, not to have disorder, anarchy. Russians are conformists. We like authority. It protects us from anarchy. Authoritarianism is for most a price worth paying. We never had your Renaissance, my friend. So we don't understand your freedom of the individual. To us it looks like chaos.'

'But not to you?'

'Perhaps not. Perhaps I understand, but—'

'But the Politburo doesn't?' Michael had uttered the phrase sharply, like a hostile interviewer asking a question.

Pachenko smiled weakly, recognising the journalistic tone, and nodded his head.

'So what is it, Alexei? What are they doing?'

They had come to a fountain—water spraying from golden dolphins and, above them, rising from behind the bronze figures of costumed young women, and then splashing down into the octagonal pool.

Pachenko turned to face his friend. 'You know what we call this?' he said. 'It's the Friendship Fountain. Those women are the fifteen republics of the Soviet Union. Surprising, isn't it, we haven't added Hungary, Rumania, Bulgaria, Czechoslovakia, Poland?'

Michael had never heard such bitterness in his friend's voice before. The Russian took him firmly by the arm and led him away.

'This is difficult for me,' he said.

'Because you're going to tell me something I shouldn't know, something I'm not meant to know?' It was more a statement than a question.

'I am a man of peace,' was all Pachenko said at first, as they quickened their pace towards an empty seat at the end of a long stretch of grass. Only when they sat down did he continue. 'I'm afraid, not only for you, my friend, but for Andrei and Novia. We—'

'The Politburo?' Michael interrupted, his journalistic instincts sharpened.

'We,' Pachenko continued, ignoring the interruption, 'we might be about to make a serious, dangerous mistake.'

'And you can't stop it?'

'I'm going to try . . . with your help, Michael.'

A young couple, walking hand in hand along the path, scarcely gave Michael and Pachenko a glance as they passed by. But Pachenko waited until they were well out of earshot before he added, almost irrelevantly, 'I'm not a dissident, you know.'

'I've never thought you were. You've been a friend, Alexei. That's what it's been about. It's meant a lot to me.'

The Russian nodded, his squared head sinking on to his chest. 'I have thought a great deal about what I am going to do. I haven't been able to discuss it with anyone—not even Varinka. . . .'

For one unbelievable moment, Michael thought his friend was going to ask about defection. As quickly he dismissed the idea. That wasn't Pachenko's way. But Michael could almost feel the Russian's distress like a pain.

'You can talk about it to me, Alexei.'

'No, it's my own problem. My own decision . . . for Andrei, Novia, Varinka. That's how I think of it. I'm worried, my friend, worried about a nuclear war . . .'

'What—with Britain? Not a nuclear weapon to our name.'

'No—not with Britain. Because of Britain.'

Michael was puzzled. Pachenko stood up, stared about in all directions, evidently satisfied himself that the groups of other people wandering along the paths had no interest in him, and then sat down again. He took an envelope from his inner pocket, and slid it down between them into Michael's hand. The BBC man took it and surreptitiously slipped it into the outer pocket of his coat.

'That's not for you. It is for your government.' Pachenko had become almost brusque, as though by his tone of voice he were dissociating himself from his own action. 'Guard it with your life. Take it to London—at once, Michael.'

'Look, Alexei, I'm a reporter, you know. Not a spy.'

He saw Pachenko wince and instantly regretted the word.

'I'm not a spy either.' It was the nearest to anger that Michael had ever seen in the Russian. 'But I *am* a friend, Michael. This is about being a friend. It is important . . . important for the peace of Britain, of Russia . . . oh, perhaps of the world.' The almost black, deep-set eyes were glowing with passion. 'Don't you understand?'

Michael nodded slowly. All right, so he was not a spy. He was still a reporter, and this seemed like one hell of a story.

'Are *you* in danger?' he asked crisply.

Pachenko shrugged. 'Could be. I don't think so. Not yet.' Then, interpreting Michael's expression, he added, 'No, you can't file it, my friend.'

'So—what does it say?'

'If you looked at the contents,' said Pachenko, 'they wouldn't mean anything to you. You must take them to your Prime Minister, or Foreign Secretary.' Again he pre-empted Michael's question. 'Not to the Embassy. That would only cause trouble. You must go to London—at once.'

'I can't think the office is going to be exactly delighted. They expect me to be in Moscow.'

'Tell them it's a big story you can't do here. You've got to come back immediately. Tell them anything.' With a half-smile, he added, 'Haven't you learnt the Russian facility for lying?'

'For God's sake, Alexei, am I doing this because I'm a reporter, or because I'm a friend?'

'Because I'm your friend. But also because it's necessary. The alternative is . . .' he looked up, his eyes almost black with sadness, 'is too horrible.'

'I'd better go.'

The men rose together, clasped each other's arm in the old Roman salutation. Just as Michael was turning away, Pachenko said, 'Perhaps you'd better post that as soon as you get to Heathrow—just in case. It might be safer than having it on you.'

Michael twisted back, startled. 'Why? Does anyone else know?'

'I don't think so. I hope not.'

'Then—?'

'You can never be sure in this country.'

Pachenko turned and made off in the opposite direction.

Only when he was walking beneath the arches of the entrance to the park did Michael transfer the envelope to his inner pocket. Then he headed briskly for the Metro.

By the time he had reached Sad-Sam, he'd decided he would have to do a radio story to London that night. It could be about anything. It didn't matter. Just so long as he had a chance to talk on the line to the foreign duty editor. If he telexed his intentions of returning on tomorrow evening's flight, he could imagine exactly what would happen. Within the hour, his own telex receiver would be stuttering back: 'Don't understand. Have not requested your return. Explain.'

He was about to turn into the courtyard of the yellowish stone apartment block that contained both his flat and the BBC office when a man, his coat collar half hiding a sharp, furtive face, stepped alongside and jostled against him. 'Mr North?' he muttered. Michael nodded automatically, although he knew it wasn't necessary. The man, whoever he was, would be sure of his identity. But as though it were part of one movement, accidentally jostling him and stepping away again, the man pushed a piece of paper into his hand. Michael didn't even glance at it. He returned his hand to his pocket as naturally as he could. Would the militiaman in his little box at the entrance have seen the encounter? Almost certainly. Surely the man would have realised that? Or didn't he care?

Michael strode towards the far entrance and took the lift to the third floor. As he flung open the door of No. 9 he called a greeting and went straight into the room on the right with telexes and the Tass and Reuter wires. There was nothing except a fatuous piece about last autumn's vintage of Georgian wines—a record for quantity and quality. He supposed he could work that up into something that would pass muster.

'Oleg,' he said, as he walked through the translator's room to his own, 'I'll be getting the afternoon British Airways flight to London tomorrow. Forgot to tell you this morning. I had a telex last night.'

'I didn't see it,' Oleg grunted.

'No—I said it came last night,' Michael repeated as nonchalantly as he could.

He sat on the corner of his desk and dialled 8196 for the international operator to book a call to London at six o'clock Moscow time. Then he dialled 2039463, the number of the British Airways office, and booked a seat on the 17·55 flight to Heathrow. After that he settled with a sigh behind his typewriter to tap out some nonsense about Georgian wine.

Voiced radio despatches Michael was able to broadcast direct from his own office using a microphone, and even a tape recorder if necessary, linked to an ordinary telephone line through a BBC 'black box'. This 'equalised', or improved, the sound transmission. It wasn't as good as studio quality, but it was quite acceptable for broadcasting, especially from Moscow.

Precisely at six o'clock his call came through. Michael sat before the microphone, a pair of headphones over his ears, and spoke to London.

'Nothing very important for you today.' His tone was casual, but he hoped the foreign duty editor listening at the other end would recognise that there was a reason for it. 'Just a little piece about Georgian wine. Everyone thinks the Russians drink only vodka, you know. Oh, it won't make your bulletins, of course. But I thought it was the kind of offbeat thing the *Today* programme might like . . . Are you there, Harry?'

'Yes, I'm listening.'

'OK, a word afterwards—about your request.' And then quickly before the FDE had a chance to interrupt, 'Right, going ahead then—in ten from now.'

In a recording channel in Broadcasting House, London, an

engineer pressed a button, a tape recorder clicked into motion and, in ten seconds, was imprinting on magnetic tape the Moscow correspondent's amused reflections on the Georgian wine harvest.

At the end, Michael paused for no more than three seconds before he spoke again. He didn't want to give the foreign duty editor a chance to interrupt. He spoke crisply, as though slightly impatient. Beneath the table, he crossed his fingers.

'I got your telex last night, Harry. I must say it's damned inconvenient pulling me back to London at this moment. But if it's only for a few days . . . well, I just hope your programme's important enough, that's all. I'll be on the afternoon flight tomorrow.'

He waited. His crossed fingers were gripping tightly. There was a pause at the London end. He could feel himself holding his breath. Come on, Harry, come on, for God's sake. Then at last, and with surprising conviction, there was Harry's voice.

'Oh, good. I'm sorry about it, old boy. But it's a rather big thing about international reaction to the new government. And Moscow's rather important in all this, isn't it? We thought we'd like you here.'

A bit weak. The new government had been in office for a month. Still . . . 'OK, Harry. Have a car to meet me at Heathrow, will you?' He sighed with relief and uncrossed his fingers.

'Sure. Any messages?'

'No. Nothing that can't wait until tomorrow.' And then to add conviction for the monitoring Russians he risked, 'But you might telex me details of the programme.'

There was a slight pause before Harry said, 'I'll do that.'

Michael closed the line and leant back in his chair. A half-smile quivered over his lips. In London, there was one very puzzled foreign duty editor, but thank heavens he'd played along. The correspondent fetched a glass and a bottle of scotch from the cabinet behind him. He'd earned a drink. Only when he felt the warming of the golden liquid slipping down his throat did he remember the bit of paper pushed into his hand earlier that afternoon. He jumped up and fumbled in his overcoat pocket. The scrap of paper bore two words only: 'Konstantin Azhimov', followed by a telephone number.

Oh no, he thought to himself, not now. He went out, past Oleg, into the corridor and along to the lavatory. He looked at the name again. Azhimov. It meant nothing. He crumpled the paper and flushed it down the toilet.

Colonel Viktor Brod of the KGB's Second Chief Directorate didn't merit the opulence of the apartments on Kutuzovski Prospekt, but he had been assigned a place of extravagant luxury in one of the better blocks on Kalinin—that enormously broad tree-lined highway that led almost a mile and a half west from the city centre.

At about the time that Michael North was providing London with an offbeat story on Georgian wines, the colonel was opening his front door to the tall, gangling figure of Stacey Mariner, an American CIA man whose college-boy face belied both his age and his experience. Brod was just as tall but much more thickset. He had once been a champion swimmer of the breast stroke, and the breadth of his chest and shoulders testified to his strength. He looked as though he could crush any normal human being between his arms like a nut between nutcrackers. He lived well and enjoyed the good life, and but for rigorous exercise he would have soon run to flab. He had a large, craggy face with slate-grey eyes, and he seldom smiled, except when he contemplated his treasures, which included a small collection of icons, or mused on the satisfaction of his own life-style. Part of this was his wife, Nada, whom he prized as though she were another icon. Tall, slim, dark, she was undeniably beautiful but had disconcertingly sad eyes. She was at his side when he greeted the American, but soon disappeared to leave the two men in Brod's study. It was lined with books, most of which he had never read.

Brod waited a moment or two and then led the way into a small room beyond. The walls held his collection of icons, and leaning against an old chest was something wrapped in cloth. The Russian lifted it on to the top of the chest and unwrapped it.

The American uttered a low whistle, but neither spoke. Mariner bent over and peered at the glowing paint and antique gold of the icon, and nodded his head appreciatively. Colonel Brod wrapped it carefully in the cloth again and put it in the chest. They returned to the study.

The Russian opened the glass door of a highly decorated cabinet and produced a bottle of vodka. He handed a glass to the American. They each downed the liquid at a gulp, and Brod poured another. Then he leant forward and switched on the portable radio on his desk. The room filled with the sound of a Tchaikovsky symphony.

'That's a real good-looker,' said the American.

Brod smiled. 'Rublev.'

'You don't say? That's going it a bit, isn't it? The same source?'

The Russian nodded. 'When?' he asked.

'I can't make a shipment for at least another three weeks.'

'That'll do,' Colonel Brod conceded. His tone was guttural. 'Pity we can't manage more than one at a time.'

'Don't be greedy, Colonel. It's the safest way. That one will fetch a fortune.'

The Russian took a deep breath, an enormous fist clutching the vodka glass. 'There's something else,' he said.

'That's too bad. We really can't do more than one at a time,' said Mariner.

'No, I don't mean icons. The other. We don't know if our man is talking to the fucking British too. Do you?'

Mariner smiled. It made his face look more youthful than ever. 'No,' he said. 'We don't have much talk with the Brits these days.'

'Your Western democracy is crazy,' Brod muttered. 'You were like—' he searched for the word—'like lovers. Sometimes you quarrelled, but you always made it up. Then the British have a fucking election and they kick you out. Now five years later they have another election, and . . . ah!' The Russian threw wide his arms in a gesture of incomprehension. 'Don't understand your politics.'

Mariner's response was lost in the sound of a Tchaikovskian climax.

'But the thing I do know about is security,' Brod continued. 'We shall deal with him soon.'

The two men eyed each other seriously. The American sat with his legs and arms crossed. Now he untwisted himself, leant down and lifted up his bulky black briefcase. He took out a packet, put it down on the desk and pushed it towards the Russian.

Brod's face was expressionless. He opened the central drawer of his desk and slid the package into it, not even bothering to feel its plumpness. It was an instalment, and probably held about a thousand dollars.

'I hope Mrs Mariner is well,' he said.

'Sure. But she's never liked Moscow.'

'You can get anything with American dollars.'

'She still doesn't like Moscow.'

Brod grunted, as though such an attitude was incomprehensible.

Mariner fingered his empty vodka glass. Brod pushed the bottle towards him, but he ignored it. 'We don't want your man picked up yet,' he said. 'Not for another week or two . . . if that's not inconvenient.'

'That's all right.'

'We shan't be interfering with our man either,' Mariner said.

The music from the radio still blared into the room.

'He's going dry anyway.' Brod tried to sound convincing. In fact, the American, code-named Eagle, had recently provided most valuable information, and Brod certainly did not want him withdrawn at present.

Mariner smiled. Brod poured another vodka for himself, raised his thick eyebrows. The American shook his head, and Brod tossed the colourless liquid back into his throat.

'Later on—you want a deal?' Brod asked.

'It would have to be something important.'

'It doesn't matter to me,' Brod muttered.

Mariner uncurled himself from his chair. 'I like Tchaikovsky—the fifth, isn't it?'

Brod shrugged as he lifted his immense frame to his feet. Mariner opened his briefcase again, and pushed a couple of bottles of bourbon across the desk.

'To make up for the American going dry,' he said.

The Russian gave a mock bow. 'Nice to see you again, Stacey. Let me know about . . .'

The American nodded, and preceded him to the front door. 'Thank God your Moscow summer is on the way,' he said.

After Mariner had left, Viktor Brod opened the door from his study to the room beyond that housed his icons—the heads of saints, episodes in their lives, scraps of history, all in mysteriously glowing colours, affirmed with gold. It wasn't a religious or historical interest, or even a devotion to art, that moved him, but a simple acquisitiveness—the sensual pleasure of possessing what was beyond the reach of most. He enjoyed just looking, quietly gloating.

The colonel was able to devote the remainder of the day to such undemanding pleasure, encouraged by the company of his wife. For him, she was primarily a sensual delight. She was always submissive. Possessing her was like possessing the icons.

It was, as it happened, the evening of the following day that was unexpectedly disrupted. A dead-letter box, regularly used by the man code-named Eagle, pitched him into several hours of frantic activity. First there had come a report from the militiaman stationed outside the apartment block where Michael North had his flat. Then there had come the confirmation from Eagle. This meant discussions with Vladimir Semensky, head of the third department of the First Chief Directorate of the KGB, and at last, when the action had been decided and all the arrangements fixed, a full report had to be made to Maxim Kharkov, the head of the KGB itself.

Only when, in his characteristically grudging way, Kharkov said, 'That's good, Comrade Brod,' did the colonel feel he could relax.

Sometime Azhimov would have to be dealt with, but not while the Eagle was flying like this.

# 2

Flight BA 711 was three hours out of Moscow. In another forty minutes it would be touching down at Heathrow. Michael North had been dutifully reading pages four and five of *Pravda*—what Russian commentators were saying about international affairs, and the main foreign news. But periodically his attention had drifted as he wondered what the hell he was really doing—coming back to London with a secret package destined for the Foreign Secretary. He had made no attempt to open it. Pachenko had said it would mean nothing to him. Yet it was obvious that it must refer to decisions taken by the Politburo. What else could it be? What else could be so important to Britain?—to the peace of the world, was how his friend had put it.

Never for a moment had he considered that the Russians might be setting him up. He would never have got into this situation with anyone else. But Alexei Pachenko was different. He now took the package out of his inner pocket and turned it over in his hand. Then he recalled what Pachenko had said: better get it posted at Heathrow. Why, for God's sake? No one knew he had it. Did they? He remembered the Russian jostling him on Sad-Sam, and the scrap of paper with the single name, *Konstantin Azhimov*.

He took a pen from his pocket and addressed the envelope to his own flat in Chilton Court, Baker Street. He pressed the stewardess button above his head. A minute or two later he heard a voice behind him: 'Yes, sir?'

He fiddled in his pocket, pulled out some change, handed her the letter and said, 'Would you mind mailing this for me? It has to catch tonight's post.' Sensing her momentary surprise, he added, 'I shan't have time myself. I'm being whisked off to an appointment.'

'Certainly, sir.'

Now, Michael reflected as he sank back into his seat, he had only to explain to the BBC. That might even mean the Director-General himself. He wasn't a man to stand any nonsense. Michael could imagine him complaining impatiently, 'You of all people ought to know better than to get tangled up like this. God knows where it might end.' That thought had troubled Michael as well. He didn't like departing from his role of objective reporter.

His thoughts were interrupted by a double chime. The captain's voice said, 'We are approaching Heathrow, and shall be landing in twenty-five minutes.'

Charlie Evans had a reputation for cutting up taxi-cabs. He was stocky and good-humoured, and one of the best drivers the BBC employed. He arrived at Heathrow with plenty of time to spare. This was his invariable habit, whatever the appointment, not because he set out unusually early but because, with enviable skill, he always pushed a car towards the limit of its performance. He drove straight into the short-stay car park. Another car followed him in, and drew up in the neighbouring bay. Its three occupants walked behind him across to Terminal One.

Charlie made for the arrivals board. The Moscow flight was on time. He had the best part of half an hour to spare, and by the time Michael North had collected his baggage and cleared the customs, it would be nearer forty-five or fifty minutes. Charlie idled to the cafeteria, collected a cup of tea and a bun, and settled himself at a table with the evening paper. He had instructions to drive Mr North straight to Broadcasting House, never mind about any idea he might have of calling at his flat first. He sipped his tea and spread out his paper. The main headline read 'BRITAIN SEEKS NEW LINK WITH EUROPE'. Charlie, like many drivers, had decided views about world affairs: he had never approved of what the last government did. 'Leading Britain down the drain,' he used to say. He could never understand people being so daft in the first place. But then the country had been worn down by unemployment. After all, he'd been one of the lucky ones.

So having got out of Europe, now they wanted to get back in again. Charlie, worldly wise, wasn't surprised to see that Community leaders were lukewarm and France positively hostile. He was looking forward to a chat with Mr North. He was a nice fellow, now—unpretentious, no side, straightforward, and a light-hearted manner that appealed to Charlie, though he was a thoughtful chap too. Charlie fetched a second cup of tea, and took his time drinking it as he turned the pages of the *Standard*.

After twenty-five minutes he checked the arrivals board again. The plane had landed. Charlie returned his BBC cap to his head and made off to the gents. As he pushed open the door three other men came in behind him. Otherwise there were only two other blokes there—one zipping up and preparing to leave, and the other in a far stall. Charlie really didn't notice. And when the fellow who had followed interrupted him just before he was going to pee to ask the time, Charlie didn't register either that the delay enabled the chap in the far stall to leave. In fact Charlie didn't register very much more at all. Before anyone else came in, he felt a swift, excruciating blow to the neck, was aware of a kind of flash, and then slumped into blackness.

The three men dragged him quickly into one of the lavatories, slammed the door behind them and locked it. Two of the men were large. The other was shorter and stockier. He was already slipping off his jacket and trousers, while the others were struggling in the confined space to get Charlie out of his navy blue serge suit. Once that was accomplished they gagged him securely and tied his arms and feet. The short one got himself into Charlie's suit. It wasn't a perfect fit, but it would pass in the crowd of people at the arrival barrier. His own suit was stuffed into a briefcase carried by one of his companions. They propped Charlie on the seat of the lavatory, leaning him against the back wall. He showed no immediate sign of recovering.

Michael had brought only one case, little larger than an overnight bag, and after he'd collected it from the carousel he went straight through the green channel. As he came out into the arrivals hall, he scanned the people leaning along the shining chrome barrier rail, saw the familiar cap with the BBC badge, and beneath it a round-faced disagreeable-looking chap holding a piece of cardboard with *Mr North* written on it. He wasn't a driver that Michael recognised, but that was hardly surprising. He didn't know them all. It was obvious the man didn't know him either, but as Michael lifted his hand and moved towards him, the man's face creased into a grin, and he bustled out of the crowd to meet the correspondent at the end of the barrier.

'Hello,' said Michael. 'Glad you're here.'

The man nodded, smiled, and took Michael's case. Then he hurried ahead with a rolling sailor's gait.

'In the short-stay car park,' he muttered.

There was something odd about the voice, but Michael ignored it in the relief of being home again.

'I suppose,' he said wearily, 'it's no good asking you to take me to my flat first? We're going straight to Broadcasting House, aren't we? I knew it.'

The driver turned round, grinning again, and said something that sounded like ' 'Fraid so.'

They threaded a path between the cars arriving to pick up passengers with their luggage, and hurried across the covered roadway to the car park. The driver led and Michael was amused that he had some trouble keeping up. He thought the man looked like one of those big bowls used in ten-pin bowling, rolling unerringly towards the end of the alley.

'You haven't driven me before, I think,' he said as they found the Ford neatly parked with the front wheels already turned slightly in the direction of the exit.

'Bill. I'm Bill,' the man said, as he opened the back door on the left side.

'No, I'll come in the front with you, Bill.'

The driver shrugged, unlocked the front passenger door, then took the case and threw it into the boot.

Michael settled himself in, and pulled the safety belt across. Bill turned the key in the ignition. As the engine fired, the rear door on the left was flung open. A man jumped in from a car in the neighbouring bay. Michael twisted in his seat but the rear door was already closed. He saw the pistol before he noticed the features of the man who held it. The cold metal was thrust into his neck.

The man in the back seat said, 'Any trouble, I kill you. Clear?' The tone was deep, rasping and accented.

'Sounds very clear to me,' said Michael, affecting a lightness that he didn't feel.

'I am not joking, Mr North.'

'I'm not laughing,' said Michael.

'Do as you're told, Mr North, you will be all right. Otherwise . . .'

There was no mistaking the menace in the voice. Michael had no intention of doing anything other than he was told. As far as he could see there was no alternative.

The car began to move slowly and smoothly. The cold metal of the pistol barrel was withdrawn from his neck, and pushed with a meaningful shove into his ribs. The man at the back was leaning forward as though having a conversation. His breath smelt. Michael winced.

From the neighbouring parking bay a car followed them out on to the M4. They turned west.

'Oh, so you're not taking me to Broadcasting House?' said Michael, more to reassure himself by hearing his own voice than anything else.

Bill made a noise that could have passed for a kind of laugh, and accelerated into the fast lane.

'Has it occurred to you,' Michael added, 'that you may have made a mistake? What on earth would anyone want with a BBC reporter? I'm not the chap, you know, who filmed you selling phoney insurance to old-age pensioners. That could only have been *Watch-Dog*.'

Bill made the same noise again. The man in the back gave another little shove with the pistol, and said, 'Michael North, BBC correspondent, Moscow. We don't make mistakes.'

'Your opinion, not mine,' said Michael, and turned to look behind him. The pistol jerked in his ribs. The other car was still following. North narrowed his eyes. It was just close enough to read the number plate. It was an old one. He committed it to memory: OPV 416Y. Presumably the car was stolen. The registration might mean nothing.

'No trouble, Mr North,' the voice rasped behind him.

Michael looked frontward again. The speedometer was registering 70. He remembered once seeing something like this in a film. The passenger in the front had managed skilfully to get the gun held by the man in the back somehow twisted into the safety belt, so that as the man fired, it suddenly pointed to the driver. The car, of course, had gone careering across the road, but the hero had managed to grasp the steering wheel with one hand and the pistol with the other. He'd calmly shot the man behind him, managed to straighten the car, and reach his foot over to the brake. Not merely improbable, he decided. Bloody impossible. It even made him laugh quietly to himself.

After about ten miles, Bill turned off the motorway, and within minutes was winding his way along by-roads. He pulled the car on to a grass verge. The second car stopped close behind them.

'We're changing cars, Mr North.' The man at the back was already out and opening Michael's door. 'Quick,' he said, showing the gun again.

Michael was bundled into the back. Bill, leaving the BBC cap behind him, took the front passenger seat. He now produced another gun and held North covered, while the car reversed out into the road, and the man at the back whipped out a thick strip of black cloth and tied it over Michael's eyes. 'Get down,' he demanded, and gave the correspondent a push, so that he was half on the seat and half on the floor. Then he felt the gun barrel nudging his ribs again.

Judging by the speed of the car and the number of corners it negotiated, Michael concluded that they had not returned to the motorway.

'What's happened to the BBC driver?'

'He's all right.'

'I hope so. Who the hell are you?' he asked.

The man grunted. 'I'm Fred,' he said. 'You've met Bill. The driver now is Joe.'

'Where are we going?'

'Doesn't matter,' Fred answered. 'But we shouldn't keep you long, Mr North.'

'Oh, that's very comforting.'

It was probably half an hour before Michael heard gravel crunching beneath the wheels of the car as it came to a stop. He was pulled out and hurried across what he judged to be a short drive. When they removed the blindfold, he was sitting on a chintzy chair in what appeared to be a country cottage.

The floral curtains were already drawn. There were two standard lamps, one of them casting a pool of bright light near where Michael was sitting. There was another chair like his own, a settee, two small Victorian upholstered chairs, a bookcase full of books, a television set and wall-to-wall carpeting. It looked as though the whole place had been hired completely furnished. Joe had seated himself in the other chair, Bill stood near one of the curtained windows, and Fred faced him.

Fred and Joe were not dissimilar; they could even have been brothers. Both were large, obviously strong, and had heavily-boned humourless features. They had all spoken with rather thick accents, and Michael had already concluded they were Russian.

Fred seemed to be in charge. In his raucous voice he made an effort at politeness.

'We are sorry to bring you here, Mr North. We need not keep you long. If you will help us.' He added more pointedly, 'I'm sure you will.'

'Naturally, if I can be of any service . . .' Michael said in what he hoped was his most casual manner.

'That's nice. You have brought something back from Moscow—'

'Ah, yes, a couple of bottles of Georgian wine.' Michael indicated the Moscow carton at the side of his chair. 'It's very good. You should ship it here, you know.'

'I am not being funny, Mr North. Don't waste time. You were given something to bring back. We want it. Who gave it to you?'

'I don't know what the hell you're talking about.'

Immediately he'd uttered the words Michael realised what a cliché they sounded.

The long hard line of Fred's lips moved in the nearest they were ever likely to get to a smile. He bent forward from the hips so that he came nearer to his hostage.

'Now, that won't do, will it? No fooling, huh!'

Michael pressed himself back into his chair, trying to avoid the unpleasant smell of the man's breath. Fred evidently interpreted the movement as a sign of fear, because he nodded his head approvingly.

'That's better.'

'No, it's your breath,' said Michael. 'It's revolting. Hasn't your girl friend told you?'

Fred grimaced. There was a chortling sound from Bill by the window. Joe merely sat looking solemn, fidgeting with his pistol.

'It'll be quicker if you just give it to us.' The menace was unmistakable.

Michael's anxiety was deepening. But then he hadn't got anything, so what had he to lose? He attempted the insouciant air again.

'My dear old Fredorovich, do you imagine that, facing the three of you with pistols, I wouldn't give you whatever I'm supposed to have, if only I'd got it?'

Fred was clearly puzzled by the syntax, but he disliked the manner. He jerked Michael to his feet. Joe alerted himself with the pistol, and Bill grinned with undoubted pleasure.

'Coat!' Fred said and, with a spinning movement, began to pull Michael's jacket from his shoulders. When he'd removed it, he flung it across the room to Bill, who sat on a nearby chair and systematically emptied everything from its pockets. Then, with a sharp pocket knife, he ripped out the linings.

'Where is it, Mr North?' Fred muttered angrily.

'I haven't got anything,' Michael shouted.

'Clothes. Get 'em off.' He stepped aside and, in the facing chair, Joe tilted the gun.

Michael calmly removed his clothes. Fred and Bill went

through them swiftly, then threw them back again. Trying to affect the same calm, Michael dressed himself.

'I shall have to claim on the Russian Embassy for this jacket,' he said. 'You've ruined it.'

'You met Konstantin Azhimov outside your apartment,' Fred continued. 'What did he give you? What have you done with it?'

'I don't know Comrade Azhimov. And I haven't got anything from him or anybody else.'

Bill pulled Michael's travelling case to the centre of the floor, and was about to burst it open.

'No, please,' Michael interrupted. 'You've got the keys there.'

Bill grinned, as though the remark were a revelation. He sorted out the key and unlocked the case. The few items of clothing, a file of papers and a book, were emptied on to the floor. Fred took the file and left the rest to Bill. As he realised nothing was there, Fred became more exasperated. He seemed fascinated by Michael's expenses form, but reluctantly conceded that was not what he was looking for. He watched while Bill cut the lining out of the case, and then probed the rest of it with his knife to make sure there were no other compartments. Eventually, he threw it aside.

Michael had resumed his seat in the chintzy chair. He wasn't happy with the Russians' frustration. Even Bill looked angry. For some moments no one spoke. Fred and Joe stared at him. He felt the silence, threatening. He tried conciliation, speaking quietly.

'Do you think if I really had anything, I wouldn't have given it to you by now? I've got nothing to gain by holding out, have I? I don't underestimate any one of you, believe me.'

Fred said nothing, only stared.

'Shall we,' Michael ventured tentatively, 'have a glass of wine?'

The offer was ignored. Fred started to stride about the room. Then he pulled up one of the Victorian chairs in front and slightly to the side of Michael. It left Joe an unhindered line of sight. At last Fred said, 'All right, what have you done with it?'

'I haven't got anything.'

'Who gave it to you? Was it Azhimov?'

'You told me it was. But I don't know Azhimov, and I haven't got anything.'

'You've got to tell us.'

'I've got nothing to tell,' Michael muttered despairingly.

'Who talks to you? Come on, North, who talks to you?' Fred slammed the arm of the chair with his fist.

'Nobody.'

The fist slammed down again. Fred's eyes glinted frighteningly. 'Who is it? Who gives you things? Who talks to you? Is it Azhimov?'

Michael again wearily denied any knowledge of Azhimov, and maintained that nobody talked to him. Then began a long interrogation. What had he done the previous day —from the moment he got up to the moment he boarded the aircraft at Sheremetyevo airport? Patiently they went over every detail again and again, until Michael was beginning to feel exhausted. Suddenly Fred gripped him by the throat. 'Who is it?' he roared. 'Who is it, you fucking bastard?' The grip of the fingers was like steel. He shook until Michael felt his bones would rattle, and then he threw the correspondent back in the chair.

Michael's hand went up to his throat. He gasped for breath. Fred was breathing heavily. He waited for Michael to recover. Then he spoke again. 'You don't tell us, we shall make you wish you had.'

Michael struggled to keep calm. 'And do you think the police . . . do you think the British Government—?'

'Fuck the British Government.'

Bill made his laughing sound. Joe still held the pistol, expressionless. For several minutes no one spoke, but Fred continued staring menacingly at the slumped figure in the chair. When at last the atmosphere appeared to have calmed, Michael tried again, this time in a tone of utter defeat.

'Can't you see,' he said, 'that if I had anything I would have given it to you by now? If I knew anything, I would have told you? Comrades, there's nothing.' He gestured with his hands in despair. 'Nothing, I promise . . . nothing.'

Fred appeared to be thinking. Ultimately he said, 'Get up!'

He led Michael upstairs to a small bedroom. 'Sleep on it, Mr North,' he said, as he pushed him roughly on to the bed. 'We shall take it in turns to sit with you . . . all night.' Then he called for Joe.

Michael was tired and exhausted, but sleep didn't come easily. It wasn't merely his own predicament that nagged at his mind, although that was alarming enough. The fact that they hadn't found the envelope, for the obvious reason that he hadn't got it with him, was no guarantee of his safety. The KGB—and he had no doubt they were the employers of the so-called Fred, Joe and Bill—had no fine moral feelings. If they wanted to get rid of him—even for no better reason than their own impatience or frustration—they would do so without qualm. He must try to be conciliatory, and as helpful as possible without endangering Pachenko. And that worried him too. Whatever it was Pachenko had given him was clearly immensely important. And did they really believe it was Azhimov? Who the hell was Azhimov anyway? Oh, my God, he thought, why didn't he stick to journalism? He should never have got mixed up in this, but again he saw no alternative. Certain decisions carried their own imperative, which was inescapable. To Pachenko it had been a desperate act of friendship. That was something Michael could never have denied. On one side there was journalistic integrity; on the other was the honour of friendship. Wearily, he tried to nudge himself into sleep. It was hopeless. Nevertheless at some time he must have dozed off because it was daylight when he felt Fred's grip on his shoulder shaking him awake. He was propelled roughly downstairs.

'There's no breakfast,' Fred announced as he hurled Michael into the chair. 'We hadn't planned that it would take so long.'

'It need not have done,' said Michael quietly. 'I haven't got anything. There's nothing I can tell you. And I still don't know Comrade Azhimov.'

Fred took no notice, but his eye suddenly caught the

carton containing the two bottles of Georgian wine. He bellowed with delight. Excitedly, he pulled them from their wrappings, and then rushed over to the window, and held the bottles aloft in the early sunlight. He shouted at Bill in Russian, and the stocky little man quickly returned from the kitchen with a bowl. Fred broke the bottles over it and poured out the liquid. He stared at them in dismay, roared a violent Russian oath.

Michael said quietly, 'I could have told you.'

Fred swung the back of his hand savagely across the correspondent's face and Michael let out a yelp of pain.

The three Russians sank into silence. Eventually, Fred pulled Michael to his feet. He put a massive hand under the BBC man's chin and forced back his neck until Michael felt it would snap. Then came a vicious blow to the solar plexus. He crumpled to the ground, winded and gasping.

Bill was commanded in Russian to 'Watch him!' and the other two left the room. When Michael got his breath back he was aware of a murmuring sound of conversation in another room. He looked up at Bill. The man grinned.

Michael said quietly, 'I haven't got it, Bill. I haven't, you know.'

The Russian grinned again.

It was ten minutes before the other two returned. Then Fred kicked the travelling case across the floor and indicated to Michael that he should put his belongings into it. When he had done so, Joe bandaged his eyes with black felt.

'Come on,' said Fred, and again Michael felt two short jabs of the gun in his ribs.

In the car he was held on the floor. He guessed that Bill was driving, and at a sickening speed along what were surely country lanes. After what seemed about twenty minutes, the car slowed to a crawl, the nearside back door was flung open, and he was hurled out. He heard his case thud down beside him as the car accelerated away. By the time he had rolled into a sitting position and torn the blindfold from his eyes, the car had disappeared round a bend fifty yards or so ahead.

He felt bruised, and his left knee was paining him, but

nothing appeared to be broken. He was on the edge of a narrow road, one which he guessed was coloured yellow on the Ordnance Survey maps. There were birch woods on each side and, ahead of him, the road was twisting and undulating. That seemed the obvious way to go. He flicked off the dirt and leaf-mould, gathered up his suitcase and set off. Soon he came upon the county sign of Hampshire, and after about half a mile reached a road junction with a signpost showing that he had come from the direction of Linch and Hollycombe. Haslemere was 4½ miles down the road to the right, and a ring of iron on the top of the signpost bore the words: Liphook, Hampshire. In spite of the pain in his knee he pressed on past new housing estates and, within another fifteen minutes, was standing in the News Shop in the centre of Liphook, surrounded by counters of chocolate bars and video cassettes and, on the newspaper display, looking at the headlines on the front page of the *Daily Mail*: 'BBC MOSCOW MAN MISSING—DRIVER TRUSSED IN LOO'. He asked a surprised assistant if he could use the telephone, and then dialled 01 580 4468. Just as the nine o'clock morning radio news was going on the air, he told the foreign news editor, Harry Wyles, that he was safe and well, if bruised, was phoning appropriately enough from the News Shop in Liphook, was proposing next to call the police, and would be back as soon as possible.

After identifying himself to the police and explaining where he was, he gave them the registration number of the car the Russians were using. He guessed they would have changed it by now, but anyway it was worth a try. He was told to stay put, and a police car would collect him. It did, in remarkably quick time. A detective inspector sat in the back with him and told him they were going to Petersfield. In less than fifteen minutes they swept past the end of the High Street and turned right into a road lined with lime trees and came to a halt outside a flint-cobbled and brick-framed building.

Five minutes later Michael was doing his best to explain to a detective superintendent what had happened, but the police officer suggested that before they took a detailed statement it might be better to try to pinpoint the whereabouts of the cottage.

'At a guess,' said Michael, 'we must have turned south off the M4 before reaching Reading. So it's in Berkshire, Hampshire or Surrey, and somewhere not more than half an hour's fast twisty driving from Liphook.'

Wall maps were consulted, areas squared off, and instructions radioed to patrol cars. Then the questioning began again, until Michael suggested, 'Look, wouldn't it be quicker if perhaps I typed it out myself?' The offer was accepted, but it was 11.30 before he was being driven to Broadcasting House.

The balding figure of foreign news editor Harry Wyles greeted him with, 'For Christ's sake, what the hell have you been doing?'

Michael recorded a radio interview with a reporter, then went down into the basement television studio to be interviewed again for television news. He agreed, with uncharacteristic tetchiness, to meet newspaper reporters at a BBC-arranged news conference in the evening. By the time a car took him up Portland Place, through the park to Baker Street and Chilton Court, his head was already dropping sleepily on to his chest.

But at last he was standing in front of the door to his own flat, his battered suitcase beside him, the keys in his hand. He let himself in, slamming the door behind him, left the case in the hall and threw open his sitting-room door.

He stared unbelievingly, and shook his head. Facing him, sitting in one of his own easy chairs, was a woman. She was naturally blonde, good-looking, and sat with slim, well-shaped legs crossed. Bright blue eyes were laughing at him.

'You know,' she said, 'you really should have better locks fitted.'

# 3

She was undeniably attractive, about thirty Michael guessed, and judging by her expensive, well-cut dress, a woman of taste. But he was too tired to appreciate her humour, and his knee was shooting with pain.

'Who the hell are you? And what do you think you're doing here?'

She smiled, with her eyes as well as her lips. On any other occasion Michael would have been enchanted.

'The name's Carol Rogers,' she said. 'And, I hope, I'm looking after your interests.'

'I don't care who you are, or what you are, just go.'

The smile was replaced by a serious, concerned look. 'Why don't you go and lie down for a bit? Then we'll talk later.'

Michael had already slumped on to his well-cushioned chesterfield. He sighed—a mixture of exhaustion and impatience. He didn't really care about the girl breaking into his flat; he didn't really care what she was meant to be doing there. He just wanted to be left alone and to sleep. He'd still got that bloody press conference. The woman was talking again. She had a soft, mellow voice. It was nice. Damn it, it was even soothing.

'I'm really here,' she said, 'to pre-empt your Russian friends. I mean, if they didn't get what they wanted from you they might try your flat. They didn't, so I thought I might as well wait for you to turn up.'

'Oh, very considerate.' He didn't like his sarcasm, but there it was. She raised an eyebrow and half smiled. 'I don't see that you would have fared any better against them than I did,' he added.

'Perhaps not, but I was in a better position than you.'

'Meaning?' He managed to sound both sceptical and cross at the same time.

She took a small two-way personal radio from her handbag and extended the aerial.

'Help's not far away,' she said. 'And—oh, by the way, the Special Branch have got the whole block under observation, and there's a man at the end of the corridor.'

'Oh God! . . . Perhaps he would like to arrest you for breaking and entering.' The blue eyes were laughing at him again. 'Oh—go to hell,' he said, and then wearily stretched himself on the chesterfield and arranged the cushions behind his head.

He thought he had been aware of odd dreamlike sounds and movements, but it was at least two hours before he stirred into wakefulness, opened his eyes and saw Carol Rogers standing beside him. She was holding a cup and saucer.

'I found some China tea in the kitchen,' she said. 'No milk or lemon, I am afraid.'

He sat up. The blue eyes looking at him were liquid and gentle. To call her pretty was perhaps too hasty a judgement. She had high cheek bones, and the features were regular and finely cut; the mouth was generous; her fair hair, with deep waves, was done in a soft, short style that looked chic. He took the cup of tea, and was already regretting his previous churlishness.

'Thanks,' he said. 'Sorry I was a bit—well, peevish.'

'You'd had more than enough to put up with.'

She returned to the kitchen and came back with a cup of tea for herself, and then edged on to the end of the chesterfield. He looked at his watch. It was 5.30. He'd have to go in another hour. He swallowed a mouthful of the fragrant, smoky tea, and was aware that they were studying each other intently.

'What were they after?' she asked.

'You mean *you* don't know?'

'Haven't a clue.'

'No, neither have I,' he lied, hoping that his own eyes hadn't betrayed him.

'The Russians are capable of anything,' she said, softly, incisively, 'but even they don't abduct a BBC correspondent for nothing.'

'Well, they didn't find anything, because I hadn't got anything for them to find.'

'Why did you come back suddenly?' she asked.

'I have to come back sometimes.' He looked away from her and drained his cup of tea.

'The BBC had no idea why you were returning.'

'A special programme.'

'I know that's what they say, but I don't believe it any more than I believe you.'

'You know,' he said, 'I think I've had enough questioning for today, even when the interrogator is someone as charming and criminal as you.'

She laughed, and raised an eyebrow.

'You did break into my flat.'

'It was approved.'

'Not by me it wasn't.'

'Now, you're not going to be peevish again, are you?'

'Well, you must admit, Miss Rogers—it is Miss, is it?—that it's all very odd.'

'Yes . . . Miss, I mean. Odd, too, for that matter, unless you're holding out. Which you are, aren't you?'

'No.' That reminded him: he must go and look at the mail in the wire basket behind the front door. But he couldn't do it now. That would be too obvious. The door buzzer interrupted them. Before he could get up Carol was already in the hall. Two men came in. They introduced themselves as a chief inspector and a sergeant in the Special Branch.

'Ah,' said Michael light-heartedly, 'you've come to arrest Miss Rogers. The charge is breaking and entering.'

The chief inspector said, 'If you pressed it, sir, it would be very embarrassing.'

Oh dear, had the man no sense of humour? Michael added, 'I'm sure she would like to make you a cup of tea. She's very good at that too.'

The police officer's moustached upper lip twitched. 'Just a few questions,' he said.

'I've made a statement that is bristling with details like a porcupine with spines.'

'I know, sir. Very helpful indeed. But one or two points arise.'

'More spines—how uncomfortable.'

The chief inspector seemed impervious. Michael caught Carol's eye. Her glance was amused, teasing.

'For example, sir, you are quite sure the three men were Russians?'

'Yes. They spoke Russian among themselves.'

'Were you threatened at all in Moscow, sir?'

'No.'

'Have you ever been?'

'No.'

'Have you always got on well with the Russian authorities?'

Michael laughed, he hoped not impolitely, but it was an incongruous, totally irrelevant question.

'You don't not get on well with them, any more than you get on well with them,' he said. 'It's not that kind of relationship. They tolerate you for their own reasons, and you put up with little inconveniences from time to time. I hadn't incurred their hostility, if that's what you mean. They have made no official complaint.'

'I see, sir. Why didn't you let the British Embassy know you were leaving?'

'There wasn't time.' That wasn't true, but Michael assumed the inspector wouldn't know.

'And why *did* you come back, sir?'

'Special programme.'

'The BBC seem rather vague about that.'

'The BBC can be vague about all sorts of things.' Michael smiled. 'You can blame it on creative bureaucracy.'

The chief inspector exchanged a glance with his sergeant, who had been scribbling dutifully.

'You haven't ever seen any of these Russians in Moscow?'

'No. I imagine you will find them in one of the Soviet warrens here.'

The inspector nodded none too surely. 'Now you've had an

opportunity to consider things a big longer, Mr North, can you think of any reason why they should abduct you?'

'No.'

Michael looked at his watch. It was twenty past six. A BBC car was collecting him at half past. He reminded the police officers that he had to go to a press conference.

'Ah yes,' said the chief inspector, 'you'll be discreet, Mr North?'

'I'll tell the story as I know it.'

'Of course. But I wouldn't mention anything about Miss Rogers and your flat.'

'I wouldn't dream of it,' said Michael, a mocking gleam in his eye. 'That's quite a different crime. Of course, I shall check over my silver.' He noted Carol's appreciative smile, but the inspector seemed unmoved.

The sergeant put away his notebook. Carol announced that she would leave with them. She stretched out her hand, and Michael shook it.

'Thank you,' he said, 'for keeping the Russians away. I don't imagine we shall meet again . . . except in court.' He saw a reflection of his own laughter in her eyes. The chief inspector shook his head, and the three of them left.

Michael immediately retrieved the mail from its wire basket. Most of it looked like junk. Ah, but there was the envelope addressed in his own hand. He took it back to the sitting room, resumed his seat on the chesterfield, and carefully slit it open. Inside was a smaller paper wallet. It held some quite impenetrable strips of film. He put them away and restored the envelope to his inner pocket. It was almost half-past six. The Foreign Office switchboard would have gone off duty. He consulted his diary for the direct-line number of the Head of the East European section.

As he dialled he wondered, for the first time, if this instrument was now being tapped like those in his Russian apartment.

A voice said brusquely, 'Makepeace.'

'Geoffrey—hello, it's Michael North. I want to come to see you in the morning.'

'I thought you might. Let's make it 9.30.'

Michael put down the receiver. Suddenly he had the sensation of being watched. He turned. Carol Rogers was standing behind him. She smiled, half mocking.

'I think I must have left my hankie on the chesterfield,' she said, quite unconvincingly. She rummaged among the cushions, then straightened up and looked at him with an inconsequential shrug. 'It's not there.' She added, 'I must have lost it.'

'You'll find it in your handbag,' said Michael, sharply sarcastic.

'Do you know, it could be.'

'Well . . .?' Michael, while acknowledging that he found her attractive, even intriguing, was tired of other people interfering in his life . . . and that included Carol Rogers.

'I'm glad *you* found what you wanted,' she said. 'I'd noticed that it was there. But breaking and entering's one thing; stealing other people's mail . . . well, it's going a bit too far, isn't it?'

# 4

Sir Kenneth Propter, Eton and Balliol, had been Foreign Secretary for only a few weeks, but he was an experienced minister in a former Conservative administration, and had distinguished himself as Opposition spokesman on foreign affairs during the past five years when the government was busy dismantling Britain's nuclear capability and abandoning NATO and the European Community. He was clever at the despatch box, skilful at laying traps, and delightedly adept at springing them. He also knew how to use publicity to the maximum advantage of himself and the irritation of his opponents. Before accepting office he had headed a highly successful advertising and public relations agency. Indeed, to him had gone much of the credit for exploiting the government's failures and fostering every breath of change in the public mood. He was tall and well-built, as befitted a rowing blue. His fresh, eager expression appeared to knock a good ten off his fifty years. He relished the task of re-establishing Britain's influence in world affairs, but didn't underestimate the difficulties. He was acutely conscious of being at a disadvantage in almost everything, but was equally determined not to let that discourage him.

Sir Kenneth was even at a disadvantage this morning—in delivering a rebuke to the Russian Ambassador. He had nothing to back up his threats. But it was a gloriously sunny May morning. St James's Park was brightly green, blossom was showering, and tulips were spreading great washes of brilliant colour. He refused to be depressed.

He received His Excellency Anton Markolevsky stiffly. The Russian had spent a long time in the West and enjoyed its life-style. He cultivated an attitude of being friends with everyone. He was said to be fond of music and football, and had certainly been pictured on more than one occasion watching Arsenal at Highbury.

Once Markolevsky was seated, Sir Kenneth went and stood half-on to the tall windows that flooded the spring light into the room. He looked a large, uncharacteristically stern man.

'I expect,' he said, 'you have guessed why I have asked you to call, Ambassador?'

The Russian raised his eyebrows and made a brief questioning gesture with his hands.

'Her Majesty's Government takes the strongest exception to the abduction of a British citizen, a BBC correspondent, by—not to put too fine a point on it—three Russian thugs.' He was already visualising the press release. It would certainly use the word *thugs*.

The Russian's friendly expression disappeared. He looked dour and displeased. 'You are making a very serious allegation, Foreign Secretary, and one which you cannot possibly substantiate. You must know that there are no members of the Soviet embassy staff who would be guilty of such a grave breach of diplomatic privilege. I have no knowledge of the cause of your complaint.'

Sir Kenneth shifted from one foot to the other. He wasn't impatient, but it would do no harm if Markolevsky thought he was.

'Oh come, Ambassador, we needn't go in for that kind of nonsense. You have read the papers, seen the television reports—you know very well what I'm talking about. Moreover, Mr Markolevsky—' he injected a tone of considered anger—'you have to accept responsibility for this outrageous act. There aren't any Russians like that in London for whom you are not ultimately responsible, even if they are members of one of your many commissions. I want them delivered to the Metropolitan Police. I hope I make myself clear, Ambassador.'

'Perfectly. If I could help I would do so, of course. I agree the act was outrageous. I understand it can't be tolerated. It . . .' He paused deliberately to give added meaning to the words that followed, 'it would not be tolerated in the Soviet Union. But . . .' He spread his hands, simulating despair. 'I cannot help. I know nothing of this. We have no responsibility. The act can only have been committed by criminals in your own community, Sir Kenneth.'

The Foreign Secretary hoped his expression showed his displeasure at the intimacy, as well as his anger at the allegation. 'I expect,' he said, 'those three men to be handed over to the Metropolitan Police immediately.'

The Ambassador raised his eyebrows and pursed his lips. 'If I could, I would,' he said. 'I think you understand, Foreign Secretary.' His mood changed. 'I had such good, friendly relations with your predecessor. We even went to Highbury together. I am sorry that our first meeting should be like this, and that you should accuse me,' his voice was rising with indignation, 'and accuse the Soviet people so unjustly.'

The Foreign Secretary expelled his breath with impatience. But the Ambassador was continuing in a gentler tone.

'The Soviet authorities have nothing against Mr North. So there is no reason why we should be responsible for this outrageous act. No reason at all. Mr North is a respected correspondent. He is a very good correspondent. He has always behaved most properly in the Soviet Union. We shall be very happy to see him return to his post. I can assure you, Foreign Secretary, you are . . . chasing a dead ball.' He smiled.

Sir Kenneth's expression made it clear that he was unimpressed.

'I have only this to say to you, Mr Markolevsky: surrender your thugs to the police. If not, Her Majesty's Government will take the appropriate action. I think you know what I mean.' Again there was the little inconsequential gesture of Russian hands. 'And,' Sir Kenneth continued, 'if you do not hand them over, when eventually they are arrested, there will be no question of deporting them to the Soviet Union. They will stand trial in a British court. Her Majesty's Government will not tolerate behaviour of this kind from foreign nationals in this country. There is no more to be said, Mr Markolevsky. Good day.'

A little earlier that morning Michael North, at last refreshed after a night's sleep, took the Bakerloo line from Baker Street to Embankment, and then strolled through the gardens in the spring sunshine, cut into Whitehall, and thence to the Foreign Office. He had first met Geoffrey Makepeace when he was serving at the Embassy in Moscow. Now he was back in London heading the East European section. He had a comfortable figure that would doubtless become portly later on, and Michael had always found him relaxed, with a sense of humour like his own. Getting to him involved a small marathon through long stone corridors that threw back the sound of his footsteps. At last the uniformed attendant who had accompanied him tapped on one door indistinguishable from countless others, and Makepeace threw it wide himself.

'Mike, how nice to see you,' he said, extending both hands. 'Now come along in and tell Uncle Geoffrey all about it.'

The first thing that Michael noticed was the wall chart with pictures and biographies of the entire Politburo. Then he saw the other occupant of the room, completely relaxed in the most comfortable chair available, legs crossed in the same way they had been at their first meeting.

Makepeace grinned. 'I . . . think you've met Carol Rogers,' he said.

'I thought I'd seen the last of you,' said Michael looking directly at her slightly mocking blue eyes, 'but now I'm rather glad I hadn't. I'm feeling better, you see.'

'Carol is . . .' began Makepeace, and then paused, wondering how precise he need be, 'well, she belongs to us . . . and someone else as well, if you see what I mean.' He gave a knowing nod of his head. 'But she's quite a Russian expert, speaks and writes it fluently.'

'And highly accomplished at breaking and entering,' Michael added with a smile. 'I'm surprised she hasn't arrested my kidnappers by now.'

'Not quite my line,' she laughed. 'But we did have to make sure that, if they had decided to turn your flat over, they would have found a reception party.'

'So, what was it, Mike?' Makepeace asked. 'What were they after?'

'This.' He handed over the envelope containing the wallet of film strips.

Makepeace slid them out gently and handled them with great care, using the edges of his stubby fingers.

'I guess,' he said, as he laid them carefully on his desk, 'it's information that has been microfilmed. Will it be in code?'

'Don't know. I wouldn't think so.'

'In Russian then?'

'I imagine so.'

'Well, it'll take a bit of time to analyse, old man, before we know what we've got.'

Carol untwisted her legs and slid to her feet, then bent over the desk and peered at the films closely. Michael found the view from behind worth his full attention.

She straightened up. 'That was a sensible precaution—' she said, 'posting them.'

Michael feigned a bow.

'Your idea?' she queried.

He was amused at how neatly she had trapped him.

'Not exactly,' he said. 'My informant's.'

'And who was that? Who gave them to you?' Makepeace asked.

'Geoffrey, a journalist doesn't disclose his sources, you know that.'

'Come off it, old man, what the hell's this got to do with journalism?'

'I suspect damn all. But let's wait until you know what it is, shall we? Then I can decide if you need to know who provided it.'

Makepeace nodded understandingly. 'Fair enough.'

'Mind you,' said Michael, 'I feel uncomfortably more like an agent than a reporter. And I don't like that, I don't like it at all.'

Carol had returned to her chair, and Makepeace was sitting on the corner of his desk swinging his legs. 'Was he a . . . well, a regular contact?'

'Not a contact, a friend.'

'That's even more interesting. Did I know him?'

'I don't know. I don't think so.'

'It was a man, was it?' Carol's voice was soft, mellow.

'I'm not daft enough to get involved with a woman—not in that country,' Michael said briskly. In spite of her attractions, he still occasionally found himself resenting Carol Rogers.

'What motive would he have?' Makepeace returned to the questioning.

'Perhaps that'll become clear when you know what's stored on the film. But I can tell you this—although, Geoffrey, you must know it only too well—that the result of the election came as a very nasty blow to the Soviet Union. They can't understand why Britain, when at last blest with true socialism, should ever want to change it. Incidentally, I was told to deliver that package either to the Foreign Secretary or to the Prime Minister, and not to pass it through the British Embassy in Moscow.'

Makepeace was biting his lower lip, considering. 'Is there nothing more you can tell me about him—your contact; I mean, your friend?'

'I don't think so. He's a family man, with the Russian sentiment about family life highly developed.' Michael thought for a moment. 'He's a good man,' he said.

'But in a pretty high position?'

'I suppose so. I guess that much is obvious.'

Makepeace nodded, swung down off his desk and settled in his chair behind it. Carol leant forward, looking at Michael intently.

'How did they know you'd got that stuff?' she asked.

'I don't know. I don't suppose I convinced the KGB eavesdroppers about the reason for my sudden return, but that wouldn't explain—' He broke off, considered for a moment. 'There *was* something,' he added. 'A bloke banged into me outside my apartment, gave me a bit of paper. It had a name on it, and a telephone number. Konstantin Azhimov. Mean anything to you?'

Makepeace drummed his fingers on the desk. 'No. Have you still got it?'

'No. I flushed it down the loo. But those three guys who

picked me up seemed to think Azhimov had given me something of value.'

'And of course he hadn't?'

'No, but I'd got this package on me at the time.'

'He couldn't have been trying to get it?'

'I shouldn't think so. Why give me the bit of paper?'

'You don't know if it was Azhimov himself?'

'Of course not. I've no idea who Azhimov is.'

'And you can't remember the number?'

' 'Fraid not.'

'Well, whether you like it or not, old man, you're involved up to your neck in *something*, aren't you?'

Michael saw Carol looking at him. He hoped his eyes were not giving him away. He didn't want to be involved. He was a reporter, and in Moscow it was important to stay that way.

'I don't see,' he said thoughtfully, 'how they can really know that I had anything at all. It's pure supposition on their part. I only hope my friend is not suspected.'

'That's something we'll have to consider,' said Makepeace. 'You may have to give him a helping hand.'

Michael ignored the suggestion. Much as he liked Geoffrey Makepeace, he resented the assumption that he was there to be made use of. He wouldn't want anything to happen to Pachenko, but he was not happy with the thought that the responsibilities of friendship could lead to espionage. He had been asked, as an act of friendship, to bring something obviously of great importance to London. He had done so, and he hoped that was that.

'Well, I suppose I'd better be going,' he said, adding with deliberate finality, 'I've completed my mission.' He noted Makepeace's sceptical smile. As if to underline the point, Michael turned towards Carol and said, 'I imagine this really will be the last time we meet.'

She gave him a dazzlingly demoralising smile, and he saw she was laughing, perhaps sardonically.

'Unless, of course, you were going to take me out to dinner,' she said.

In other circumstances that was not an invitation Michael

would pass up, but he was determined not to be entrapped by the machinations of the Foreign Office.

'I wasn't planning it,' he said crisply.

'*I* don't get invitations like that,' Makepeace moaned. 'I'm married.'

The three of them laughed.

As he was going through the door, Carol called softly, 'By the way, if you see a guy following you—don't worry. It's not the KGB this time. But someone's got to keep an eye on you.'

# 5

From his office on the third floor of the dirty mustard-coloured building that was No. 2 Dzerzhinsky Square, Maxim Kharkov could see the statue of Feliks Edmundovich Dzerzhinsky, the Polish aristocrat who had said he stood for 'organised terror' and who had founded the organisation of which Kharkov was now the chairman, the *Komitet Gosudarstvennoe Bezopasnosti*—the KGB. The statue showed Dzerzhinsky with a goatee beard. Kharkov had once been tempted to grow one himself; instead, he became content with a ragged, Stalin-type moustache. His mouth-line was hard, the face square. He may not yet have been responsible for as many deaths as Dzerzhinsky, Menzhinsky, the bloody dwarf Yezhov, Beria, or even Andropov, but there was still plenty of time. Kharkov was ambitious. He even saw himself as a new Stalin, and was prepared to be ruthless for it. He returned to his huge desk and jabbed out the Cuban cigar he held in his stubby hand. It was one small death that should have occurred, and had not, that was occupying him this morning. It was the reason for summoning the head of the third department of the First Chief Directorate, Vladimir Semensky, from his office in the enormous half-moon-shaped building on Moscow's ring road. Semensky's department had specific responsibilities for the United Kingdom. It was also the reason for summoning, from the Second Chief Directorate, Colonel Viktor Brod.

The two men entered through the oak double doors together. Kharkov remained seated at his desk. He jerked his head in the direction of two hard chairs.

'What went wrong?' he growled. 'Vladimir Borisovich—what went wrong?'

Semensky was a thin, wiry, tense man with a bony face and

square-framed glasses. Kharkov had never been sure of him.

'North had nothing.'

'You mean your bloody apes didn't find it.'

'I wasn't told what we were looking for,' Semensky said acidly. 'But, Comrade Chairman, I am certain North had nothing at all.'

Kharkov pulled at his moustache, and looked directly at Colonel Brod, by far the largest man in the room. Brod's slate-grey eyes returned his chief's gaze unflinchingly. He was in a difficult personal position; it was important to be confident, authoritative. Anyway, Azhimov was inevitably coming to the end of his usefulness. There was a limit to how much he could be allowed to pass to the Americans, in spite of anything his American counterpart might do, and Brod had done very well out of the icons. You couldn't have it like that for ever. He glanced at Semensky. He felt nothing for him, least of all sorrow. He spoke with a guttural assurance.

'Azhimov contacted North outside his apartment,' he said. 'Something passed between them.'

'And how do we know the Brits haven't got it?' Kharkov asked.

'We don't,' said Brod quickly.

'They haven't got it from North,' Semensky said nasally.

'Why did those fools let him go?' Kharkov gave another tug to his moustache.

'Had they any alternative—in Britain?' Semensky blinked behind his spectacles. Kharkov had never been outside the Soviet Union.

The chairman banged his stubby fist on the desk in frustration. He understood Semensky's implication, but was not prepared to make allowances.

Semensky fidgeted. 'The ambassador has made it clear that North will be welcome to return to Moscow,' he said, with a certain defiance.

'Of course,' growled Kharkov. 'If your apes let him go, the best place for him is here, isn't it? We shall know what to do with him when the time comes.' He turned towards Brod.

The colonel made the kind of sound that was meant to imply that he would have pleasure in dealing with Mr North whenever it became necessary.

Kharkov stretched his arms on the desk in front of him and leant forward threateningly. 'You'd better find out where he got the information from, Comrade Viktor Leonidovich.'

Brod was unmoved. 'Of course, Comrade Chairman,' he said. 'I shall deal with Azhimov at the right time.'

Kharkov nodded. Now, ignoring Semensky, he adopted a more conciliatory tone with Brod. 'London may have been alerted,' he said, 'but we've got to make sure there aren't any more leaks. It's important, vitally important, that the Brits shouldn't learn anything else.'

'If they're dependent on Mr North,' Brod said, 'they won't.' His lips twisted in the nearest they ever got to a smile, and Kharkov nodded approvingly.

'But,' Kharkov went on, 'he has to get the information in the first place. There's a limit to what Azhimov is able to discover. There may be another source, comrade.'

'If so, I shall know,' said Brod with assurance. In fact, if it wasn't Azhimov, then he didn't know who it was. There might have to be some disconcerting action if he was to protect his own skin.

Kharkov got up from his desk. He was shorter than either of the other men but stocky. He went over to the window and looked out at his fanatical predecessor standing atop the green mound in the square. Semensky and Brod knew it was time to go.

So far as the media were concerned, the mystery of Michael North's abduction remained unsolved. He had done the inevitable radio and television interviews, in which he had declared that his kidnappers had repeatedly asked for a package he was supposed to have brought back from Moscow, but that, as he had got no such package, they ultimately let him go. And the police had, so far, failed to arrest the three Russians concerned. It was assumed that they had taken refuge within the diplomatic immunity of the Embassy, where they would remain until the Russians judged it safe to let one or more of them return to the Soviet Union. From the Foreign Office there was complete silence.

Michael discussed with his editors the possibility of accepting a different posting immediately, but finally decided he would like to finish out his term in Moscow, assuming the Russians would let him return. He didn't see how they could very easily refuse. In any event, he had personal reasons for wanting to go back which he disclosed to no one—the need to satisfy himself that Alexei Pachenko was safe. For Michael the integrity of friendship was as important as the integrity of his journalistic ethic. He was resolved that from now on all his activities in the Soviet Union should be purely journalistic, and he only hoped the two would never conflict. His resolution was reinforced by a telephone message he received, asking if he would be good enough to call on Sir Dick Randle at Century House, 100 Westminster Bridge Road, at three o'clock.

Sir Dick (he had never used Richard) appeared in *Who's Who* as Deputy Under-Secretary at the Foreign Office and Superintending Under-Secretary for Records and Research, both of which titles Michael knew were intended to hide his real identity as Director-General of the Secret Intelligence Service—MI6.

Sir Dick was very tall, lean and ascetic-looking, his hair receding from a high and wide forehead, his face falling away into a sharp triangle. He had a habit of stroking his aquiline nose with his forefinger when he was thinking. In the twenty-storey glass block that was Century House, where he had his office, he received Michael effusively. When the introductions were over, tea and biscuits had been brought in and cigarettes offered, which Michael declined, Sir Dick came quickly to the point.

'That material you brought back from Moscow,' he said, 'is very important. Where did you get it?'

'In Moscow,' Michael said laconically.

'Yes.' It was a thin smile. The tall figure of Sir Dick hovered near the window like a crane. 'Yes, I know all about your journalistic ethics, Mr North. But,' and his voice honed to a sharp edge, 'this is a matter of national security. I'm going to suggest to you that you have a duty over and above that owing to your craft.'

Michael was immediately irritated. He said shortly, crisply, 'That's for me to decide.'

Again the thin smile. Sir Dick appeared unmoved. He angled himself down into an easy chair, and pointed his long fingers together.

'Let me explain,' he said tolerantly. 'Whoever your friend is, he has access, I would say, not merely to the Politburo but to the Soviet leadership itself. More than that, he has facilities for putting on to microfilm a very large amount of material. Incidentally, it was, as you supposed, in Russian, not in code. Did he tell you anything about it?'

'Only that I was to deliver it to the Prime Minister or the Foreign Secretary, and that it was important for the peace of Britain, of Russia, perhaps of the world.'

'So it is, Mr North.' Sir Dick fluttered his hands, and ended with one finger stroking his nose. He repeated thoughtfully, 'So it is. He must be quite a remarkable man. It goes without saying that he is a brave man. He undoubtedly took a very considerable risk. Has he ever passed anything to you before?'

'Never. It is, as you will know, Sir Dick, difficult for an Englishman in Moscow to have a real friendship with a Russian, but this is such a friendship. We have a mutual interest in fly-fishing.'

Sir Dick nodded his head and stroked his nose. He had noted North's earlier irritation and didn't want to encourage it again. So far as the man's identity was concerned he could afford to wait. It was essential not to lose the possibility of North's co-operation.

'Yes, yes,' he said, 'that is unusual. And he asked this of you as a friend, nothing else?'

Michael nodded.

'Well, then, unless he is protected by his own position, he could be in danger. Do you suppose he . . . he wants to defect?'

'I don't think so. In fact, I'm sure he doesn't. His loyalty is to the Soviet Union.'

'It's a loyalty that hasn't stopped him giving away a lot of very important information.'

'What is it?' Michael asked.

The thin smile cracked over Sir Dick's lips. 'I think it's enough, Mr North, to say that it could make the difference between peace and war.'

Again Michael felt a mild irritation. For God's sake, he'd brought the stuff back, he'd been abducted and roughed-up by three Russian thugs, and now here was this lanky spy chief virtually telling him to mind his own business. Well, it was his business.

'That's not enough for me,' he said brusquely.

'Oh, I only meant for the moment, Mr North,' Sir Dick said soothingly. 'If you can help us—and I hope you can—of course you will be fully briefed.'

Michael had no wish to help them. That would probably put Pachenko in even greater danger, not to mention himself.

'I think I've fulfilled my role,' he said.

Sir Dick nodded, considering. 'Look,' he said, 'if you don't want us to know the identity of your friend—and I can understand that—would you be prepared to try to persuade him to defect?' Before Michael could interrupt, he added hastily, 'He could be in danger. You might be able to save him. You wouldn't have to worry about how it's done. We'd look after that.'

Michael had no doubt whatsoever about his responsibilities. Without showing the anger he could feel just beneath the surface, he said only, 'No, Sir Dick. I'm a reporter, not one of your agents.'

The Director-General of MI6 stretched out his long, thin legs, and nodded his head understandingly.

'I was afraid you might say that. The trouble is you have got yourself involved. Moreover the Russians know you have—or, at any rate, suspect you have.'

'Yes,' said Michael firmly, 'I've done more than I should have. But that's an end of it. Look, Sir Dick, if the Russians could really pin something on me—quite apart from any danger to myself—and I don't notice you expressing much concern over that—the BBC would never be able to get another correspondent into Moscow. We'd lose all our credibility.'

There was silence between them. Sir Dick stroked his hollowed cheek. 'You see,' he said, 'the information he has sent to us is not complete. I suspect it couldn't have been; that decisions still have to be taken. It is important—and as your Russian friend so rightly said, certainly for the peace of Britain, possibly the world—it's important that we find out what those decisions are. If he won't defect, then—well, we still have got to get the information. We *have* to know what those decisions are.'

'It's no good looking at me. Why don't you get one of your resident spies to do it? Legals you call them, don't you?'

The Director-General tut-tutted, but not seriously. He replied, however, with deadly earnestness.

'Our residents are known, just as we know theirs. If one of ours should make contact with your friend it might prejudice his own freedom of manoeuvre, might bring suspicion upon him. The work needs to be undertaken by someone unknown to them.'

'Well, that rules me out, anyway.'

'No, because that contact is evidently not suspected. And you're his friend.'

'Well,' said Michael obdurately, 'I am not doing it. Once and for all, I'm not going to do your spying for you.'

'H'm . . . Yes, your Director-General said that's what you'd say.'

Michael took a deep breath. 'That's despicable—utterly despicable.'

Sir Dick raised an eyebrow. He was not used to being spoken to in that manner.

'I thought it was courteous to make the offer.'

Michael controlled his anger, breathing deeply. He said decisively, 'I don't think we have anything more to say to each other, Sir Dick.'

'Perhaps not . . . for the moment.'

Michael didn't even wait for the MI6 chief to proffer a hand to shake. He turned abruptly and left. A few moments later, Sir Dick, standing thoughtfully by the window, watched Michael emerge on to the pavement and look about irritatedly for a taxi. Pity he'd taken that line; otherwise, seemed quite a sensible chap. Odd really that he'd never married—personable enough, good-looking; those brown eyes ought to have appealed to some woman. Unless he was queer, of course. That would be difficult. The Russians had a way with quiet ones. There was nothing in North's record to suggest it, either at university—where you'd expect it to show up—or since. MI5 had produced an extremely full dossier. Sir Dick turned away, as he saw a taxi draw to the kerb. Oh well, it was over to Number Ten then.

By the time he was pushing against the almost immovably heavy doors of Broadcasting House, Michael had simmered down. Nevertheless, he had decided he would ask to see the Director-General immediately he got to his office. It wasn't necessary. There was already a note on his desk saying, 'The Director-General would like to see you on your return.'

Henry Annersley was the first Director-General of the BBC with a technological background. The press had dubbed him 'the hard-headed northerner', a description which seemed to have some physical justification, because he had a broad, almost bald head, strong features, and a stocky frame. He was a Yorkshireman, product of a redbrick university, and had entered the BBC as an engineer. It would be wrong to say that, from the beginning, Henry Annersley had decided to be Director-General, but he had certainly been determined to get to the top. Director of Engineering was in his sights, but after a few years he did an unusual thing. He moved out of engineering into broadcasting journalism, and became a current-affairs producer. Persuading Appointments Department and Current Affairs to accept him had been difficult, but he was a determined man. He persisted, and he won. As he saw it, there was only one Director of Engineering, but there were a number of directors and managing directors who had emerged from a journalistic and current-affairs background. He was now in his early fifties—a no-nonsense man—regarded perhaps with a little suspicion by the establishment, but he knew exactly what he wanted for the BBC, and he wasn't going to be prevented from achieving it.

His office was an oak-panelled room on the third floor in the bows of the building. He sat at his wide, modern desk with his back to the tall windows, but jumped up as Michael entered, waved a short arm at the U-shaped complex of chairs and settees, and said, 'A drink, Michael? I'm going to have one.'

Michael asked for a gin and tonic. Annersley poured himself two fingers of scotch, and sat near to his correspondent, at an angle.

'The bastard wanted you to do a bit of spying for him, eh?'

'Yes, he did, DG. It made me cross.'

'Quite right. But what was it, what *did* you bring back, Michael?'

'He wouldn't tell me, except that it was of great national importance, wasn't complete, and that they needed more information.'

'Why the hell did you bring it back? You're experienced enough to know the dangers.'

Michael swilled his gin and tonic in his glass reflectively. 'I know, sir. It doesn't seem all that sensible, but—well, my contact's a friend, and he was so distressed and worried. He seemed as much worried for his own family. It was an act of friendship, not an act of espionage.'

'A distinction which the Russians are not likely to recognise. Nor, it seems, the government here.'

'Well, they're going to have to,' Michael answered sharply. 'DG, it's important we don't get our reporting mixed up with espionage. We'd never—'

'Of course,' Annersley cut in. 'I'm glad you took a strong line. But I hear you want to go back. You've only got another six months anyway. Is it safe?'

Michael said he thought it was. The Russians had nothing on him; they might even be feeling a little embarrassed and self-conscious.

'Anyway,' he added, 'I want to make certain my friend is quite safe.'

The Director-General wasn't sure that was a very good reason, but his telephone buzzed before he could say so.

'Humph?' he grunted into the mouthpiece. 'Oh? Hello, John, what is it?' There was a pause while he listened, an odd snort, another pause, and then he said, 'Yes, yes, very well. We'll be there.' He put the phone down, returned to his seat, and took a gulp of whisky before he announced, 'That was the Prime Minister's principal private secretary. We've been summoned—both of us—to see the PM tomorrow morning—ten o'clock.'

The Director-General of the BBC and his Moscow correspondent were led up the main iron-balustraded staircase of 10 Downing Street. Its walls were hung with engravings and photographs of all the prime ministers since Robert Walpole. They were shown into the white drawing-room. Michael's reporter's eye noted the gilt Adam furniture, the gold damask curtains and settees, the glittering pendants of the chandelier, and saw in the same glance that, as well as the Prime Minister waiting to greet them, there was also the lanky figure of Sir Dick Randle. Introductions were made, coffee and biscuits were brought in and placed on the slender table between the two facing settees in front of the fireplace.

The Prime Minister, Lionel Bryce, was tall, although not as lankily so as Sir Dick. He was a distinguished-looking man in his late fifties, with a full head of grey hair, although it was his strong, jutting chin that had been a greater attraction to the caricaturists. In difficult times he'd been pictured 'taking it on the chin' and, in the recent election success, 'leading with his chin'. In his earlier political career he'd been a darling of the party conferences with an instinct for the clever or colourful phrase. He still had a flair for publicity, which had served his party well, but with the passage of years he had acquired a reputation for astuteness. The more extravagant dress of his younger political life had been replaced by expensive elegance.

When his guests were seated, the Prime Minister poured the coffee himself, and passed the plate of biscuits, selecting a chocolate bourbon himself because, he said, he had always adored them as a child, and was never allowed enough of them.

He stirred his coffee vigorously, took a couple of mouthfuls, and then said with a smile, 'Thank you for coming, gentlemen. I'm sorry the notice was so short, but perhaps we don't have a lot of time.' He turned deliberately to Michael North. 'I gather our Russian "friends"—' he put the word ironically into inverted commas—'were a bit disconcerted by our election victory.'

'Yes, they were, Prime Minister. They'd been getting on so well with your predecessors.'

'Of course. Five disastrous years, gentlemen—no nuclear deterrent, no American umbrella, no NATO, even no Common Market. Still, I don't have to tell *you* that we're in one devil of a mess. Another year, and this country would have been part of the Soviet bloc.' With a jutting of his chin, he looked straight at the BBC's Director-General. 'Mr Annersley, your Moscow correspondent has brought back, condensed on to microfilm, an account of discussions in the Politburo itself. The change of government here means that either they have to abandon their plans for Britain altogether, or they have to speed them up, to take advantage of us before we can recover. So they have been carefully assessing the possibility of European or American reaction to whatever they decide to do. This assessment is based on information from their own intelligence network. As a result of that assessment they have decided to speed up their plans. What exactly they intend to do, and the timetable for it, are still unknown to us. But we can have a fairly shrewd guess.' The Prime Minister looked from Annersley to North and back again. He leant forward earnestly. 'Gentlemen,' he said gravely, 'I don't exaggerate when I say that what is at stake could be the survival of Britain itself.' At the corner of the same settee Sir Dick Randle slowly stroked his aquiline nose.

If this was just leading up to another request for North to put his own life in danger, trying to pass information from his contact, then, Annersley decided, it wasn't on. He wasn't having any nonsense. No Prime Minister was going to put pressure on him. They'd have to find another way.

The Prime Minister sensed that a forthright interruption was inevitable, and quickly forestalled it.

'What,' he asked, 'do I do if Soviet warships try to sail into British ports, if their military aircraft invade British airspace? That, gentlemen, is what it is all about. An isolated, ill-armed Britain is a great temptation to the Soviet Union.' He swallowed the rest of his coffee at a gulp. 'We have got to know precisely what they are planning. And we have got to know the timetable.'

Annersley had heard enough. This time he jumped in quickly, 'And you're asking North to find out, pass the information back? Prime Minister, it's not on. You can't ask a BBC correspondent to become a spy.' When he was being obstinate Annersley's voice plainly betrayed its northern origins. 'Anything like that would destroy the BBC's independence, turn it into an arm of government. That is something which I have to resist.'

The Prime Minister nodded, and took another bourbon biscuit.

'I understand, Director-General. I only wanted you and Mr North to be aware, not only of the seriousness but the importance, the national importance, of this whole business. I have no wish to compromise the BBC, or to threaten its independence . . . More coffee?'

He poured it out anyway.

'Then,' said Annersley bluntly, 'what *are* you asking?'

The Prime Minister smiled. 'I'm not asking Mr North to become a spy. I am not asking him to be anything other than the BBC's Moscow correspondent, but I am asking—in the national interest, you understand—for his very reasonable co-operation.' Seeing that Annersley was about to protest, he added quickly, 'He will not be personally involved. I give you my word. We shall send in our own special agent. The agent will be responsible for making contact, for discovering if Mr North's friend is prepared to defect and, failing that, get the information we need and pass it back to London. You, Mr North, will not be involved in any of this at all, so your position will not be compromised in the least. But some co-operation from you, as distinct from involvement, will be necessary.' The Prime Minister turned towards Sir Dick Randle.

Sir Dick cleared his throat politely. 'Sending in a special agent,' he said austerely, 'has its difficulties. Anyone new arriving at our Embassy in Moscow, or any sudden arrival of a businessman or some other specialist, would, in the present circumstances, be viewed with suspicion. So our agent has to arrive in such a natural way that no suspicion is aroused. As I see it, gentlemen, there is one way that can be done.'

The Prime Minister sat back with quiet satisfaction. Annersley and North were studying Sir Dick intently.

'The Russians have no objection to your return, Mr North. Indeed, the Russian Ambassador has told the Foreign Secretary that you have an excellent record in Moscow and they would be pleased for you to resume your duties for the BBC. They haven't really any alternative without admitting their own involvement. Of course, I imagine they'll keep a close eye on you, but that's to be expected. I suppose they always have.'

Michael nodded.

'So, why did Mr North come home so suddenly?' Sir Dick continued, uncrossing and recrossing his flamingo-long legs. 'Well, to record a special programme, I know. But the Russians still have their suspicions about that. They know there was no telex calling you back. Those suspicions need to be allayed. They can be, quite easily. Mr North came home suddenly . . . to get married. At last, the young lady had said "yes".'

After a glance from Sir Dick to the Prime Minister and back again, Michael laughed sceptically.

'Oh, of course,' Sir Dick continued seriously, 'we shall pretend it was a "secret" wedding. All the publicity will be after the event, and we can arrange that quite easily.' He smiled thinly. 'Your bride, Mr North, will be Miss Carol Rogers. I don't think any sensible man would complain at that, h'mm?'

Michael's exclamation was half indignation, half mirth. If he did feel incensed, at least the situation appealed to his sense of humour. His Director-General made no sound at all. He stared at Sir Dick with disbelief.

The MI6 chief continued hurriedly, 'Miss Rogers is totally clean so far as the Russians are concerned. As Mr North's wife she would be above suspicion. It's him they're interested in. They certainly would raise no objection to her accompanying Mr North. BBC correspondents have had their wives with them in Moscow before. It's, er, ahem, fortunate Mr North is not married.'

He looked rather pleased with himself. For that matter, so did the Prime Minister, who now seized the chance to voice his own support.

'Gentlemen, it's a matter of national, international importance. Your Russian friend was right, Mr North, in saying that the peace of Britain, perhaps the peace of the world, is at stake. That's how vital it is. And you would not be involved in espionage at all. You would retain your integrity.'

Michael chuckled. 'Prime Minister, this is preposterous. Of course I can't agree to this nonsense.'

'Whatever it is, Mr North, it is not nonsense,' said the Prime Minister with a pugnacious jerk of his chin. 'I can't force you to do this. Of course not. I wouldn't dream of it. But a great deal is at stake. If this country should suddenly find itself plunged into war, war which might have been avoided with your co-operation . . . but no, to be fair, I can't guarantee that. Even with your help, anything might happen. But at least, Mr North, we would be in a better position.' The Prime Minister ran his fingers through the thatch of his grey hair, the only gesture that had suggested any nervousness so far.

'It won't work,' was the blunt opinion expressed by Henry Annersley.

Sir Dick fluttered his hands. The Prime Minister looked grave. 'It might not,' he said. 'But it's the best chance we have. That's why, frankly, I appeal to you, Mr North, to try to make it work.'

Before Michael could reply, however, Sir Dick Randle interjected, 'There would be no danger for you—not as I see it. Any danger would be incurred by Miss Rogers.'

Michael recognised that for the unfair cut it was—designed to make him feel it was cowardly to refuse. He tried not to let it influence him.

'Might I ask you, Mr North,' the Prime Minister pursued, 'if your Russian friend showed any particular anxiety?'

'Yes, he did. To be fair, Prime Minister, he was distressed and worried, and clearly he had been through an agonising time before deciding to ask me to bring that package to London.'

'Well, then . . .?'

Michael considered. Annersley looked as though he was going to speak, but kept silent. Michael was aware of the Prime Minister and Sir Dick Randle staring at him.

'I don't think,' he said, 'my friend can be persuaded to defect. But supposing Miss Rogers gets the information you want, how does she get it out?'

Sir Dick looked benign. 'There would be no difficulty about that. Although the decision would be hers. She is skilled, highly trained.'

Michael got up from the settee, momentarily oblivious of his surroundings, as he thought about the proposition. He stood in front of the fireplace, staring at Samuel Scott's *View of Westminster* that hung above the marble mantelpiece. He looked through the pigment, the blue clouded sky, the light low on the horizon by the bridge, and saw Alexei Pachenko and himself—the pair of them sitting on the bench in the grounds of the Exhibition of Economic Achievements, and Pachenko saying he was afraid, afraid for Michael, for the British people, for his own children. 'We might,' he had said, 'be about to make a serious, a dangerous mistake.' Michael could still see the distress in Alexei's eyes. 'This is about being a friend,' Alexei had said. Michael was beginning to feel that, at any rate, he had a duty to friendship. That was more readily understandable than a duty to his country, which raised all sorts of complicated propositions in his mind. He turned away from the painting.

'I don't know,' he said quietly, as though he were thinking aloud, 'it's not impossible. It could work. It . . .' He broke off and turned to his Director-General. 'What do you think, sir?'

Henry Annersley knew very well what he thought. He thought it was a damn fool idea, but lest he should be accused of neglecting the national interest—a not uncommon accusation levelled at broadcasters—he said only, 'If you do this, Michael, it will have to be under my conditions. I am not prepared to have the BBC's journalistic integrity endangered.' He clamped his mouth shut with finality.

Michael returned to the settee. 'I had decided to go back to Moscow in any event, Prime Minister.' The humour of the situation was beginning to appeal to him. 'Very well, Miss Rogers can return with me.'

Even before either the Prime Minister or the Director-General of MI6 could express their appreciation, Henry Annersley butted in. 'It's on condition that North's work in Moscow shall not be inhibited in any way; that there shall be no attempt, from this end, to interfere with his coverage.'

'Mr North will be unaffected,' said the Prime Minister calmly. 'Naturally, he will be free to report from Moscow in the usual way.'

'Yes,' said Annersley, 'but, in this whole affair, I must be free to publish what I judge to be in the public interest.'

There was a disapproving tut-tutting from Sir Dick, but the Prime Minister stroked back his hair, and then tilting his chin in the direction of Henry Annersley, said, 'Unless there was any threat to national security.'

'That is a risk, sir, you are going to have to take,' said Annersley pugnaciously, and then added, reasonably, 'but no Director-General of the BBC is knowingly going to put the nation's security at risk.'

'Quite,' said the Prime Minister pointedly. 'Well, I think we understand each other, Mr Annersley. You have my word that the integrity of the BBC will not be endangered.'

They stood up and shook hands, and the Prime Minister said with relief that he was very grateful to Mr North for being so co-operative.

Sir Dick Randle untwisted himself from his corner and leant against the mantelpiece. 'Of course,' he said, 'we will arrange for the "marriage" to have taken place in a register office, and then let the secret out. You must, perhaps, be prepared for some interviews. We shall want to make it as good a story as we can.'

Michael was now distinctly amused. 'What about our parents?'

'I'm sorry, but they can't be told. It'll have to come as a happy surprise. I can't imagine,' Sir Dick added with an attempt at humour, 'that either of you are going to be unacceptable, can you?' He paused. 'Afterwards, well, that's a different matter. Then they can be told.'

Oh well, thought Michael, the old man would blow his top, but—so what?

With a sudden access of good humour as they all shook hands, the Prime Minister once more emphasised the national importance of what they were all undertaking.

As Michael and his Director-General began to descend the stairs, Sir Dick called from above.

'Oh, Mr North—many congratulations.'

# 6

Early that same evening the telephone rang in Michael's flat. He barely had time to say hello before the voice at the other end said in a seductively sarcastic tone, 'It looks as though you're going to have to take me out to dinner after all, doesn't it?'

Michael laughed. He'd already made up his mind that he was going to make the best of the situation.

'Come round for a drink,' he said, 'and I'll book a table somewhere. I'll see that you don't have to break in this time. By the way, I'm dropping the charge.'

There was a chuckle at the other end of the line.

'Of course, I'd pick you up,' Michael continued, 'but I don't even know where you live.'

'You don't have to.'

'I see. Do you know when we . . . er, got married?'

'I think yesterday.'

'Where?'

'Very secretly, of course. At St Pancras Register Office. That's being arranged.'

'Oh, highly appropriate. Roman martyr, wasn't he? And damn all's known about him.'

'I'll be round in half an hour.'

She was, almost to the minute. She looked lovely—Michael had to admit it—in a blue floral dress, classically cut; her hair, naturally blonde, was short but soft, with deep waves above the forehead, and her eyes quite startlingly blue. He thought they might be mocking him.

'When do we have to be prepared for the stories?' he asked, as he poured her a gin and tonic.

'I think tomorrow. I'll be round early. It would be better if you didn't go into the office.'

They chinked glasses. 'Here's to us,' he said. Then, as an awful thought struck him, 'Oh, my God—what about our parents?'

She smiled, not the least disconcerted. 'My father's Permanent Secretary at the Ministry of Health. So he's easy, and he'll be able to deal with Mother. We live in Sussex. I'll give you all the details later. But yours—near Honiton in Devon, I believe; father a doctor; mother, enthusiastic gardener and county councillor—they might be more difficult. I'm afraid you're going to have to deal with it, Michael.'

It was the first time she had used his name, and he liked it.

'Well, at any rate, they ought to be pleased that I've found a "wife" at last. They've been worried about my single state for long enough. But what am I going to tell them about you? What do you do?'

'Well, once upon a time, I worked for Sotheby's. I know about Impressionist painting, and even more about Russian icons. You can say I still work for them. That can be fixed too.'

They settled at opposite corners of the chesterfield, and chatted on about their family backgrounds until Michael, suddenly looking at his watch, muttered, 'If the old man's had a surgery tonight, it'll be over by now. He'll be the more difficult of the two, so I think I'd better take him head on. He didn't take the kidnapping all that smoothly. Told me to get out of this damn fool job, and be done with it. I should have gone in for medicine. He's always believed that. Anyway, I rely on you to make sure I don't go wrong.'

Carol raised her glass and looked at him over the rim. 'Good luck,' she murmured.

After the immediate greetings were over, Michael braced himself. 'Father, I've got something important to tell you . . .'

'You're leaving that daft job of yours?'

'No. No, listen, Father. In the next day or so you'll see stories—and it's bound to get in the local rag—that the real reason why I returned so suddenly from Moscow was to get married. There may be pictures of me and my bride—Carol

Rogers. But, Father, I want you to go along with it—do you understand?'

'Married? Go along—what the hell do you mean?'

'Well, it'll all become clear in the end, Father.' He glanced at Carol. She was chuckling quietly to herself and watching him.

'For God's sake, are you married, or aren't you? And why the hell didn't you tell us?'

'That will become clear, Father. But look—I knew Carol for about a year before I took on the Moscow job. We'd thought of getting married then, but—well, we didn't. And that explains this very sudden, secret—'

'The hell it does. I don't understand a damn thing, my boy. Who is she? Why haven't you told us about her before? You haven't got a bun in the oven, have you?'

'No, of course not. She's a lovely girl, Father. You'll like her.'

This time Carol's chuckle was audible.

'For God's sake, my boy, why didn't you tell us you were getting married? Why have we never met her? Don't like this hole in the corner stuff, Michael. Your mother won't like it.'

'She's been wanting me to get married long enough.'

'Yes—properly. Why should you keep it all from us like this?'

'Look—there's a lot that's impossible to explain at the moment. You're just going to have to trust me. Please. What you have to say if you're asked is that you've known about it for some time—it's all a lovely romantic story. You're very pleased. Father, please go along with the stories. It's *very* important. That's why you've got to trust me.'

'I don't understand a bloody thing, Michael.'

'All right, Father, you don't have to. No—I'm sorry to sound like that, but I promise you, you'll know everything eventually, and then you *will* understand, truly you will. And you'll approve. You'll say I did the right thing. But please, in the meantime, just accept it as a *fait accompli* and be very happy about it. Look, Father, I need your help on this, please.'

After a little more argument, his father ultimately capitulated. 'All right then—God knows how I'm going to explain to your mother—but I'll do as you say.'

'That's marvellous. By the way, she's a jolly good fly-fisherman.' He saw Carol crinkle her brows, mystified. 'Yes, casts beautifully. Now, look—I shall shortly be going back to Moscow, just to complete my assignment, that's all. I've only got six more months to do. Carol will be coming with me. Then, when we get back we'll both—' he looked towards her and she nodded affirmatively—'we'll both come down to see you. We can all go fishing.'

At last he put down the receiver. 'Phew,' he said, 'I can do with another drink.'

Carol got up and poured it for him. As she resumed her seat, she said, 'What's this about fly-fishing?'

'You mean you can't?'

'You know I can't. I've never really fancied standing up to my pussy in cold water for the odd trout or salmon.'

He laughed. 'Oh, you don't have to. Just up to your knees. Or, if you're lucky, even from the bank. But I'm sure you'd be adept at covering the rise,' he chuckled.

She looked mystified. 'It's not me, Mike.'

'It's going to have to be.'

'Why, just because you do?'

'No—although that would be nice. No, but if you want really to get to know Alexei Mikhailovich Pachenko—that's his name by the way; for you only, that was agreed—the way to do it is standing up to your . . .' he cleared his throat, 'thighs, casting a fly. He's very keen. It's also a safe place to talk.'

She began to laugh gently. 'I've learned to fly; I've learned to parachute; to drive a long-distance lorry; to shoot, of course; and I've been taught karate and unarmed combat; I've even been down in a diving bell—didn't like that at all—and now . . . oh, well, I suppose it could be worse. But how am I going to learn? We haven't got much time.'

'Look, we'll get these damn-fool interviews out of the way, and then I've got just the man for you—Conrad Voss Bark. He's an ex-colleague, but I never knew him in his BBC days. Before my time. I've met him since, of course. Great reputation as a fly-fisherman. Fly-fishing correspondent for *The Times*. Lives in Devon—on the Cornish border—helps his wife, Anne, with fly-fishing courses. She runs the hotel —Arundell Arms, perfect fisherman's place. You'll love it. I'll give him a ring, and tell him it's urgent. If you have to spend all day and all night casting—he'll manage it.'

'God, what I do for my country. You sound horribly enthusiastic, Michael.'

They laughed. Then, as she drained the last of her gin and tonic, she suddenly became serious.

'By the way, how is it you've never married? You're not—?'

'No, I'm bloody not. I suppose it's as you say—not many women want to stand up to their pussies in cold water.'

'You're that keen, then?'

'I'm not fanatical. But I enjoy it. The perfect cast is sheer poetry.'

'I hope Mr Voss Bark makes me feel the same, that's all.'

'He will.'

The first call came the next morning about ten o'clock from the *Standard*, and was quickly followed by the *Sun* and the *Daily Express*, who wanted pictures with the bride. Soon other newspapers were also ringing, as well as his own colleagues from television news. Michael invited them all to the flat for twelve noon. The whole situation was so false to him that it was difficult to appreciate the reality of it to others. But given that it was true, he had to admit, it was really a rather good human story. The Moscow correspondent who was mysteriously kidnapped and roughed-up by the Russians, really came home—not with a spy-package as the Russians alleged—but just secretly to get married.

The cameras flashed; the questions showered. How long had they known each other? How did they meet? Was she going back to Moscow with him? What did they have in common? To that one, Michael almost answered, 'Fly-fishing,' and then imagined the demand for pictures of them both on the Test, and so quickly changed course and, with a disarming smile, said, 'I suppose, being in love.' The answer was reinforced with a little giggle from Carol who patted his arm affectionately.

Then someone said, 'Do you think the Russians kidnapped you because they didn't want you to marry Carol?'

'Oh, I hadn't thought of them as jealous rivals,' said Michael, and everybody laughed.

Afterwards there were a few more questions about the original abduction: was he *sure* they were Russians, because the Embassy continued to deny it? Hadn't he really any idea why they took him? Was he worried about going back to Moscow?

Michael replied that he was sure the Russians now realised that they had made a mistake, and they had said he would be welcome back in Moscow. He was looking forward to taking Carol there.

Eventually it was all over. Carol had been splendid—light-hearted and laughing with happiness. When the last reporter had gone, the pair of them laughingly collapsed on the chesterfield.

'My God,' Michael said, 'what a hoax. They'll murder us if they ever find out. I reckon in any event we deserve some champagne.'

# 7

In Moscow summer was beginning. As the aircraft banked on its approach to Sheremetyevo international airport Carol peered through the window to see, sliding beneath her, a random pattern of green forest and blue lakes. Edging away on the horizon was the ochre-coloured splurge of Moscow itself.

Beside her, Michael was looking thoughtful. Already she had noted how a sudden seriousness would alternate with his more nonchalant manner. She found it appealing. But that didn't influence her immediate resolution, which was to fulfil her role with professional efficiency. Anything less would be unfair to him and might jeopardise her chances of success.

In spite of her knowledge of the Soviet Union and her proficiency in the language, this was her first visit to the country, and Michael had assured her that she was coming to Moscow at the best time of the year. 'It will be green and bursting with blossom,' he had told her. 'Muscovites may be a grey, drab lot, but they're crazy about flowers.'

From the moment a girl in the blue suit of Aeroflot led them from the foot of the aircraft steps to the airport bus, Carol was surprised at the efficiency of the terminal's routine. Border police, wearing green caps, stamped her passport in a small glass booth, customs forms were filled in, porters helped with the luggage, and then, in a surprisingly short time, there was the BBC Volvo with its Russian driver. When she expressed her surprise to Michael, he said, 'It's uncharacteristic.'

In the aircraft he had told her about the apartment, and said that, for the benefit of the bugs, they would have to share the same bedroom, but she needn't worry, there were separate beds. Finally he had warned her that he couldn't even be sure that the Volvo wasn't bugged. Any private conversations would have to be in the open air or in noisy places. In those last minutes of the flight she had struggled to think of any personal words that still had to be spoken. From the moment the aircraft came to a stop on the apron she knew her training had to take over.

They sat hand in hand in the back of the car as it plunged immediately into unspoilt countryside. The impression made upon their driver could be important. Soon they had turned on to the Leningrad Highway, and as they sped towards the city, Michael pointed out to her the major landmarks, from the huge sculpture of anti-tank barriers that marked the place where Hitler's armies were fought to a standstill, to the eighteenth-century Petrovsky Palace and the massive Dynamo stadium. She made the sounds that she imagined appropriate for any new wife on her first visit to the Soviet capital.

In spite of the tree-lined roads and the sudden splashes of flower beds, by the time the car turned in through the archway of Dom 12/24 Sadovaya-Samotechnaya—an arrival duly noted by the militiaman in his sentry-box outside—Carol was already sensing a closed-in oppressive atmosphere. She looked at Michael, gave his hand a slight squeeze. He smiled distractedly. He was wondering how the Russians were going to treat him, whether they were convinced they'd made a mistake, or if they would embark on a series of irritating harassments. Many correspondents had suffered them in the past. What was it Gogol had said? 'No Russian likes to admit before others that he is to blame'? In fact, Michael doubted whether they really thought they were. There was still the mystery of Konstantin Azhimov.

The car drew to a stop in the inner yard. At the far end were the swings of a children's playground. Michael led Carol to the corner entrance of the L-shaped apartment block. It was built, like much of Moscow, of yellowish stone. The driver followed with their luggage. Michael dismissed him and took the lift to the eighth floor. The solid wood door of No. 72 opened on to a small lobby.

'Welcome home,' he said with enforced heartiness. 'I suppose I should really carry you over the threshold, but—'

She laughed, and ran in excitedly, or at least she put on a convincing display of excitement. She made a hasty tour of exploration. By Russian standards the flat was luxurious, with a central hall off the lobby, a spare room alongside, a large living-room facing the side street and also looking on to the ring road, with an adjacent bedroom, and then a kitchen and bathroom. Michael watched her looking round appreciatively.

'It's a cut above most modern blocks,' he said. 'Built by German prisoners of war, and I reckon there were one or two craftsmen among them.' He pointed to the high ceilings with their pleasing mouldings and medallions. Then he hurried into the hall to telephone the Aragvi restaurant at 6 Gorky Street. For their first night he had promised her an expensive meal in what was probably Moscow's most popular restaurant. 'But it'll take a long time,' he warned her.

On their way, however, they stopped at a Metro station, and from one of the hooded public telephones he dialled Alexei Pachenko.

'It's . . . Peter here,' Michael said, speaking Russian. 'Can we all meet for a meal? Yes, Varinka as well. Say, Thursday night—our favourite place?' He almost added, 'I've a surprise for you,' and then checked himself.

'And what did that mean?' asked Carol, as he put down the receiver.

'Well, to begin with, it meant Wednesday and not Thursday. Restaurant dates are always for the day before. And "favourite place" is our code for Baku. It's a splendid place, with small discreet rooms. Of course, tables may be bugged, waiters may make phone calls to get the bugs switched on, but not at our table. Alexei will have fixed the waiter. The restaurant's in Gorky Street, so we'll call in and book. You'll like Alexei, and Varinka is—well, she's quite beautiful, but rather sad looking.'

Carol nodded admiringly. 'Very impressive,' she said. 'I couldn't have done it better myself.'

When they were shown to their table at the Aragvi, Carol

said that she was sure he really came there for the waitresses—hospitable Georgians with dark and lustrous eyes. The meal, as Michael had prophesied, did take a long time, in spite of the fact that they ordered the speciality of the house—chicken *zatsivi*. He insisted, however, on preceding it with some Beluga caviar, served on small pieces of bread. But the delay was not only attributable to the traditionally slow service of Moscow restaurants. There was another reason—a man who, until their arrival, appeared to be eating alone—Wyndham Taylor.

Michael introduced him as the American friend who was frequently more English than the English—thanks to Yale followed by Oxford—but who earned his living as Cultural Attaché at the American Embassy.

As they all sat down again, Michael murmured, 'Wyndham, who most of us call WT, has helped me a great deal in understanding Russia and the Russians. What's more, his books on Dostoevsky and Tolstoy should be compulsory reading for anyone interested in Russian literature. And as if that's not enough, he knows more about the country's music than anyone I've ever met. So be suitably awed in the presence of WT.'

The American, who appeared to be in his late thirties, seemed neither embarrassed by the eulogy nor teased by Michael's humour. He acknowledged it all with a pursing of the lips and an almost imperceptible shaking of the head, at the same time studying Carol through large horn-rimmed glasses. They gave him an owl-like appearance.

'I would have thought,' he said, 'that the mere sight of Carol would have convinced our Russian friends that there was no better reason for hurrying back to Britain.' There was hardly a hint of his American origins, so well had it been overlaid by Oxford English. 'Oh, we've heard all about your exploits on the BBC's Russian service. What *have* you been up to, dear boy?'

Michael gave his own crisp version of what had happened, and ended by asking, 'Do you know anyone called Konstantin Azhimov?'

'Azhimov, Azhimov,' WT repeated, 'can't say that I do,

old boy. But the name's familiar. I wonder why? And what *did* you take to London, you wicked fellow?'

'Nothing,' said Michael. 'But I bumped into a chap called Azhimov—if that's who he really was—just before I left. That's what alerted the KGB, and you know what they're like once they get an idea into their heads.'

WT considered. He looked ascetic and wise, but all he said was, 'You'll have to watch your step, young Mike, won't you?'

The smiling buxom waitress had mixed up their dishes, and Michael had to pass over to WT the chicken *tabaka* he had ordered.

'Ah, you see how easily they make mistakes,' said WT. 'It's almost inherited, you know.'

'Yes, but she's Georgian,' Michael chided.

'True, true—but I think they're no better,' said WT. 'Remember Stalin was a Georgian.'

'We're not talking about mistakes then,' murmured Carol. 'He was obsessive—and a lot more besides.'

'We must be careful,' said WT, 'or we'll be discussing the consequences of the Russian Revolution, and that's really not a fit subject for your first night in Moscow.'

As the American ate the chicken in prune sauce he had ordered, Michael asked, 'Was there any reaction here to the London stories?'

'Not a word.' WT studied him thoughtfully. 'I'm surprised you came back—only for six months.'

'Well, why not? It gives the BBC a chance to line up my successor. And I haven't done anything. I think the Russians know that.'

WT looked at him sceptically.

'Besides,' Carol interrupted, 'I'm looking forward to seeing some Russian icons.'

The American raised an eyebrow above his thick hornrims.

'There are plenty to see,' he said. 'You're interested?'

'I used to deal in them.'

'Really? You must see the Dionissis—lovely, long introverted figures.'

'I know,' said Carol. 'They called him the Ponderer.'

Again WT lifted his eyebrows. Then he said, 'Well, you'll have a feast here, Carol—a veritable feast.'

They chatted on about the sights of Moscow, the American authoritative about the places she must not miss, and periodically digressing into reflections on the Russian character. When they eventually parted, Carol told Michael, 'I like your American friend, but he sounds as though he should have come from an old family in one of the English shires.'

'I think that's why I like him—he's an original.'

By the time they had reached the apartment on Sad-Sam, the long, light evening had turned dusky with twilight. Michael rummaged in the mail box at the entrance. There was only one letter. When they got into the hall, he saw that it was unstamped and had been delivered by hand. So whoever had delivered it must have had a pass, otherwise he wouldn't have got beyond the 'milliman'. He slit open the envelope. Inside was a single sheet of paper. On it was written only, 'Imperative we speak,' followed by a telephone number, and the name 'Konstantin Azhimov'. He passed it to Carol, but held up his finger to indicate silence. She wrinkled her brows, as Michael muttered quietly, 'You or me?'

There was nothing Carol could do until the meal with Pachenko. So she spent much of the next day—Tuesday—wandering about the old city with its grey cobbled squares, its ornately stuccoed buildings, its towers and spires and golden domes. But first there was a meeting with Duschinka, plump and looking like a Russian doll, with a round solemn face that surprised by the brightness of its smile. She was a combination of maid, cook and housekeeper, assigned by the UPDK to look after them.

Introductions over, Michael took Carol across to the BBC office. It was reached through the end entrance of the block, and by taking the lift to the third floor to No. 9. There she met Oleg, the translator, who uncrouched himself from his typewriter and extended his arm for a formal handshake. He asked if she was a journalist too, and Michael replied, 'No, she is just my wife.' Oleg made a polite little sound, as though to say, 'Yes, I know.'

Then she left Michael to read *Pravda* and make his routine calls, although one of them would be far from routine. They had decided that he should call Azhimov from a public telephone. Carol embarked upon her wanderings, which led, as she had determined they would, to the Kremlin, and the three cathedrals—of the Archangel, of the Annunciation, and of the Assumption. They housed some of the most remarkable icons she had ever seen, and afterwards she took one of the chequer-banded taxis to south of the Moscow river to see yet more icons in the Tretyakov Gallery.

Michael was apprehensive about his telephone call. If there was to be a meeting, then he would pull in another correspondent to come with him. But as it happened there wasn't time to arrange one.

The voice at the other end of the line identified itself immediately: 'Azhimov.'

'No names please. But I'm the person to whom you wrote saying, "Imperative we speak".' Michael spoke quietly and, although only shielded by a hood, there was little chance of being heard. He was speaking from the entrance to a Metro station, people bustling along the pavement behind him and Moscow's scattered traffic swishing past.

'Ah,' said the Russian voice. 'You know Brod?'

'No.'

'Colonel Viktor Brod, KGB.'

'What about him?'

The Russian swore. Michael thought he heard a sound in the background.

'Difficult,' Azhimov said. 'You make inquiries.' Then he muttered quickly, 'Stacey Mariner . . . Andrei Rublev,' and rang off.

Michael assumed the man had been interrupted, but how was it he was prepared to talk on the telephone in any event? And what did those names mean? He knew one of them only. Stacey Mariner he'd met on the diplomatic circuit. He was something to do with intelligence at the American Embassy. Could be CIA, Michael supposed. But Colonel Viktor

Brod of the KGB, and Andrei Rublev, meant nothing to him.

He was still pondering the mystery when Carol returned and found him sitting in the living-room of their apartment, scotch in hand, looking abstractedly through the double-glazed window towards the ornate clock of the puppet theatre.

'I've had a marvellous time,' she interrupted him enthusiastically. 'I suppose vodka and tonic is not done in Moscow, is it?'

Michael smiled, and got up to pour her a drink. 'So where've you been?'

'Icon gazing. Mike, they're marvellous. The iconostasis in St Michael the Archangel is a magnificent gold fretwork holding some of the most famous of the icon painters—Ermolayev, Zolotarev, Milyutin. Unbelievable. Then in the Assumption, there are five tiers of them from the eleventh century to the seventeenth, encrusted with precious stones. But I think my favourite was at the Cathedral of the Annunciation. It's not very big. In fact it's the smallest there. Most of the icons are by Theophanes the Greek, but in the third row are the most fabulous works of Andrei Rublev. There's one of St Michael the Archangel which—'

'Who did you say?'

'St Michael—'

'No, no . . .'

'Andrei Rublev? He's fourteenth-century—probably the most famous of the Russian icon masters. Do you know, they still argue about the symbolism of his *The Holy Trinity*? I saw it in the Tretyakov today—marvellous.' Suddenly she halted the spate of her enthusiasm as she noticed how preoccupied Michael had become.

'Rublev,' he repeated. 'How very odd.'

She looked at him, puzzled. 'What is it, Mike?'

'Come on.'

He hurried her out of the apartment and down to the street. They set off briskly, and only when they were strolling more leisurely in the nearby Hermitage Gardens, did he say, 'Rublev was the name Azhimov gave me.'

He told her about the brief conversation, and the way it had suddenly been brought to an end.

'So obviously,' said Carol, 'he was interrupted. He couldn't tell you all he wanted to, and so he just gave you the essentials—the names.'

'Well, I guess I could see Mariner without too much trouble,' Michael mused, 'but Brod is going to be more difficult, probably impossible, and Rublev . . . well, there isn't a hope, is there?'

'Of course, it's just possible he was referring to a living person with the same name.'

'He must be. So the question still is: who the hell is Andrei Rublev?'

'Perhaps he *was* referring to the painter, after all. Perhaps there is a connection between Brod and Mariner and the old master.'

'I think the other is more likely.'

Carol shrugged. 'I suppose so.' But she wasn't convinced.

As they turned to walk back, Michael remarked, 'The Politburo will have met today. Tuesdays and Thursdays.'

'Like British Cabinet meetings.'

'Except you can never find out what happens at the Soviet kind. The trouble is, I don't know if Azhimov is my affair or yours. Somehow he doesn't sound like a dissident. I don't know why. He just doesn't. One of those would have probably set up a meeting by the clock.'

She looked mystified.

'The clock at the puppet theatre,' he said. 'The one where the animals come out on the hour. It's a favourite rendezvous with foreign correspondents. But Azhimov was known to those thugs in London. They thought *he'd* passed the package to me—or at least that's what they suspected. So Azhimov must be a spy. And who's getting at him? Mariner? Brod? Rublev?'

'So perhaps I ought to be speaking to him, Mike.'

'Not yet. Let's see Alexei first. After all, he's your . . . your target.'

*

'The advantage of Baku,' Michael said, as he and Carol entered, 'is that, by Russian standards, the service is prompt. But they don't hurry you—you're made to feel at home.'

The place had an almost oriental atmosphere with brass lamps, walls hung with carpets from Azerbaijan and stained-glass windows. The Pachenkos were already there. The Russian jumped up to greet them, but the wide smile froze when he saw Carol. Varinka stood beside him, taller. Her oval face and large eyes instantly reminded Carol of the gravely beautiful faces of some icons.

Michael saw Pachenko's sudden hesitation, the doubt in his eyes. He said with brimming enthusiasm, 'Alexei, Varinka—my surprise! This lovely girl is my wife. Carol—Alexei—Varinka—Carol.'

Alexei's smile relaxed. He threw wide his chubby arms, as though he was going to embrace them both into his own family. There were embraces all round. The Russian's genuine pleasure at seeing his friend again was clearly accentuated by his relief. 'But why didn't you tell me?' he chided.

'I didn't tell anyone,' Michael said. 'You see, it was a bit of a surprise to me. But when I had to go home so quickly, I thought—well, I'd try again. I'd been asking her long enough. And this time, she said "yes".'

Varinka had been studying Carol's face—the wide forehead, the high cheeks, the widely spaced blue eyes. She said with quiet sincerity, 'You are very lucky, Michael.'

A family atmosphere had been so quickly established that Michael was beginning to wish that it were true. Alexei insisted on *champanskoye*—not really very good, but the Soviet Union's best. They drank to lasting happiness, and Michael saw the teasing laughter in Carol's eyes. He wondered what she was really thinking.

'Ah, ah—all is well, all is so well,' Alexei said happily.

'Yes, yes, all is well,' Michael replied, throwing his arm round Carol's shoulders. He was telling Alexei that the package had been safely delivered, just as the Russian was saying that he was unsuspected.

Alexei chatted on about Moscow in the summer, telling Carol about the places she should visit. How long was

Michael here for? Only another six months? There was so much for her to do. Carol was spooning Baku's *piti* from its clay bowl and then, on Alexei's recommendation, ordered *golubtsy*—a chopped meat and rice dish cooked in grape leaves. 'Baku is famous for its *golubtsy*,' he told her, and then turned excitedly to his wife: 'Where else should we send Carol, eh?'

'I've already been to three of the Kremlin cathedrals,' Carol said. 'The icons are marvellous.'

'You like icons, eh?'

'Carol is really quite an—'

'No, I'm not an expert,' she laughed. 'I just know about them.'

Alexei thought for a moment, but before he had made a decision, Varinka said, 'Viktor collects icons. I'm sure he'd like you to see them.' Was she sure? Varinka wondered, but felt carried away by the atmosphere. Why shouldn't Carol see them?

'Yes,' said Alexei, a little more seriously. 'It's a small collection, but quite good.'

Carol looked at him and thought she saw a momentary doubt in his deep-set eyes.

'Viktor?' Michael queried.

'My brother-in-law,' Alexei answered. 'He's married to Varinka's sister, Nada.'

Michael thought he detected a certain unwillingness in his friend's manner, as though he were wondering about the wisdom of such a visit.

'I'd love to see them if it's possible,' Carol interrupted.

'Yes, yes, of course.' Alexei brightened again. 'I will fix it for you, Carol. He is Colonel Viktor Brod, of the KGB.' He spoke the man's name with a certain tone of disapproval, turning his eyes away from Carol at the same time. So he didn't catch the sudden glance of surprise between Carol and Michael.

'Of course,' said Michael, restoring the light-heartedness of the occasion, 'I didn't marry her because of icons. Don't know anything about them myself. No,' he said, patting Alexei's arm warmly and smiling at Varinka at the same time, 'the only reason I really married her is because she's a damn good fly-fisherman.'

Alexei became animated instantly, and his chubby hand gripped her arm. 'You fish?' he said. 'Wonderful. We must all have a fishing expedition.'

'Oh, she casts a very pretty fly—sheer poetry,' said Michael, confident that Conrad Voss Bark had done his job well.

'I'm longing to see the flies.' Carol affected excitement. 'In England we fish the dry fly a great deal—the Greenwell, the Pheasant Tail—do you have anything like those in Russia?'

Alexei threw up his hands. 'Ah, we don't fish the dry fly much. We spin. So I,' he grinned, 'I am a bit of a rare one. I show you Russian flies. Oh yes, we must have a fishing expedition. This weekend's too early to arrange. The weekend after—yes? At Zavidovo. I have a *dacha* there. Michael you will have no trouble, fixing through the UPDK. They arrange for you.'

'Of course,' Michael replied, maintaining the enthusiasm. 'That will be wonderful.' He raised a glass of wine. 'To next weekend.' Then turning to Carol, he added, 'Varinka does not fish, but she produces the most wonderful picnics.'

A few moments later, Alexei excused himself, and muttering, 'Me too, I think,' Michael followed him to the toilet. Immediately they were away from the table, Alexei said, 'There is nothing new. They argue, two factions.' He smiled grimly. 'Doves and hawks, eh?'

'Is it all right about Brod? I mean . . . someone in the KGB,' Michael asked.

'I wondered at first. I think so. Anyway, it's innocent enough . . . icons.'

Michael whispered, 'Do you know a Konstantin Azhimov?'

Alexei looked surprised. 'Yes.'

'Who is he?'

'What you would call a civil servant.'

'Why should he be trying to contact me?'

Alexei shrugged. 'Be careful, Michael. You should not get involved.'

'On the telephone he mentioned Viktor Brod to me—just his name.'

Alexei looked puzzled, even worried. 'I'm unhappy,' he said. 'He may want to use you. I think you must be very careful, Michael.'

'It can't be anything to do with . . .'

'No.'

'But, Alexei, I was kidnapped in London by Russians. They thought I was carrying a package given me by *Azhimov*. He was seen trying to stop me outside the apartment before I left.'

They'd begun slowly to return to the dining-room. Alexei's eyes seemed to sink even deeper into their sockets. 'This is bad,' he said. 'But they don't know anything. Poor Azhimov . . . I don't know what he thinks he is doing.'

'He mentioned the American, Mariner, too—just his name. And Andrei Rublev. What was he trying to tell me?'

Alexei shrugged. 'I don't know. There are icons by Rublev. I don't know a Rublev.'

'You are looking so solemn, both of you,' said Varinka as they returned to the table. Alexei laughed the mood away, and his wife began telling Carol about their children, Andrei and Novia.

When at last they parted with bear-like embraces from Alexei, darkness was falling at the end of a long June evening. It wasn't cold, and Michael and Carol decided to walk home. It wouldn't take more than half an hour. The traffic was light, the streets emptying.

'They're lovely,' was Carol's verdict on the Pachenkos.

'You know what I meant now when I said he was my friend?'

She nodded, and took his arm. Michael told her about their conversation.

'Rublev must be the old master. That's the connection with Brod—he collects icons.'

'But he wouldn't have a Rublev, would he?'

'No, of course not. There are very few of them surviving. But I've a feeling that the sooner I see Colonel Brod the better.'

'I'll get the fishing expedition fixed through UPDK tomorrow,' said Michael. 'I feel a bit guilty about that. I shan't be coming, of course. This is your chance with Alexei.'

'I know.'

'He was worried—worried about the Azhimov business. God, it's all very well, Carol, but I'm beginning to wonder where reporting ends and bloody spying begins.'

Carol said nothing. She had been less than fair with Michael. They all had, including the Prime Minister. It was inevitable that he should become involved. She didn't see how it could be avoided. Her personal feelings mustn't matter.

He said ruefully, 'Espionage is a story. Perhaps it's a hell of a good story.'

She gave his arm a squeeze. 'We'll try to keep it separate, Mike,' she said.

The next morning he was reminded of how difficult this was going to be. He was in his room in the BBC office making a couple of routine telephone calls when Oleg announced that there were two men to see him—from the KGB.

They were dressed in grey and looked grey, with set, peaked, grey faces. If they remained completely still they might almost have come out of Madame Tussaud's. They looked very strong.

The slightly taller one said, 'Welcome back to Moscow, Mr North.'

'Thank you. What can I do for you?'

'Why have you come back?'

'Why not? I was told I would be welcome—officially.'

'So you are—officially. But we don't like journalists who turn to spying, Mr North.'

'I should think not,' he said casually. 'And you wouldn't be so silly as to suggest that's what I've been up to, because you know very well it isn't.'

The second sentence didn't please either of them. After an uncomfortable silence, the taller one spoke again.

'You were seen with Konstantin Azhimov. What did he give you?'

'That's what your friends in London kept asking me. I

don't know Konstantin Azhimov. It's true I was approached by a man outside my flat, and it looked as though he wanted to speak to me. I wouldn't let him. I hurried past him, and came in here. I don't know who he was. And nothing passed between us. That's where you've made your mistake.'

Their faces remained sternly expressionless.

'Then why did you go to London?' the spokesman asked.

'I had a telex calling me back for a programme.'

'Mr North,' he said icily, 'there was no telex.'

'Have it your own way.'

'And there wasn't any programme broadcast in London either, Mr North.'

'That's true. We recorded it for future use.' Michael smiled. 'I also went home to get married.'

'And does your wife like Moscow, Mr North?'

'She thinks it's lovely. And she adores Russian icons.'

'Oh. It would be a pity, Mr North, if you got your pretty wife into trouble, because of your own . . .' he searched for the word, 'misdeeds.'

'I've no intention of misdoing anything.'

The casual air obviously irritated the KGB man. He snorted, and added, 'I suggest you keep away from Konstantin Azhimov, Mr North. It might be dangerous otherwise.'

'That won't be difficult. I don't know him. Look – I'm fed up with the whole misunderstanding. I've never met him. He never gave me anything. I never took anything to London. And I don't like being roughed-up by your thugs over there because none of you has got the sense to know you've made a mistake.'

He could see their jaw lines tightening.

The spokesman said grimly, 'We don't make mistakes, Mr North. Remember that, please. We hope you enjoy the rest of your assignment in Moscow. And we hope your wife will be very happy here, too.'

They turned stiffly, and went out. At the door, the taller one repeated, 'We don't make mistakes.'

# 8

The trees down each side of Kalinin Prospekt were in full leaf. Summer dresses were beginning to appear among the crowds that jostled on the broad pavements, and a few men were risking shirt sleeves. The concrete and glass apartment blocks, more than twenty storeys high, cast jagged shadows across the pavements and the greensward. It was late on Monday afternoon, and the BBC Volvo, Russian driver at the wheel, was taking Carol for tea with Colonel Viktor Brod of the KGB. A brief note delivered to the BBC apartment on Saturday had given her details of the arrangement. The driver knew precisely where he was going, and after leaving the car by the kerb even accompanied Carol in the lift to the colonel's front door. It was opened by Mrs Brod.

She looked almost the twin of Varinka, but her eyes, large and luminous, seemed sadder. Her manner was hesitant, but her greeting was warm. She led the way into a sumptuously furnished lounge, with thick oriental carpets. She hoped Carol liked Moscow, and would be happy here, and what a coincidence it was that she had met Varinka. Tea was served and then they were joined by her husband. He extended a hand and attempted a smile, but the large rugged face was reluctant. Carol felt dwarfed as much by the massively broad swimmer's shoulders and chest as by his height. The English words tripped and tumbled awkwardly from him as he uttered the usual pleasantries. He gave the impression that they were unpleasant for him, and Carol wondered what it was that had attracted his wife. She remembered the momentary doubt she had seen in Alexei's eyes when the visit was first proposed and how he had looked away from her when, in a somewhat disapproving tone, he told her Brod's name and job. Already she didn't like the colonel, and wondered why Nada did.

'Interesting,' he said to Carol, 'that you should meet my brother-in-law.'

She smiled brightly. 'An advantage of the diplomatic circuit.'

'Of course,' he said without conviction. 'And I am pleased to meet anyone so interested in icons. But Alexei may have exaggerated. My collection is a very small one.'

'You are a very fortunate man, Colonel. I envy you,' she lied, again turning on a dazzling smile. 'I don't think a colonel in the British army would be able to afford to collect Russian icons.'

The man grimaced. 'The Soviet Union has advantages,' he said.

She stared at him unflinchingly with her bright blue eyes, and wondered if he was disliking her as much as she was disliking him.

Nada moved nervously and poured out more tea. Was she really as sad as she looked? Carol stared back at the hard-hewn figure of the colonel. Of course his rank did not necessarily place him in the KGB hierarchy; it might be an army rank, and his status in the KGB could be higher. But high enough to be able to collect Russian icons as well as afford a luxurious life-style?

'What is your interest?' he asked, almost fiercely, as though he were interrogating a prisoner.

'I used to work for Sotheby's,' she said.

'Sotheby's?'

Carol explained, and said that her real expertise was in Impressionist paintings, but she had acquired some experience in icons and, she hoped, some knowledge too. All the time she was speaking she was aware of his grey eyes—the colour of slate—watching, piercing.

At length, he said, 'Come,' and led the way out of the room, through his book-lined study to a small room beyond. Nada remained behind.

The floor was covered with Afghan rugs. There were two upright, nineteenth-century chairs, a small table and an old chest. Ranged in orderly lines on the walls were about fifteen icons.

Carol uttered a slight cooing sound, and went closer to peer at them. She saw immediately that most were not of first-rate quality, or by famous masters, but then she wouldn't expect them to be. Many icons were the work of 'schools', and several of the colonel's were undoubtedly anonymous, but all were quite fine of their kind. She would have loved to possess them herself. Her pleasure was unmistakable, and she could feel his satisfaction behind her.

'My best,' he said, 'is this . . . a Ushakov—genuine.'

For once there was a sort of smile on his face. Simon Ushakov was the last of the great Russian icon painters. It seemed inconceivable that Brod should possess one, but as she peered at the saintly face, roundly modelled with light and shade, she saw that the icon could easily be by Ushakov. She was about to voice her surprise when the door opened. Nada stood there.

'It's the telephone,' she said.

Brod grunted and excused himself. Nada hesitated, and then, seeing Carol bending towards the icon, closed the door and followed her husband.

Carol gave a practised glance at her surroundings. The table had a single drawer. She tried it. It was locked. Briefly she listened at the door, and then moved swiftly towards the chest. Slowly she lifted the lid. There was a diminutive creak. A number of things inside were wrapped in cloth. She undid the folds of the topmost item. It was an icon—apparently of remarkable quality. She stared in disbelief. This was one she could identify, especially after her recent visit to the Kremlin cathedrals and the Tretyakov Gallery. It had all the appearance of a Rublev. If it were not by the master, it was a superb imitation. But how could Brod possibly have acquired it? They weren't to be had. Hurriedly she covered it, and lowered the lid of the chest. When Colonel Brod returned, she was peering at the last icon on the line.

'You like them?' he asked.

'Oh, yes. You are very lucky, Colonel.'

He made a grunting sound of affirmation.

'I didn't think,' she added, innocently, 'that there were private collections in the Soviet Union.'

As he clenched his lips she wondered if he were regretting having allowed her to come. At first she thought he wasn't going to respond.

Ultimately he said, 'There are many misunderstandings about the Soviet Union. Those of us with the most service to the State are well rewarded.'

'I'm so glad to hear it,' she said lightly. Then she added with the same innocence, 'The other day I was looking at the Rublev icons in the Kremlin cathedrals and in the Tretyakov. They are wonderful. I don't suppose you have ever had the chance of acquiring a Rublev, Colonel?'

His face was inscrutable.

'No,' he said. 'That would be impossible, Mrs North.'

She gave a little toss of her head. 'I imagine so. There must be some things not even privilege can buy.' She had kept the sarcasm out of her voice.

'Privilege,' he said seriously, 'is reward. It is earned.'

'Yes, I'm sure,' she replied, with the same insouciance.

She returned to the icons, noting work that especially pleased her, and this aroused in him the nearest thing she had seen to enthusiasm. At any rate, she concluded, he knew something about the icons he collected. The mystery was how he ever acquired them in the first place, and that was not something he was likely to divulge.

Finally she turned to him and said, 'Thank you very much, Colonel. This has been a most interesting and pleasurable visit.'

He gave a slight bow, attempted a smile, and led her back into his study. There he paused.

'Mrs North,' he said, 'is your husband not interested in icons?'

Pretending not to notice the significance of his remark, she said, 'No, he's not the least bit interested. Fly-fishing is his interest. Mind you, I'm not bad at that myself.'

'Mrs North,' he said again, 'we would like you to be very happy in Moscow. But Mr North worries us.'

'Oh, really, why?'

He looked straight at her. She held his gaze steadily, as ingenuously as she could.

'We were surprised,' the colonel answered, 'at his unexpected departure for London.'

'That was to marry me,' she interrupted. 'I gave in at last.'

'Your husband is a fortunate man,' he replied formally. 'But we believed he took something with him, given to him by a Soviet citizen who is a traitor.'

'Oh, I can't believe that,' she said, as though seriously worried. 'Not of Michael. He wouldn't do that.'

'I hope not. It would be very serious.'

'Of course it would, Colonel. I can't understand why you think he should be involved.'

'Because he has been seen with a man called Azhimov. We believe this man has been passing information to the Americans and now to the British.'

'But not to my husband, Colonel. I can assure you he would never get mixed up in anything like that. He is just a reporter, and British reporters are proud of being independent of the government. But you know that, Colonel. Why don't you arrest this man Azhimov?'

'Oh, we shall, Mrs North . . . at the right time.' His huge square face was impassive, the eyes unwavering. 'I am very glad to hear what you say about your husband.'

He led her back to the living-room. She said goodbye to his wife, and left.

When Michael and Carol drove through the gates of the British Embassy that evening, two old women in baggy grey clothes, scarves round their heads, were sweeping the wide pavement with small rush brooms.

'Do women do everything in this city that men don't want to do?' she asked.

'Pretty well.'

The Embassy stands on the south bank of one of the long curves of the Moscow River. It is a fine Venetian-looking building put up in spacious grounds during the nineteenth century by a sugar baron, and its position immediately opposite the Kremlin had proved a periodic source of irritation to the late Josef Stalin.

The occasion of Mr and Mrs North's visit was informal

drinks with the Ambassador and some other members of the embassy staff. The fine weather enabled them to stroll through the immaculately kept gardens, and safely discuss the details of her visit to Colonel Brod and her discovery, in the chest, of an icon that had all the appearance of being the work of Andrei Rublev. The Ambassador was immediately suspicious that anyone—even a high-ranking official of the KGB—should own an original Rublev. All the surviving Rublevs were probably known, and anyway what was it doing wrapped and hidden in a chest? Ultimately it was decided to send a coded telex to the Foreign Office for subsequent transmission to Sotheby's, inquiring about the likelihood of a Rublev coming on to the market, and asking for information about recent icon sales, especially in the United States. The introduction of the 'American dimension', as Michael called it, was Carol's idea. If Azhimov, in referring to Rublev, had been talking about icons, why did he mention Stacey Mariner as well as Brod? What had *he* got to do with it?

The Ambassador was wary. First, he was concerned about the possibility of Michael getting involved; and secondly, he didn't see what Brod, Mariner or icons had got to do with Carol's primary mission—she had sketchily briefed him about this as they stood by the tennis court and the Ambassador complained that Michael always beat him when they played. Carol wasn't sure of the relevance of the icons either. She just felt instinctively that there must be a connection. She, too, was worried about Michael's involvement; she wasn't immune to feelings of guilt, though he had, after all, taken the first step himself when he had carried the microfilm to London. She was surprised at his casual manner. He seemed almost not to care. Unless that was a mask. How well did she know him?

By Wednesday Carol had received a reply from Sotheby's. There had been no large icon sales recently, but a few Russian icons had been dribbling on to the American market, most of them quite good but anonymous works. There had, however, been one by a master but, hardly surprisingly, not a Rublev.

None of these individual sales had been handled by Sotheby's. The old-master icon had been studied by their American expert, and he had been suspicious of its origins. It had nevertheless exceeded its expected price.

So the only significant icon sales had been in the United States. Carol was beginning to feel that she needed to talk to Stacey Mariner . . . or to Azhimov. She tried ringing the number that Michael had been given. There was no reply.

She discussed the situation with Michael that evening as they idled slowly through Alexander Gardens, certainly the most beautiful park in central Moscow, and hard by the Kremlin wall. The lime trees were in yellow leaf, the flower beds ablaze with colour, the evening air heady with scent.

'Why not forget the bloody icons?' Michael said. 'They can't have anything to do with what you want to know.'

'I'm not so sure. If Rublev, Brod, Mariner are an irrelevance, why are the KGB worried about you? They wouldn't care if it was just information about icons, would they?'

They paused under the white bridge that divided the gardens—the bridge over which Napoleon had led his troops towards their fatally brief stay in the Kremlin.

'I suppose we could throw a party—have Mariner to it—or WT,' said Michael. 'That might be better. He might know about the Mariner connection. Or,' he suddenly brightened, 'maybe it *is* a different story. But a good one. I think it's time we had a chat with Bob.'

'Who's he?'

'Robert J. Cresswell. He's the *New York Times* correspondent. Lives next door to us on the eighth floor. We really should have seen him before now. You see, foreign correspondents just have to work together in Moscow.'

Carol was instantly alert. 'I want to know where those icons that have been dribbling on to the American market came from. There can't be that number of American collectors. And let's find out what he knows about Mariner.'

They returned to their car, drove home, and immediately knocked on Cresswell's door. Carol thought he looked too young and almost too handsome. He greeted her enthusiastically, told Michael, in English style, that he was a dark horse, and why hadn't they met before? Come to think of it, why had Michael been in hiding since his return? Or—looking at Carol—perhaps he could understand it. Beneath his bubbling manner, however, he appeared serious enough, especially when, once they were at street level, they told him that they suspected there was a big story of some kind about icons. They didn't mention Azhimov, but Michael said he had been passed a tip naming Mariner and Brod as having something to do with it. Brod collected icons, and Carol explained how she had discovered the hidden Rublev, and how Brod had denied ever having the chance to acquire one. Cresswell promised to get inquiries started in the States, and said he would see what he could dig up on Mariner and any connection—other than an unsavoury professional one—he might have with Brod. Then they returned to Cresswell's flat and he toasted them in Stolichnaya vodka—'By far the best,' he told Carol. 'The stuff is filtered through quartz sand and charcoal made from birch wood. You'll never get a hangover drinking it.'

The next morning Michael immediately phoned Wyndham Taylor and arranged for the three of them to meet for lunch in the main restaurant at the Metropole. It turned out to be an occasion which left Carol puzzled.

WT was waiting for them at the top of the stairs. The whole place reminded Carol of Vicki Baum's *Grand Hotel*, all palm trees, mirrored walls and glittering chandeliers. She half expected to see Greta Garbo drift across the vast space to a secluded table in the corner.

Once they were seated at their own table, she was fascinated to see WT take from his inner pocket what appeared to be a fountain pen and, unobtrusively, run it all round the underside of the table.

'You can't be too careful,' he said seriously.

Michael smiled. He'd seen the trick performed before, and was a little surprised that Carol hadn't been provided with a similar device by the British Embassy. She was looking thoughtful.

Between their Moscow-style borsch and the beef Stroganoff, Michael predicted, there would almost be time to read

*War and Peace*, but at any rate they had plenty of opportunity to talk about what Moscow had to offer in the spring. This led, as naturally as they had hoped it would, to Carol's enthusiasm for the icons she had seen in the city's museums and cathedrals, and then to her innocent question. 'Have you seen Viktor Brod's collection?'

WT considered, looking more like an owl than ever. 'Viktor Brod?' he muttered. 'Name's familiar, but should I know him?'

Carol reflected that his reaction was similar to the response he had made when Michael had asked about Azhimov.

'He's a colonel in the KGB,' she said.

'Indeed. Then I don't know him. Not one of my contacts, you might say. KGB colonels are not usually culture vultures.'

Michael added by way of explanation, 'He's Alexei Pachenko's brother-in-law.'

WT had, to Michael's knowledge, only once met Alexei. It had been an apparently casual encounter in a restaurant rather like the American's first meeting with Carol. At the time Michael had been delighted. WT had been a good friend to him; so had Alexei. What better than that the three of them should know each other? He had even said something jokingly about a happy Anglo-Soviet-American *troika*. But the evening hadn't gone well. Alexei had withdrawn into himself. Michael had felt his own humour was falling flat.

Afterwards Michael attributed Alexei's manner to anxiety—arising from the caution that any Russian, especially a distinguished one, needed to show in contacts with citizens from the West. But he noted that Alexei never mentioned WT to him, and gradually he came to feel that there was no point in trying to get together again.

On this occasion, in response to Michael's information, all WT said was, 'Oh, is he?'

'And he has quite a collection of icons, including a Ushakov,' Carol interspersed brightly.

'Well, you know what it is,' WT murmured airily, 'privilege, my dear. The people might just as well be living under the tsars. Today, they're Communist tsars, that's all.'

The tables were widely spaced, the midday diners, to Carol's practised eye, appeared to be visiting tourists or businessmen, including foreign ones, and a scattering of officials. It wasn't likely that their conversation would be overheard, but it hardly mattered if it was.

'Could you find out anything about Brod, do you think?' Michael asked. It was the question of a journalist.

'Why, is he a story, Michael?'

'He might just be a rather big one.'

'They're all in bribery and corruption, old boy. There's nothing new in that.'

'If that's all it is, then I may not have much of a story, but I think there's more to it than that.'

WT looked somewhat aloof. 'And what is the story?'

'I wish I knew. I'm sniffing. But it's probably got something to do with icons.'

'Michael, old fellow,' said WT exaggeratedly, 'don't go landing yourself in the Russian borsch now.'

'But can you find out anything about Brod?'

'Rather doubt it. Not on my net, you know.'

'But he might be on Stacey Mariner's net,' Michael ventured. 'I've only ever met Mariner at a cocktail party. Tell me about him.'

'Special duties, that's Stacey.'

Carol was about to interrupt but thought better of it. Perhaps it was as well not to arouse even WT's suspicions. She must appear only as Michael's wife, nothing else.

'That means intelligence, I suppose,' said Michael.

WT stroked his pointed chin, and peered through his horn-rims.

'CIA?' Michael added.

'Well, you must know that well enough. I'm sure the Russians do. There are unwritten rules, you know.'

They smiled knowingly at each other.

'And would Mariner know Brod?' Michael asked.

'Ah, that I wouldn't know.'

'But you could find out?'

'You know,' WT mused, 'the Stroganoff might be an old standby, but the Metropole do it quite well.' He paused, and then added, 'Yes, I might be able to—if it's important. But aren't you getting yourself into rather deep water, old boy?'

'I told him,' Carol said ingenuously, 'that even if it all does turn out to be a big story, it's not worth it if it makes the Russians suspicious. I don't want my new husband beaten up again.'

Michael gave her a sidelong glance before crisply asking the American, 'Does Mariner know anything about icons?'

This time the owl-like gaze was distinctly wary. WT arranged his knife and fork meticulously at the side of his empty plate. At length he said, 'I don't know, Mike. Should he?'

'Well, if he did, you would have been bound to talk to him about them, wouldn't you?'

'I suppose I would— yes. Then I guess he doesn't. Mind you, I don't know Stacey that well. Intelligence and culture . . . you know, not a good idea to get them mixed.'

Michael had one more stab. 'Did you remember anything about Azhimov?' he asked.

'I can't say I have. I feel I should know the name, but—no, nothing.'

'Well, I don't know about him either. I just wish the Russians had been convinced.'

Michael prodded away for a few more minutes until he had satisfied himself that either WT didn't know any more, or wasn't prepared to tell him. Then it was Carol who asked about new plays running in Moscow.

'Oh, far better to go to see Tchekov or somebody. The new things are deadly boring. Full of Party ethic and all that kind of thing. Interminable. Although sometimes you'll find something more adventurous at the Taganka or the Sovremennik. They try. But nothing I could recommend at the moment. Why not the Bolshoi? Very traditional, but very spectacular.'

'It's planned,' said Carol.

And so the conversation ran to the end of their meal. After they had parted on Karl Marx Prospekt, Michael asked her, 'What did you make of that?'

'Your friend wasn't being as frank as usual.'

'I don't know.'

'Oh, I do. If he doesn't know Brod, I'm damn sure he knows what he's up to—and his connection with Mariner.' Michael was waving his hand in the air at an approaching chequered cab as Carol added, almost to herself, 'I wonder what cultural attachés at the American Embassy do?'

There was no further development by the time Carol was ready for the two-and-a-quarter-hour drive to Zavidovo where, Michael informed her, Western diplomats, other foreigners, including correspondents, and top Soviet citizens could all be found hunting, shooting, fishing, and generally having a good time. The weather remained fine, and it was already getting much warmer. She was horribly conscious that this was going to be her first essay in fly-fishing without the reassuring figure of Conrad Voss Bark beside her. Nevertheless, as she drove north along the wide Leningrad Highway, she felt reasonably confident. For the journey Michael had provided her with the best map available—one produced by the Americans—and had himself drawn the Zavidovo area in detail, showing her how to reach Pachenko's *dacha*.

This was on rising ground up a narrow track between conifers and birch trees. And there was Varinka, smiling like a madonna, to greet her, with Andrei and Novia beside her. But where was Michael? Alexei threw his arms wide in dismay. Why no Michael? And Carol could see that, for a moment, he was worried. She explained as convincingly as she could that there had been an unexpected story, and London wanted him to make a number of inquiries. Alexei looked unconvinced, but accepted the explanation. The children hugged her warmly, and Alexei brought out a small box of flies—Russian flies—and was explaining their merits to her. Soon they were driving back down the lane towards a fast-running stream. Her immediate impression of the whole area was of rivers and streams with lovely rising banks and wooded slopes, and low hills beyond.

Although she had become proficient at casting, she wasn't altogether sure that she really liked fishing, but this afternoon she was determined to enjoy it. She stood well upstream of

Alexei, but was grateful that, after some forty-five minutes, she had caught nothing, for then she had an excuse to stop fishing and move downstream alongside the Russian. She knew that he also wanted to talk. Varinka was well out of earshot, reading her book on the bank, and the children were flying a kite higher up the slope.

Alexei had admired the easy accuracy of her casting, and he looked up with surprise as she joined him. 'Giving up so soon?' he said.

'They're not taking today. I leave them all to you.' For some time she watched him in silence, and then she said casually, 'Your brother-in-law has a very nice collection of icons. Thank you so much for arranging my visit.'

Alexei made a little gesture with his chunky shoulders.

She added, 'He must be very privileged to acquire such a collection.'

The Russian looked at her solemnly. 'I don't know how he's got them,' he said in a tone that suggested no great affection.

'Could Azhimov have been referring to them when he mentioned Rublev on the phone to Michael?'

Alexei moved uneasily as his line hissed out over the water. 'Has Michael spoken with him again?' he asked anxiously.

'No.'

'I don't know what he meant.' The sentence had a finality about it. Alexei didn't want to discuss Viktor Brod and his icons.

Carol didn't reply. For some moments she watched him silently, listening to the sibilance of his line, a counterpoint to the chuckling sound of the swiftly running stream.

Then, as if the thought had just come to her, she said, 'I know about the stuff Mike took to London. That's another reason—apart from being his wife—that I'm here.'

Alexei stopped in mid-cast, and his line snaked disconsolately on to the water. He reeled in, staring at her—with dark, thoughtful eyes.

She continued, 'Michael is worried in case you are in any danger.'

He shook his head.

'You're safe?'

'I think so.' He turned away and resumed casting.

'They suspect Azhimov?'

He nodded. 'He's been passing stuff to the Americans. That's known. Perhaps to the British. But he would never have access to the material Michael took to London.'

'Then they don't know what it is?'

'Not yet.' Again his line fell back to the stream through lack of attention as he turned to her, and said in a troubled voice, 'Oh, Carol, this has been very hard for me. Michael knows.'

'I know,' she said, so softly that he must have only just heard her above the sound of the water.

Again he reeled in, and looked at her with a sad smile. 'Do you know what it was?'

She returned his gaze, directly and frankly, so that he would know he could trust her.

'Yes,' she said. 'I know—in detail. More than Mike knows. More than he was told.'

Alexei's head barely moved in a nodding acknowledgment. She saw that he understood. She added, 'It's difficult for Mike. He's a reporter. He mustn't get other things mixed with that. For him it's a question of ethics.'

'Yes,' he said. 'That's not something Russian reporters would understand. But I do. And you?'

'Michael knows I have "other" interests. I have my own work to do.'

'Which is?'

'You,' she said.

He still had not resumed fishing, but held his rod skyward as he stood thinking. The dark eyes looked troubled, the face sad.

'It is for them,' he said, jerking his head in the direction of Varinka and the children playing on the bank. 'It is for my own country.'

Carol knew then that there was no possibility of Alexei defecting. He would never leave his family, and it obviously wasn't going to be possible to get them all out at once.

They were both silent for a while, and then, as though he

had been party to her thoughts, he said, 'There is nowhere else I could ever live. But I am worried . . . I am worried, Carol, about what we may be about to do—worried for Andrei, Novia, for the future.' He hadn't resumed his casting, but stood still, made anxious by his own thoughts. 'Russia has always suffered,' he said reflectively. 'Our people are used to suffering as a way of life. Their expectations are limited. They always have been. It's part of the tradition —even of the old Orthodox Church. The life was the life to come, not the life now. That is why we can do things that horrify the West, that threaten your values of personal freedom and liberty. Russia doesn't understand such values. They have not been part of our history. But I am worried about the present, Carol. For their sakes.' He tipped the end of his rod back towards the family group on the bank.

Carol moved closer to him, reached out and touched his arm in a brief gesture of affection and understanding.

He gave her a quick smile of gratitude, and they stood for some moments immersed in their own thoughts, as the stream swirled about their legs.

Then she said, 'Have the Politburo decided what they're going to do—and when?'

'No. As soon as they do, you will know. Then you must go to London at once. By then, only the American president—' He left the sentence unfinished. 'We have,' he continued, 'what you call doves and hawks in the Politburo. Konevsky is the hawk. He is backed by the Head of State Security, Maxim Kharkov. They want to do immediately what had been planned if Britain had not changed its government.'

'Which was?'

'Occupation of the United Kingdom. It had been planned to happen over a few years, as you became more and more separated from the rest of Europe and America reverted to its traditional isolationism. The problem they now face is: can it still be done?'

'And the doves?'

He smiled grimly. 'The Foreign Minister, Yuri Groznov, and the Defence Minister, Nikolai Ogarovich . . . We must continue meeting. Michael and I have already arranged a series of secret meetings—just because of our friendship, nothing else. He will tell you.'

'I know about them,' she said.

He resumed fishing, and she stood silently beside him. After another fifteen minutes, he reeled in his line, and gestured despairingly with his chubby hands. 'You're right,' he said, 'nothing is taking today. There are no fish.'

Carol laughed. It was as much by way of relief as anything else. She decided to risk a further question.

'Are you,' she said, 'very close to your brother-in-law?'

Alexei was packing up his fishing gear. He stopped and looked up, almost startled.

'No,' he said flatly.

'You don't like him, Alexei?'

He nodded. 'I don't trust him.'

'Could he harm you?'

'He could. But he . . . he would have to be very careful he did not harm himself too.'

'Because of your position?'

'Because I have . . . the cards.' He smiled wanly.

As they collected their things together, he said to her, 'Be careful Carol. It is important that you are able to return to London.'

Carol nodded. After a pause she tried again.

'Russian icons have been creeping on to the American market.'

'Oh.'

'Could they have come from here?'

He shrugged, but all he would say was to repeat his warning, 'Do be careful. You have to get back to London.'

They turned away from the stream and made their way up the bank to where Varinka and the children were laying out a picnic on the grass.

Carol drove herself back from Zavidovo on Sunday afternoon, making good time along the almost empty road. As she approached the city limits, however, she immediately reduced her speed to sixty kilometres. She wasn't going to give the authorities an excuse to book her for a motoring offence.

That would be too inconvenient. Suddenly she realised that she was looking forward to getting home, if the bugged apartment in Sad-Sam could really be described in such comforting terms. Perhaps it was Michael she was looking forward to. Then a glance in her rear-view mirror confirmed that two black cars were closely tailing her. She checked her speedometer. Fifty kilometres. But police cars were bright yellow. These were Volgas, used by—Her thoughts broke off, as one of the vehicles drew alongside. She glanced at it to see a square, stern face. The car maintained its position, driving close to her. The other one remained behind. The man in the passenger seat made several short pointing jabs towards the kerb. Then the Volga accelerated and swung sharply across her bows. Carol had to brake hard to avoid a collision. When she stopped at the kerb, she was within six inches of the other car's rear bumper. She glanced up to her mirror. The second car had stopped closely behind her. She was trapped. She remained in the driving seat and checked that the door was locked.

Two grey-suited men got out of the leading car and came and stood alongside. One of them tapped on the side window. Carol gave him a dazzling smile, and lowered the window six inches.

'Did you have a good weekend, Mrs North?'

The speaker was a bit more than average height, with broad shoulders, an almost expressionless face, and short cropped hair. His companion stood by the end of the bonnet.

'Thank you,' she said. 'Except your driving nearly spoilt it for me.'

The man did not smile. He merely inclined his head.

'I hope you're enjoying married life in Moscow, Mrs North?'

'I am, thank you. The old city is lovely.'

Again he inclined his head. 'You're interested in pictures?'

'I've been to most of the galleries by now—yes.'

'I know. But you gave us the slip the other day.'

She smiled, as vivaciously as she could manage. 'I didn't know you were following me,' she said.

'We like to look after you.'

'Soviet citizens are not followed in Britain,' she replied, purposely sounding a little hurt, 'and I don't expect to be followed in the Soviet Union.'

'Perhaps you don't take as much care of your visitors,' the man said, humourlessly.

'I'm sure you mean to be kind.'

He nodded politely, and she thought he had probably taken her seriously.

'Mrs North,' he said, peering into the gap of the window, 'we are only anxious to see that you don't get into any trouble.' He paused. 'Like helping your husband,' he added.

'Oh, I couldn't help him. I don't know the first thing about reporting. I'm just taking advantage of six months in Moscow to be a happy tourist.'

'So we see. That's very good, Mrs North. We want you to enjoy yourself . . .'

'Well, then . . .' Carol prepared to raise the window and end the conversation. The man put out a large hand to restrain her, and bent down again.

'Why didn't your husband go out to Zavidovo with you?' he asked brusquely.

'Because he was working.'

'Doing what, Mrs North?'

'Oh, but surely you know.'

He gave no sign of recognising her sarcasm.

'What was so important he couldn't take the weekend off?'

'Some story he was following up, I believe. I'm sure you must have checked on his inquiries.'

'Yes, we have.'

'Then you know,' she answered brightly.

'We know it wasn't enough to keep him from a weekend in the country.'

'It's a matter of news values, I guess. British ones are different from Russian. I don't always understand them myself,' she laughed.

The man nodded solemnly. He drummed his fingers on the roof of the car. 'It would be a pity,' he said, 'if such a lovely young wife had her marriage spoilt because of her husband getting into trouble.'

She ignored the menace and said, as innocently as she could, 'Oh, there's no chance of that. He's just a correspondent like all the others.'

'Yes, Mrs North, we know,' the man said slowly and portentously. He jerked his head at his companion standing by the bonnet, and the pair of them walked off to their own car. They didn't drive away immediately, but waited a full five minutes, leaving Carol trapped and unable to move between the two Volgas. Then, very slowly, the car in front moved off. Carol checked her mirror, and followed. Both cars stayed with her until she drove past the militiaman, through the archway into the inner yard of the apartment block.

She parked and locked the car, and ran over to the corner entrance. The lift seemed to take an age to reach the eighth floor.

'Michael!' she called, 'Mike!' as she let herself in and rushed through the lobby into the hall. But even as she shouted his name she knew he wasn't there.

She walked slowly into their living-room, on the corner of the block, trying to stifle the cold feeling of fear. There was no sign of him—no clue either there, or in the spare room as to where he could be. Everything looked normal, except . . . he wasn't there. She picked up the phone and dialled the BBC office number. There was no reply. Perhaps he'd gone to the television station. She was on the point of dialling, then checked herself. The call would be monitored. It would arouse KGB suspicions about her own involvement. She cursed quietly to herself. If he was at Ostankino, the television station, then there would be a telex in his office—a copy of his to London, and a copy of the BBC telex to Gostel, booking the circuit. She hurried down again, across the yard to the end entrance, and up to No. 9 on the third floor. She threw open the door of the telex room on the right of the corridor. There was nothing on either machine. She rushed along to Michael's office. There was no copy telex on the clip on his desk. She shuffled through the papers lying there, looking for a sign. There was nothing. Surely he would have left a note somewhere, if . . .

She slumped into the chair behind his desk, and told herself to be calm. This wasn't behaving like a professional at all. Why shouldn't he be out, and why—if it was purely a business arrangement between them—should he leave her a note? She failed to convince herself.

Slowly and thoughtfully she made her way back to the flat. If she phoned the British Embassy that would give everything away. If there was something she should know, they would get in touch with her. And if anything happened to Michael, sooner or later, they would know. Or would they? Again she found it hard to reassure herself. Perhaps he had just gone for a walk—why shouldn't he? She rang the bell of Robert Cresswell's flat next door, but there was no reply. Perhaps they had gone out together. Now, that made sense. Well, it was a possibility, but . . . her recent encounter with the KGB men thrust reasonable explanations from her mind. That kind of cat-and-mouse cruelty was characteristic. They'd probably got him all the time. Suddenly she really did feel guilty at involving Michael in the first place—but, she told herself, there had been no alternative. She tried to read. It was impossible. She put the Brahms piano quintet on the stereo, and after a few minutes took it off again. It seemed only to irritate her. Her watch told her she had been at home for more than an hour. She went to the cabinet to get herself a drink, and then decided against it. She must be sensible, and calm. If she were always going to react like this, then . . . She left the thought unfinished. But where was he? In heaven's name, where was he?

Ten minutes later Carol heard his key in the door. She rushed into the hall to meet him. He had scarcely got through the lobby.

'Oh, thank God you're back,' she breathed, and flung her arms round him, hugging him close to her.

'It's all right,' he said softly, as he ran his fingers through the short, fair waves of her hair, and then drew back sufficiently to be able to kiss her.

There was more than gratitude in her kiss, and she didn't want to let him go. At length he took her hand and led her into the living-room. She collapsed on the settee, and he poured them both a gin and tonic before he joined her. They touched glasses, and for the first time she smiled. Her bright blue eyes were moist. He touched her cheek.

'You must always leave me a note,' she said quietly. 'Where've you been?'

'I went along to *Pravda* to see one of the editors. Just a chat—part of the general background. I find it useful occasionally.' He looked at the woman beside him with unabashed pleasure. Her eyes had lost their anxiety. They were glowing. She smiled, and it was no longer that slightly mocking smile that was so characteristic of her. He put their drinks down. Then taking both her hands, he looked at her. But all he said was, 'Carol,' and then kissed her.

She put on a bright, false tone specially for the listeners concealed in their walls.

'I was stopped on the way home,' she said, 'by some very kind men from the KGB. They just wanted to be sure I was having a good time—enjoying myself in Moscow. I couldn't understand. They seemed to think that I might be helping you, darling. But I explained that I was no journalist. But it was nice of them, wasn't it?'

She saw his brown eyes cloud with concern.

'Oh yes,' he said, 'they're very considerate.'

They raised their glasses, and silently toasted each other. Then she chatted about how she had failed to catch a single trout in the streams at Zavidovo.

That night they shared the same bed for the first time. And before they went to sleep, feeling drowsy, happy and content, Carol broke into a little chuckle.

'Oh, I do hope the bugs enjoyed that as much as we did,' she said.

# 9

By 8.30 the next morning, Michael was in the office checking the overnight tapes. There was nothing of importance, and an hour later he and Carol were idling in a pale and slightly chilly sunlight down Tsvetnoy Boulevard. After about half a mile they turned right into Petrovsky Boulevard, part of the boulevard ring—a series of tree- and shrub-lined parks that encircle the inner city. Only in these surroundings could she give him a detailed account of her conversations with Alexei Pachenko. So much, she thought, for Michael not becoming involved. That was a hypocritical pretence by her London masters. She'd known that from the beginning. It didn't seem to matter much then, but now—well, things were different. She was as committed to Michael as she was to her mission. They walked hand in hand, and she enjoyed his sidelong looks of sheer admiration. There was nothing now that she was not going to tell him.

'You know what it's really about, Mike?' she said. 'Nothing less than the Soviet occupation of Britain.'

'But that's—'

'Impossible? It would have been six years ago. But now? We're out of NATO. We're out of the Common Market. We've got rid of our own nuclear weapons, and we've kicked the Americans out of Britain. What have we got to stop it?'

'We've still got an army, a navy and air force.'

'H'm. The Soviet judgement is that we'll get no help from Europe, and the Americans won't want to know. After all, why should they—the way we've treated them?'

'So, what don't you know?'

'The detailed plan, and the timetable. It hasn't been decided. We've got to get it back to London.'

'We?' he smiled.

'All right, I'm sorry, darling. I.'

'I guess it's we,' he said.

She squeezed his hand. 'I'm certain of one thing,' she added. 'You're right about Alexei. There's no chance of him defecting.'

'I think I'd be worried,' Michael said, 'if I had a brother-in-law high up in the KGB.'

'I'd even be worried if he were an office boy. But Alexei didn't seem too concerned. He said he had the cards.'

'He'll need five aces.'

They turned round, but their conversation was interrupted when they reached the end of the boulevard by Carol suddenly tugging back on Michael's hand. They stopped as they were about to step into Trubnaya Square. He followed her gaze.

There, standing by a building which now houses a government committee but was once the famous Hermitage restaurant, was Wyndham Taylor. But it wasn't the sight of the American that caused Michael's mouth to drop open.

Carol saw his look of astonishment. 'Who's he talking to?' she asked.

'I'd like to know,' he said sharply. 'It looks very like the man who stuffed that scrap of paper into my hand outside the apartment. He's got that same thin, weasel face.'

'Azhimov?'

'Yes—if that *was* Azhimov. I'm sure it's the same man.'

He drew Carol back into the boulevard. After a few moments the two men began slowly to walk along the side of the square. Then they stopped, the thin-faced one turned back, and they parted.

Michael and Carol waited until both were out of sight. Then they walked back to the square and turned left into Tsvetnoy Boulevard, as they made their way slowly homewards.

'Well, I'm damned,' said Michael.

'Either that man's not Azhimov,' said Carol, 'or your friend—'

'Has been lying,' Michael interrupted. 'Why should he . . . why the hell should he?'

'Warning him not to talk to you?' Carol ventured.

'If that's the case, then it means that the icon story—whatever it is—would be damaging to the Americans.'

'That's one possibility. Another is that it would endanger Azhimov himself, and the Americans want to keep him alive for the information he's passing to them.'

'If weasel-face *is* Azhimov?'

'Either way, it looks as though your friend is not being altogether frank.'

Michael was puzzled. He saw no reason why WT should mislead him, unless he had misjudged the man from the beginning. Oh, hell—was this really a story? Or was Carol right, and that somehow it was an inextricable part of her own mission? It was too late to wish he had not got mixed up in it at all. He was committed and, as he looked at Carol, he was glad of it.

They'd almost reached the end of the boulevard where it joined Sad-Sam when, suddenly, as though aware of his thoughts, she said to him with surprising firmness, 'I've made up my mind about one thing, Michael North. When I go back to London, you're coming with me. I'm not leaving you in Moscow.' He gave her a non-committal smile. 'After all,' she continued in a much lighter tone, 'it's not fair on a young wife, is it?'

When they got back the *New York Times* man, Robert Cresswell, was leaning against one of the children's swings at the far end of the yard, waiting for them.

'Hi!' He lifted his arm and beckoned them over. 'Say, I hear you went fishing, Carol. What did you catch?'

'Nothing. But how did you know?'

'Things get around here in Moscow. You can't keep anything secret. Don't you know about the bugs? Ah, it's all right,' he said grinning. 'Oleg told me. But where have the bride and groom been this morning?'

'Having a little marital chat away from the walled ears and the busy Duschinka,' Michael answered. 'There's nothing happening, is there?'

'Not much, but I'm glad you've turned up.' He glanced at

his watch. 'We've got a meeting in half an hour—usual place. Meanwhile, I've found out something about those icons. There've been a few sales in the States, as you said—not named stuff, but good . . . some Moscow school, some Palekh village. Would that mean anything to you, Carol?'

She nodded. 'They would be worth quite a lot if genuine.'

'Yeah, well, there's something odd about those sales.' He gave the swing a gentle push. 'The icons were all bought anonymously.'

'That's not unusual in international art sales,' Carol said.

'Sure, I know. But a reporter can usually find out who the secret purchaser is, or at least get a good idea. But not a single buyer has been found. So what's happened to the icons? No one knows. And they haven't turned up in any public collections—or the well-known private ones.'

'And Brod or Mariner?'

'I'm not likely to get anything on Brod—any more than Michael—am I? But Mariner—he's a smart guy. CIA, I guess. But I haven't nailed a link between Mariner and icons, or Brod. But then I haven't really got into Mariner yet. Give me time. If there's a story there, we'll get it.' He grinned confidently.

Carol looked thoughtful. 'So what have we got? Some very good quality but not top-rate Russian icons come on to the American market. They're sold, although not by the biggest auction houses, and fetch good prices. The buyers are unknown and the icons disappear.'

Michael had been leaning casually against the other stanchion of the swing. He straightened up alertly. 'How did they get to America? Where did they come from?'

'Now that's another funny thing,' said Cresswell. 'According to the guy who's worked on this, they each had a Russian provenance, but pretty thin. Old Russian families—that kind of thing. When he started probing, he got the push off.'

'From whom?' asked Michael.

'FBI, CIA—who knows?' The seat of the swing had idled to a stop, and Cresswell gave it another little push. 'I guess I'm going to see Mariner, and ask him straight out, "What do you know about icons, Stacey boy?" At least his expression will be worth seeing.'

Carol and Michael exchanged glances. They hadn't yet told Cresswell about the mysterious Azhimov, but Carol was already guessing that Azhimov, Brod and Mariner all had something to do with those icons getting on to the American market. And the Rublev she had seen in Brod's chest—well, that was going to be the biggest prize of all. That would explain why Azhimov had mentioned the old master's name. But why was he talking at all? Suppose he was the channel for the icons, and suppose something had happened between him and Brod?

'Penny for them, beautiful?'

She looked up, startled, into Cresswell's boyish face.

'Oh, just thinking, Bob. I was wondering,' she said, 'whose side Mr Mariner was on.'

Cresswell shrugged and made a gesture with his hands that seemed to say, 'Who knows?' Turning to Michael, he said, 'Come on—dissident time.'

The 'usual place' he had referred to earlier was the clock on the puppet theatre just around the corner—a huge fantasy house with twelve windows from which fairytale characters are summoned on the hour by the flapping and crowing of a golden cock. It is a favourite place of assignation between Russian dissidents and Western correspondents. Cresswell had received the call in his apartment a couple of hours ago. A voice had simply given the time and added, 'Usual place.'

As Michael and Cresswell reached the rendezvous, a dissident contact they had met before was walking past the theatre. They fell into step alongside. On two or three previous occasions, he had been the source of information about the treatment of several of the country's leading dissidents, whether they were being held in a psychiatric hospital, a prison, or a labour camp. God knows how he got the information. He invariably had it typed as a statement in English.

The three of them threaded their way through the carelessly strolling Muscovites, and Michael reflected how odd it was that Russians always seemed to be jostling or pushing, even when, as here, there was ample room on the pavement.

'It's about Lukovsky,' said the man.

Pytor Lukovsky was one of the Soviet Union's leading physicists. For some time his outspokenness had been tolerated because of his eminence. But a speech he had made in Hungary had been the last straw. He dealt with the ethical choices facing scientists, and said that morally he could no longer serve the motherland in the way he was being asked. At no point did he reveal what was expected of him, or the nature of his research. But at the same time he smuggled to the West a paper criticising Soviet treatment of a number of prominent dissidents. From the moment he returned to the Soviet Union Lukovsky disappeared.

'We have got a full account of what has happened to him.' The dissident's hand went to his inner pocket. 'You will give it to other Western correspondents?'

'Sure we will,' said Cresswell.

'He's in Gorky,' said the man. 'Not badly treated yet. They're trying to "persuade" him to work.'

'What on?' asked Michael.

'It's in the statement.'

The man handed it to Cresswell. 'I must go,' he added. 'There is no more we can say now.'

They turned into the park by Samotechnaya Place.

'Do you know anyone called Azhimov?' Michael asked. The dissident slackened his pace. 'Konstantin Azhimov?' Michael added.

The man shook his head. 'Not Konstantin,' he said. 'There was an Igor Azhimov a long time ago.'

'One of you?' Michael queried.

'No—not really. Painter.'

'Say,' Cresswell interrupted, 'what's this about an Azhimov guy?'

Michael silenced him with a lifted hand, and asked the dissident, 'What happened to him?'

'It was long before your time in Moscow. He was a popular painter. He painted the right things—socialist realism it was called. Then, in one exhibition, there were two different paintings—abstracts. He was criticised, of course. But he was allowed to go on painting, because most of his work was the right stuff. For his last exhibition, he insisted on leaving the paintings covered until the opening. Then, one after another, he pulled off the coverings. They were all abstracts —decadent Western rubbish, the critics called it. That was the end of him. His union card was taken away. No one bought his paintings. He disappeared. No one knows what happened to him. I heard once that he was in some remote part of Azerbaijan. Why, what have you discovered?'

'Nothing,' said Michael. 'I'd heard his name, that's all. I thought it was Konstantin, but perhaps not. I thought he was a dissident.'

The man shook his head, and then walked quickly away from them. The two correspondents turned about and headed briskly towards Sad-Sam.

'What is all this about Azhimov, Mike?'

'A bloke by that name has been trying to contact me. I'll let you know. Meanwhile, we've got quite a big story.'

'If those engineering sods don't pull the plugs.'

Alexei Mikhailovich Pachenko, like several of the Soviets' top brass, had a luxurious apartment on Kutuzovski Prospekt—a seven-lane boulevard that leads south-east from the Moscow River towards Minsk and the rural homes of many of his leading countrymen. His brother-in-law, Colonel Viktor Brod, felt that his own position really merited the extra accolade of Kutuzovski, but he was not dissatisfied with the extravagance of his own apartment. Besides, he had his collection of icons; and it was hard for a man of his giant stature not to feel superior in the presence of the chunky but much smaller figure of Alexei Mikhailovich. This evening was a family occasion. He was sure it was no more than that. The two sisters enjoyed each other's company. He seldom saw Nada looking livelier than when she was with Varinka. But Brod never felt he had much in common with the more ebullient and yet thoughtful Alexei. Of course, the man always kept a good table and good wine, and there were servants to help, including one who was on Brod's own staff.

For his part, Alexei neither trusted nor liked his brother-in-law. Moreover, he knew that Brod's penchant for the good life owed something to American generosity. Indeed, he knew a good deal more about this than Brod could have suspected, but preferred in Nada's interests to ignore it. He never much enjoyed these occasions, although he indulged them for Varinka's sake.

Tonight there had been a tension beneath the surface all through the meal and the family conversation. He was sure he was not imagining it, and he could see that Viktor also felt it. Several times he noticed the puzzled look in his wife's eyes, and saw it reflected in Nada's expression too.

Towards the end of the evening he and Viktor retired to the study with a bottle of bourbon.

'I know this is your favourite,' said Alexei with a twinkle.

Brod nodded his massive, rugged head. The implication had not escaped him, but he swilled the golden liquid in his glass appreciatively.

'It's one of those things,' Alexei added pointedly, 'that the Americans do well. Although the real connoisseur, Viktor, would go for a Scottish single malt.'

Alexei was deliberately testing the strain. Brod resented the superior tone.

'I know scotch,' he said gruffly.

'Yes, but the single malt, Viktor. That is different altogether.'

'You have some?' said Brod accusingly.

'No, but I can get some.'

'You have your own contacts.' There was the merest hint of menace in the tone.

'It can be bought quite properly,' Alexei said calmly.

Brod only grunted, and took a swig at his bourbon, and then helped himself to a cigar and painstakingly lit it. He blew out a cloud of smoke before he spoke again.

'I'm not sure I should have let that North woman see my collection.'

'But why not? What's the harm in it?'

'Her husband. You know about him?' Then he added pertinently, 'You know him, Alexei.'

'Yes, I know him. I know some other foreign correspondents too. It's useful. Even you would agree, eh?'

Brod made a growling sound that could have been assent or dissent, and rolled the cigar across his mouth. He looked round the book-lined walls suspiciously.

'Oh, it's all right,' Alexei chuckled. 'They're deaf tonight.'

Brod wondered at such confidence, but he often wondered about his brother-in-law and his source of influence and power. He was never quite sure how far he dared go, and for a man of his overpowering strength that was an irritant.

'Kharkov is cross because North wasn't dealt with in London,' he said, and swallowed his bourbon.

Alexei shrugged.

'I may have to deal with him here,' Brod added.

'What for?' The little Russian held his chubby hands together and stared directly at his brother-in-law.

'You know he took something to London? It was important. Vital.'

'I know you all think he took something.'

'He was seen receiving it.'

'What, from Azhimov?'

Brod raised his thick eyebrows in surprise. He was unsure how much Alexei knew, not only about this, but about his own involvement. But he couldn't know about the icons—how could he? Slowly he nodded his head.

'Do you know what it was supposed to be?' Alexei asked.

The colonel didn't exactly. That was something else that angered him. And he was annoyed that he couldn't bluff in front of Alexei.

'Not precisely. But it was something vital from the Politburo itself.'

'Would Azhimov have access to that?' Alexei looked at the KGB man shrewdly. There was almost mischief in his dark eyes. He was probing the limit of Brod's knowledge.

'You tell me,' Brod grunted.

Alexei pursed his lips and made a little gesture of doubt with his hands. 'Perhaps. Perhaps not,' he said. 'Depends how clever he is. A really clever man can find out anything—even in the Soviet Union, Viktor.' His gaze didn't leave the colonel's face. Now he took a bigger risk: 'Is he still talking to the Americans?' he said.

Brod was startled. His slate-grey eyes squinted, trying to hide his surprise. How much more did Alexei know? He grunted affirmatively.

'I suppose he serves his purpose?' Alexei added.

'He'd be stopped if he didn't,' Brod said brusquely.

'But he has his other uses?'

Brod shifted his huge bulk uneasily and poured himself another glass of bourbon. He stubbed out the cigar, half smoked. He was disadvantaged, and that was not a feeling he enjoyed. He decided to attack. 'What do you mean, Alexei?'

The Russian shrugged. 'He must have some use,' he said, 'or else he's passing the Americans stuff that doesn't matter. You wouldn't let him do it otherwise—would you?'

It looked as though Alexei was smiling. Brod took an angry draught of his bourbon.

'He's my concern,' he said with finality. 'I know how to deal with him.'

'Oh, I've no doubt, Viktor. But . . .' He left the sentence unfinished.

'But what?'

'Don't get the wrong man, will you?'

'You know what Kharkov said?' Brod responded belligerently. 'He said there was a limit to what Azhimov could discover. There might be another source, he said.'

Alexei was unperturbed. 'Well, if there is, you will know it, brother.'

'That's what I told Kharkov. "I shall know it," I said.' Brod banged his fist on the nearby table.

Alexei thought what an ugly and unpleasant man he was. He had never understood why Nada had married him. Nevertheless, he replied gently, 'I'm sure you will, brother.'

The self-assurance, the superiority, the simulated affection, all irritated Brod. Moreover he was beginning to feel the effects of the night's drinking. He got up from his chair, glass in his hand, towering over the figure of his brother-in-law. Words spilled out of him in hoarse anger.

'Get the wrong man? I won't get the wrong mother-fucking

man, brother. But you—don't you be so concerned about your Mr fucking North. Ah . . . that's something he might not be doing much longer—fucking that pretty wife of his. Ho!' He broke into a drunken laugh, pausing only to swill down another glass of bourbon, and then spluttered as it burned in his throat.

Alexei leaned against the bookshelves, watching. For some moments the great figure in front of him didn't stop laughing. It was as though the man were watching some bawdy pageantry of his own thoughts. Alexei felt an involuntary shudder, but it was more of disgust than anything else. He had no reason to feel intimidated, either by the man's strength or his influence. He waited until the laughter had subsided. Then he spoke quietly.

'Kharkov says many things. He's a man with ambition.'

Brod nodded his head vigorously. 'Don't we all know it?'

'He was saying the other day,' Alexei continued, 'that he wants a clean-out among the top ranks of the KGB.'

Brod swung round to face his brother-in-law. His grey eyes had lost their menace; they were looking watery.

'He was saying . . . he was saying,' Brod repeated drunkenly, 'what was he fucking saying? A clean-out, was he? A clean-out . . . that's what he wants . . .' He stopped and stared at his empty glass as the significance of what Alexei had said at last penetrated the alcoholic blur. He shook his head. His brain momentarily cleared.

'What did he mean? Alexei, what did he mean?'

'What does Kharkov ever mean?'

Brod thumped the table. His empty glass jumped and rattled. But whatever he was going to say was stopped by the door opening. Nada stood there, her face for once relaxed, almost happy.

'Viktor,' she said, 'it's very late. We really should be going. Whatever you two have been talking about must have been very amusing—judging by your laughter.'

Brod nodded and ambled to his wife. 'Time to go,' he said, hardly appearing to know what he was saying.

Varinka was standing behind her sister. Alexei saw her despair as her glance took in Brod's drunken condition.

Perhaps she heard, perhaps Nada heard, but Alexei spoke too quietly for Brod to hear.

'There's nowhere to go,' he said. 'No way out of it—that is the tragedy. No exit.'

# 10

The Prime Minister stood alone, leaning against the marble mantelpiece in the Cabinet room at No. 10 Downing Street. He stroked his jaw thoughtfully, wondering about the Soviet Union's intentions, and if, without the nuclear threat, war could be avoided. Above the mantel hung the only picture in that long panelled room—the portrait of his first predecessor, Robert Walpole. From his day to the present a succession of prime ministers had, often in this room, taken the decisions that had shaped the destiny of the country. In the last five years they had been decisions which had steadily isolated Britain from the rest of the Western world. Lionel Bryce was determined, in the next five years, to reverse the process. Today he seriously wondered if he was going to have that opportunity. That was why he had summoned an emergency meeting of the Cabinet.

Until this moment, apart from the Security Service, only the Foreign Secretary, the Home Secretary and the Secretary of State for Defence had shared with him the information that Michael North had brought back from Moscow. The intervening period had been used to make a number of surreptitious preparations. Surveillance of Soviet government staff working in Britain had been intensified. There were a half-dozen men against whom enough was known to order them to leave the United Kingdom. Maintenance work on all defence installations, and especially on military aircraft, had been stepped up. A complete assessment had been made of food and fuel stocks in the country. Naval vessels had either returned or were on their way back to home waters. Leave in the armed forces had not been officially cancelled, but those men due for leave found that, for some not wholly convincing reason, they were unable to take it at present.

The Prime Minister had a complete picture of the state of the country's military preparedness. Now the time had come to take the whole Cabinet into his confidence. Already he, with the Foreign, Home and Defence Secretaries, had agreed on certain measures that would need full Cabinet approval. No papers, however, had been circulated, and there was no agenda, but tucked in each of the red-leather folders that bore the words 'Cabinet Room—1st Lord' was a fact sheet, dealing with the strength of the three services, the disposition of units, their military readiness, and the stocks of food, fuel and other essential goods and services.

Earlier that morning the Prime Minister had seen the MI6 chief, Sir Dick Randle, and had learned that no further report had been received from Moscow, and could not be expected until the complete information the Government wanted was available. Any attempt at communication in the meantime would only arouse suspicion.

Without looking out of the tall windows that gave on to the garden, with Horse Guards Parade beyond, Mr Bryce sensed that it was a grey day. The Cabinet Secretary came in, they exchanged a few words and the Prime Minister took his seat at the centre of the table, the portrait of Walpole behind him. He looked grave, and felt it, as he nodded to his colleagues as they came in and went straight to their traditional seats. He gave a special tilt to his chin in the direction of the tall, athletic figure of Sir Kenneth Propter, the Foreign Secretary, as though to imply, 'This is it.' Sir Kenneth smiled faintly.

The Cabinet Secretary went over to the double doors leading to the ante-room, and beckoned in the Chief of the Defence Staff, and the three Service chiefs. The other members of the Cabinet exchanged questioning looks, and withdrew from their boxes red folders of Cabinet papers. As they settled down, the Prime Minister waved a dismissive hand. 'You won't want those,' he said. He stroked back his thatch of grey hair, and sat waiting for his colleagues' attention.

With something of his old sense of the dramatic, the flair that had made him popular with the party, he said, 'I have called this emergency meeting because we may have to face war with the Soviet Union.'

Only the stern set of his features told his colleagues that he was not being dramatic for the sake of drama. Slowly and deliberately he explained that information had recently come into the Government's possession which proved that, had the previous government remained in power, the Soviet Union had determined on the eventual occupation of the United Kingdom.

'With the change of government,' he said, 'the Soviets take the view that, unless they are to lose the chance of adding Britain to the Eastern bloc, they will have to speed up their plans. Soviet naval vessels are already in the North Sea; others are being readied in the Baltic. Military aircraft are massing in East Germany. Russian intelligence has concluded that Britain cannot look either to Europe or the United States for help. That is also the view of our own intelligence services. We are on our own.'

The Prime Minister paused. He looked up, noticing how the light from the windows caught the brass pendant spheres of the great chandeliers. He sensed that someone was about to interrupt the tense silence, and so he went on quickly.

'We have a little time. How much I don't know. Perhaps a few weeks; perhaps a few days. But the final decisions have not yet been taken. The Politburo have yet to decide on a timetable for their plans. As soon as they have, we shall know, and we shall have the full details.'

He leant forward, 'We have to use that time to prepare for the defence of these islands. Of course, it is for the Cabinet to decide, but my own view is that we should not take the public into our confidence yet. There is much to be said for fast, secret preparation, and when we know a little more—that will be the time to tell the people. There are, of course, certain decisions we shall take, about which the House must be told.'

There was a slow nodding of heads round the table. Someone leaned forward and poured some water from a cut-glass carafe into his tumbler. The sound was a momentarily deafening cascade in the heavy silence of the room.

The Prime Minister explained that he expected the Soviet Union's first move would be a series of demands upon the British Government which, needless to say, would be totally unacceptable. Britain's rejection would be the excuse for Soviet action.

His colleagues were too stunned for many questions, and the Cabinet quickly moved to a consideration of action to be taken. The chiefs of staff were asked to assess likely invasion points and to prepare detailed defensive plans. An emergency committee would meet immediately under the Home Secretary to plan for the rationed distribution of food and the provision of essential services. Plans would be made to place factories on a war footing. The cancellation of all leave would be announced, and troops would be moved into defensive positions. For the time being these would be described as military exercises. In all departments of government plans would be laid to place the nation on a war footing immediately Soviet intentions were known.

The Prime Minister adjourned the meeting at one o'clock. It had been decided that he, rather than the Defence Secretary, would make a statement to the Commons that afternoon about certain essential decisions that had been made. The emergency meeting of the Cabinet would resume at five o'clock.

Those MPs who had not heard the radio during lunch time, or looked at the news agency tape machines in the library corridor of the House of Commons, learned that the Prime Minster was going to make a statement that afternoon from the notice held in a brass clasp on a stone portal in the Members' lobby. But Prime Ministerial statements early in the life of a new government were not unusual, and no one expected that today's would be overwhelmingly important. Nevertheless the chamber always filled for a statement from the Prime Minister, and today was no exception. By the time the clocks, set in the carved oak galleries at either end of the chamber, jerked to 3.30, the green leather benches were full. A group of members stood beyond the bar of the House, just in front of the swing doors that led to the Members' lobby.

The press gallery above the Speaker's canopied chair was full. But there was really no sense of occasion.

It was about another couple of minutes before the bewigged Speaker called, 'The Prime Minister', and the tall figure of Lionel Bryce rose and stood before the despatch box. He stretched out his arms, gripped each side of the brass-encrusted box, and looked aggressively in the direction of the Leader of the Opposition, sitting on the front bench on the opposite side of the table that divided them.

Although the Labour leader, Tom Henson, was also in his fifties, he still managed to look, with his flushed fresh face, something of an angry young man. This afternoon it looked as though he could scarcely contain his anger and indignation. He sat on the edge of his seat, clutching a copy of the Prime Minister's statement which, by customary courtesy, he had been handed in advance.

The Prime Minister began by apologising to the right honourable gentleman that it had been impossible to let him have a sight of the statement more than a few minutes previously.

Bryce had always enjoyed the House, and he still did, even on such a grave occasion as this. Moreover, he had the satisfaction of knowing that he had a very comfortable majority, and that Henson, having had five years of supremacy, now led, from the extreme left, a party that was once again seriously riven between right and left.

'As the House will be aware,' the Prime Minister continued, 'the present government was elected on—among other things—a commitment to restore the defences of this country to something like their former strength and again to seek alliances with Western Europe and the United States of America. This will be an immediate priority.'

There was a mumbling of 'Hear hears' from the benches behind him. MPs on the other side of the House fidgeted restively.

'The previous government,' he went on, 'has deprived this country of its most effective deterrent—the submarine-based nuclear weapon.' There were shouts of protest from the hard knot of Labour left-wingers sitting below their gangway on the opposite side of the House. Bryce gave them a contemptuous glance and then ignored them. With what some newspaper columnist was bound to describe as leading with his chin, he thrust out his jaw and lifted his voice above the interruptions to declare, 'This government is taking immediate steps to restore our nuclear capability.'

There were shouts of, 'Warmonger . . . shame,' and even, 'killer', to which the Speaker deliberately turned a deaf ear. This was no moment to interrupt a Prime Ministerial statement. Bryce waited for the interruptions to die down, and then he said, 'Work is to begin immediately on our Polaris submarines to convert them again to carry a nuclear weapon. The American Trident missile, which the previous government cancelled, is to be reordered immediately.'

The Leader of the Opposition was fighting to remain calm, his right hand screwing his copy of the Prime Minister's statement into a ball. His supporters, however, had erupted into noisy abuse. Several times the Speaker had to call for order. The Prime Minister sat down, waiting for the noise to subside. Labour backbenchers instantly jumped to their feet, only to be ignored by the Speaker, who again shouted for order. Lionel Bryce rose once more. If only the coming weeks were going to be as easy as this.

'Of course,' the Prime Minister continued, 'there are right honourable and honourable Members opposite who would be content for this country to abandon all its defences.' He shouted against the uproar, 'They are too blind to see the possibility of a threat from any direction, and least of all from their erstwhile friends in the Soviet Union. But, I must tell—'

He got no further. The Speaker was shouting, 'Order! Order!' Left-wingers were baying abuse; others were crying, 'Point of order, Mr Speaker.' The Speaker ignored them as, patiently, he sought to restore some sense of decorum to the House. At last the Prime Minister was able to continue.

'In the light of the government decision to begin immediately to convert the Polaris submarines to take the Trident missile, my right honourable friend, the Foreign Secretary, has already left for the United States for talks with the American Secretary of State.' (The Russians should understand what that meant.) 'I shall keep the House fully informed, Mr Speaker.'

He sat down to cheers from his own side and angry shouts from Opposition backbenchers. It was some minutes before the lean figure of Tom Henson was able to stand at the despatch box.

'Is the right honourable gentleman aware,' he began, 'that his . . .' he paused to search for the word, 'his frightening words this afternoon will be read with dismay by peace-loving people everywhere?' His supporters yelled loud 'Hear, hears'. 'Is he further aware,' he continued, 'that he sees threats where no threats exist? He and his right honourable friends told us that if we got rid of the so-called nuclear deterrent, the country would be victim to any aggressor. What aggressor?' The cheers behind him rose to a crescendo, and he managed a thin smile at his supporters. 'The only danger to this country,' he shouted, 'is from the right honourable gentleman and his war-mongering friends.'

Jeers and counter-jeers broke out. The Speaker let them ride for half a minute, and then he rose and called, 'Order! Order!' It had little immediate effect. The Prime Minister sat stolidly ignoring it all. He was not prepared to be drawn into a slanging match; the issues were too serious. Anyway, he felt little short of contempt for the Leader of the Opposition.

At length Tom Henson spoke again, wringing the words out angrily. 'Can the Prime Minister confirm,' he said, 'that all Service leave has been cancelled?'

The Prime Minister jumped up and sat down just as quickly, because all he said was, 'Yes.'

Opposition backbenchers cried, 'Why? . . . Why?' until ultimately Tom Henson was able to ask, 'Can the Prime Minister say why?'

'Yes. Because all three Services are to take part in important military exercises.'

Again anger erupted along the Opposition backbenches. For a few moments the Prime Minister wondered whether, after all, he should tell the House what he had told the Cabinet that morning, but ultimately decided it was best left for another occasion. He could see Henson screwing himself up with anger, and responded with a gentle smile.

Some of his own backbenchers rose to support the action he had announced, and Labour left-wingers condemned it furiously. It was half-past four before the Speaker moved MPs on to the business of the day.

A calm, unruffled and determined Lionel Bryce walked briskly to the Prime Minister's room in the House to deal with some routine matters before returning to No. 10 for the adjourned Cabinet meeting. At the same time a fidgety Tom Henson was calling a meeting of the Shadow Cabinet and reluctantly coming to terms with the realisation that there was very little or nothing that the Opposition could do.

In Fleet Street the front page of the last edition of London's only evening paper was being hurriedly changed to carry the headlines:

BRITAIN TO BUY TRIDENT
FORCES LEAVE SCRAPPED.

# 11

Summer had come to Moscow. Even the crispness had gone from the air. The trees were in leaf in the boulevards and parks, and the stalls round the Metro stations burgeoned with flowers. Duschinka had commented enviously on the bright summery dresses in Carol's wardrobe and held them hopelessly against her roly-poly figure. 'I'll send you something nice when we go back to England,' Carol had told her. Outside, Moscow girls had put on cotton frocks, in the colours and fashions of the West a decade earlier, and men had discarded their jackets. The customary greyness receded before a wave of faded colour.

Carol and Michael strolled, hand in hand, like tourists over the cobbles of Red Square. Snaking about a third of the way across was a queue of people shuffling slowly towards the great red granite and black porphyry slabs of Lenin's mausoleum. Carol, in her fashionable clothes, was conspicuous as a visitor from the West. They idled slowly from the magnificent extravagance of the domes and towers of St Basil's Cathedral over to the Kremlin itself. It was surrounded by a wall of red brick, castellated in a series of gapped V-shaped teeth. The walls, still on a line laid down in the fifteenth century, enclosed about seventy acres sloping from the top of the hill down to the Moscow River, and comprised a small city of cathedrals and palaces, churches and chapels, towers and cloisters, theatres, museums and state buildings. It was where Moscow began. They were neither of them, however, much aware of their surroundings, except for the two distant figures, unseasonably wearing long grey coats, that were assiduously following them. Carol and Michael had been too busy talking quietly about themselves, about the relationship between them, and the paradox represented by their developing affection for each other, Carol's mission, and Michael's work.

They talked, too, about what they had come to call 'the affair of the icons' and Carol's conviction that it was somehow part of the bigger design with which she was concerned. Michael was more doubtful. If Brod, Mariner and Azhimov were mixed up with the icons—genuine or fake—that found their way on to the American market, then it seemed like a good story, if only they could get to the bottom of it, but he couldn't see how it could be remotely connected with the information that was coming from Pachenko.

They had reached the tree-lined walk at the base of the Kremlin wall, the burial place of a number of Communist heroes. The young green leaves filtered the sunlight into a jig-saw pattern. They were looking at each other. Michael was thinking how lovely she was, and found himself staring at the way the breeze lifted the blonde waves of her hair. In spite of the danger he was happy. It was then that the man came up to them.

'Mr North?' he asked, although it was more like a statement than a question.

Michael nodded automatically.

'This is for you,' the man said, and handed Michael an envelope. He walked off quickly in the opposite direction.

Instinctively. Carol looked behind. In the distance were the two grey-coated men.

'Do you know him?' Carol asked.

'No.'

'Was he the same man who approached you on Sad-Sam?'

'No. You've seen the weasel yourself.'

'We'd better have a look at it,' she said practically.

They turned about and walked towards the Spassky gate, the entrance to the Kremlin. Michael led the way briskly along the footpath sloping towards Cathedral Square. They turned beneath the domes of St Michael the Archangel, sat on the first available seats inside, and Michael hastily slit open the envelope.

Carol glanced quickly and professionally in all directions.

The cathedral glowed dimly with colour—the murals of battle scenes and old princes, the tombs of tsars, and the gold fretwork of the iconostasis. But she was noting only the other figures in the building, and satisfying herself that they were tourists. Then she looked down at the sheet of paper Michael unfolded. On it, in Russian, was typed: 'Meet me 1500 hours tomorrow, Sokolniki Park. I can explain what you want to know. I shall be sitting on park seat indicated. You will say, "It's lovely June weather". I shall reply, "It is better in July".' The message was signed, 'Konstantin Azhimov'.

On a second sheet of paper was a meticulously drawn map. From a circular hub near the entrance to the park, a number of avenues led outwards like the spokes of a wheel. From one of these, on the map, had been drawn a route to what was evidently a secluded birch grove, and the position of the seat was marked.

Carol uttered a low chuckle. 'How the Russians love codes,' she said. 'They always have.'

'So Mr Azhimov is thoroughly indoctrinated?'

'If that is from Azhimov.'

Michael furrowed his brow as he stuffed the sheets of paper and envelope into his pocket.

'Well,' Carol continued, 'how did he know he could find us in Red Square?'

'He followed us.'

'It was a different man.'

'So what? Which one was Azhimov? But whoever he is, he wants to talk. He's the only person who's likely to tell us about the icons, and Brod, and Mariner.'

'H'm,' Carol mused. 'I think your friend WT could tell us, but he doesn't want to.'

They got up and left the cathedral. Outside it seemed unnaturally bright. They walked slowly about the Kremlin paths for the next half-hour, discussing Azhimov's note. Carol was anxious lest it was a deliberate attempt to set Michael up, but he didn't think so. Azhimov had clearly been trying to get in touch with him. All right, he'd been discovered in this by the KGB. It didn't alter the fact that he had still tried. How else explain the telephone conversation that he had had to cut short? There was no reason to assume that this wasn't his follow-up. He would have known that his earlier cryptic conversation had set them wondering. Now he was offering to explain what they wanted to know.

'And we've been tailed all morning by those two grey-coated zombies,' Carol said.

'So they saw the contact,' Michael replied. 'They can't know what's in the note.'

Carol was still anxious. 'There's nothing the KGB can't know.'

'Oh, come—be rational, Carol. Besides, do we want to know about the bloody icons or don't we?'

She flashed him an affectionate smile. 'Of course we do—but that's my concern.'

'The note was given to me,' said Michael tersely. 'And if it's just another story then that's my concern, and Cresswell's.'

He grinned triumphantly, but Carol didn't share his light-heartedness.

'I could keep the appointment,' she said.

'Like hell you could.' He took her arm as he turned to look at her. 'There's no way that makes sense, Mrs North. You must not get involved, except with Alexei. He's your source, and we mustn't do anything to endanger that. So we can't have you getting mixed up in reporters' stories about an icon scandal, can we?' His whole tone had suddenly become casual again, and he gave her an exultant look, as though to imply, 'Well, that's settled'.

Since the night she returned from Zavidovo, Carol had found it increasingly hard to take a rational view of her own mission, or to divorce it from the growing importance of her relationship with Michael. If a choice had to be made she was no longer certain that she would make the right one. It was complicated by the fact that Michael had now abandoned his neutrality, and was as much involved as she was.

They emerged into Red Square, the sprawling mass of the GUM store opposite. The queue of people still shuffling towards Lenin's tomb included two or three couples in their bridal dresses. As they crossed the cobbles, Carol looked back to see the two grey coats coming out of the Spassky Gate.

'All right,' she said, suddenly decisive. 'Keep the appointment. I shall tail you . . . just to make sure everything's all right.'

He patted her arm. 'You fill me with confidence.'

She saw the teasing laughter in his eyes, and could have wished they were anywhere other than Moscow.

'I'll deal with you back in London.'

'It'll be a pleasure,' he said, as he propelled her briskly towards the red hulk of the History Museum.

There are more than fifteen hundred acres of Sokolniki Park, and even after the roundabouts and the other amusements of a fairground, a dance hall and a skating rink have been fitted in, there are still many acres that have not changed much in the few hundred years since tsars flew their falcons there and hunted hares and foxes.

Michael and Carol had taken the Metro red line to Sokolniki station, and there they parted. Once he was in the park, and had passed the amusement area on the left, it was easy, with the help of the sketch map, for him to identify the pathway. It led off to the seclusion of birch groves, shimmering in their new leaves. He threaded his way between the trees, and there, remote at the end of a short ride, exactly as marked, was the seat. Michael hurried forward. Sitting very upright in the left corner was a little man with a weasel face. Michael sat himself about a foot away from him.

'It's lovely June weather,' he said.

There was no reply, and the man didn't even look at him. Michael repeated the phrase in his best Russian. Still no answer. Oh, to hell with code words.

'North, Michael North,' he said quickly. 'Comrade Azhimov? Konstantin Azhimov?' He paused, and added again, impatiently, 'It's lovely June weather.'

The man said nothing. He merely sat there. Michael put out a hand to touch his arm. As he gripped the coarse material of the jacket, the man fell forward. The knife was still lodged to the hilt between his shoulder blades, blood seeping out through his clothes. The body fell over on to the ground.

For a moment, Michael stared in horror. He was unable to move, unable to think. Then he jumped up, immediately alert. He looked around, and started to run back along the path. As he did so, men came out of the trees. Others were running along the path towards him. He turned, to head back into the forest, and almost immediately was on his face on the ground. He hadn't seen the figures that had sped from the trees beside him or the foot that was thrust in front of him as he began to run. He felt a knee in the small of his back, and two men roughly jerked his arms behind him and snapped on a pair of handcuffs. He was then pulled to his feet.

As he stood there, gasping to get his breath, Michael noticed that all but one of the fifteen to twenty men were in plain clothes—the drab garments of the KGB. The single exception wore the uniform of a major. It was this man, with a rubicund, complaisant face and hard blue eyes, who ordered Michael back along the path. When they reached the body, he barked an order to one of the men. The fellow bent down, rolled the dead man over, and began to go through his pockets. Within seconds he had pulled out the internal passport that all Russians carry. He announced, 'Konstantin Andreivich Azhimov.'

The major came and stood within a foot of Michael's face. The man's aftershave was obviously a cheap Western import. Michael found it faintly sickening. All he thought to himself was: So Carol's fears were justified. It *was* a set-up. Then he was immediately anxious for her. My God, if they'd picked her up as well!

The major wagged the passport in Michael's face. 'So why did you kill Comrade Konstantin Andreivich Azhimov, Mr North?'

Michael ignored the question. 'How did you know my name is North?' he asked.

The major smiled, and Michael reflected that the man looked, incongruously, more like a farmer. It was only the eyes that belied the joviality.

'It is my job to know such things,' he said. Then turning to his underlings, he snapped, 'Get that body away. And you, Mr North, had better come with us.'

Michael acknowledged the remark with a smile that wasn't as convincing as he would have liked it to be.

'If a crime has been committed, and it looks as though it has,' he said, 'shouldn't you be calling the police?'

The major burst into a laugh like a car back-firing.

'Some murders are for the police, Mr North. Others are too important for them.'

'This,' said Michael, affecting as insouciant an air as he could manage, 'is an important one, is it?'

'You should know. You killed him.'

They had begun bustling him along to the nearest of the main avenues that led from the entrance of the park out to the circumference. There, in a line, were the inevitable black Volgas. He prayed he wouldn't see Carol sitting in one of them. If they had got her, that's where she would be, and they'd make sure that he saw her. As they approached he looked frantically along the row of vehicles. There was no sign of her.

The major pushed Michael into the back of one of the cars and got in beside him. 'You have been a very foolish man,' he said.

The Volga moved off, and Michael knew they were heading for Dzerzhinsky Square.

Carol had committed the Azhimov sketch-map to memory, and had been careful on entering the park to make sure that she was not being followed. She had got within view of the seat in the birch grove just as Michael was about to sit down. It was then she had seen other figures moving in a circle between the trees. Her instant reaction had been to cry out to warn him. But even with the intake of breath before her shout, she stopped. That was no good. If he was surrounded it wasn't going to help him and, if she hadn't been seen, it was only going to give herself away. She drew back into the trees, and lowered herself to the ground, taking care to make sure there was no sound of cracking twigs. She believed all the men to be in front of her. She threw leaves over her hair, and then lifted her head slightly, so that she still had a view of the seat. There was no alternative but to lie still and watch and wait.

'Oh God, Mike,' she muttered to herself, 'what am I doing? Why did we come? Darling, why did we come? Christ, I should have known.' And even as she murmured the words to herself, she realised that she had known. All the time her experience had told her it would be like this. She should never have allowed Michael to dissuade her. But if she tried to help him now, there would never be any chance of getting Pachenko's information back to London. To be realistic—however personally painful—the best chance she had of being any use to Michael, was to make sure that she was not discovered.

Then she saw the body fall to the ground, Michael jump up, stand staring, and begin to run. She sank herself against the earth as the men closed in. She watched him fall, and saw him pulled to his feet again, handcuffed. She remained crouched among last year's leaves until everyone had gone. Then carefully she made her way back to the nearest avenue, saw the Volgas, and watched them all away. Now she had to get to the British Embassy as quickly as possible—either the Metro or a taxi.

She had saved herself, she had kept herself available for whatever information Pachenko had for her, but at what cost? She might never see Michael again. She tried to shake the thought away as she ran towards the nearest gate, almost colliding with a passerby. Instinctivly she started to apologise in Russian, then stopped in astonishment.

'It's WT!' she exclaimed.

Carol recovered herself quickly. Her brain raced. She made a number of rapid assumptions, and before WT had got over his own surprise, she said tersely, 'You saw—what happened?'

The American blinked at her behind his spectacles. He looked both bewildered and uneasy.

'Happened?'

Carol was sure he was off balance, playing for time.

'You weren't there?' She did her best to appear calm, unflustered, pushing her assumptions as far as they would go.

'Where?' he asked.

She saw that he was getting back to normal.

'Don't you know?' she pressed on.

Now much more himself, he said, 'My dear Carol, it's lovely to see you, but what are you talking about?'

'The park—weren't you in the park?'

'Yes. But, I'm afraid, my dear, you aren't being any clearer.'

Carol looked straight at him. She couldn't be sure. But she was unlikely to get any further now.

'Michael has been set up,' she said. 'Provided with a dead body. The KGB have taken him away.'

WT appeared immediately concerned. 'A dead body?'

'Yes—in the park. I thought perhaps you'd seen it. Mike was supposed to be meeting Azhimov. When he arrived the man was dead on a bench. The KGB were waiting.'

'But this is terrible.'

'I thought perhaps you might have seen—'

'There are fifteen hundred acres in there,' he replied.

'I know, I'm sorry, I . . .'

'But you're not,' he said. 'That's what's remarkable—you don't seem flustered, worried, or anything.'

'I'm good at hiding my feelings,' she said laconically. Then added pointedly, 'Where were you?'

'I was at the Sokolniki Palace of Sports. Something to do with figure skating, my dear. It all comes under culture, I believe.'

Well, she thought, that was reasonable enough. She stared hard at him, trying to make up her mind.

He took her arm and they moved off together. 'I presume you're on your way to the Embassy,' he said. Carol nodded. 'Not even the KGB will hold him on that—without proof.' He didn't sound convincing.

'The KGB can do anything,' was all Carol said.

'I was walking across to the Winter Athletic Stadium. But that can wait. My car's back here at the Sports Palace.'

'Then would you drive me to the British Embassy?'
'That,' said W T, 'is precisely what I intend to do.'

No. 2 Dzerzhinsky Square is a dirty ochre colour—a solid nineteenth-century building that, before the Revolution, had been the head office of an insurance company. Now it is the headquarters of the K G B and site of the infamous Lubyanka prison. Attached to it, and matching uneasily, is a newer building, put up by German prisoners of war, most of which is occupied by the prison. It was to this building that Michael was taken.

He was led immediately along corridors, with guards placed every few yards, to an interrogation room. It was almost bare, except for table, chairs, and the inevitable portrait of Lenin on the pale green wall. Michael was made to stand opposite, while the contents of all his pockets were emptied on to the table. Then he was pushed into a chair. Just behind it stood two grey-green uniformed guards. The major settled himself on the other side of the table.

Slowly he picked up every item—the set of keys to Michael's apartment, car keys, wallet, diary, passport, and finally, two sheets of paper, one of them the sketch-map of the route in Sokolniki Park, the other, Azhimov's note. He smiled faintly, and felt in the right-hand pocket of his uniform for a box of matches. He struck a match, held it to the papers, and watched them burn. He stretched out his hands to the edges of the table, leant forward and beamed at his prisoner.

'These items,' he said, indicating the other things on the table, 'will be taken from you, and kept safely, Mr North. If you are released, they will be restored to you.'

Michael affected politeness, perhaps because if he dared to think about the situation he would be frightened. 'Major, would you kindly explain why I'm being held? And what reason have you for abducting a British citizen?'

Again the smile; only the eyes were humourless and grim. 'The answer to both questions should be obvious,' the major said. 'Not even a British citizen and a guest of the Soviet government is immune from the consequences of serious crime. It was fortunate, Mr North, that we were on the spot so soon after you had killed poor Azhimov.'

'Am I to be charged, or do you intend to convict me without a trial?'

'All that will follow in due course, Mr North. I don't think we need keep you from your "apartment" any longer.' He glanced up at the two men behind Michael's chair. 'Take him away,' he said brusquely.

Michael was grasped roughly by the arms and frog-marched out of the room. They hurried him along corridors to a central area and then thrust him into a narrow, steel-plated lift. He knew the cells were below ground, many of them beneath the road that ran behind the Lubyanka. Within a few moments, he was bundled out, and marched into a central hall with cells ranged round all sides. At one end was a huge steel door, with two men standing rigidly beside it. Suddenly he was jerked to a stop. The door that faced him was flush, except for one spy-hole at eye level. One of the guards unlocked it and pushed him inside. The door clanged shut.

Michael stood where he came to rest—roughly in the centre of the floor, which was made of some red-coloured composition. The cell was about ten feet by eight. He stood still, trembling slightly, and trying to think clearly. High in the white-washed wall facing him was one small barred window, but it gave no natural light. The only light was a bright bulb above his iron bedstead. This held a mattress, one blanket and a pillow. The only other furniture was a stool. There was a shelf on one wall holding a tin plate, mug and metal spoon. It was painted a very pale green, as was the wall beneath it. There was also a radiator. He walked across and felt it. It was lukewarm, barely sufficient for comfort even in the present weather. At least he had been allowed to keep his own clothes and wrist watch. That, he was sure, was unusual. He consoled himself that it was a good sign. Perhaps . . . but no, it was no good being unrealistic. His prospects were bloody grim.

He knew that millions of people—ten or twelve million under Stalin alone—had been killed, many of them in this very prison, men and women who, for one reason or another, had incurred the displeasure of the Soviet government or its secret intelligence service. People were still shot at Lubyanka.

He gripped his hands tightly in his lap and clenched his jaw muscles. He must, he told himself, maintain a high personal morale. He would be as light-hearted as he could; show them that he did not, could not, take their allegations seriously. But what was the chance of successful intervention from outside? Carol would have gone straight to the British Embassy. Already the Foreign Secretary and the Prime Minister would know what had happened. A protest was probably on its way. So what? It would cut no ice with the Russians. They would ignore it, do whatever they wanted to do. Unless . . . there was some kind of offer, some deal that could be made. Michael had to admit that he couldn't think of one. He ran his fingers through his hair in desperation. But perhaps somewhere there was a Russian or an East German who could be exchanged? It was the only hope.

Then he heard a faint click. He looked up. He saw, in the tiny spy-hole, the guard's eye, watching him.

# 12

Carol, like any other tourist, stood in front of the looped garlands that surrounded the statue of Pushkin. A base of five pink steps led to the carved plinth, and on top of it was the bronze figure of the poet, his head slightly on one side, his long cloak open, his right hand tucked into the breast of his waistcoat. She wasn't there because of any great personal interest in the Russian poet, but because it was the next prearranged place for a meeting with Alexei Pachenko. It was the day after the events in Sokolniki Park. She had been especially careful when leaving the British Embassy to make sure she was not being followed, going to the trouble of taking unnecessary rides in taxis and the Metro. It was important for her, but even more for Alexei.

There were baskets of flowers at the foot of the statue. Strange, how these same people . . . Her reflections were suddenly interrupted.

' "I have outlived all my aspirations, The dreams I loved are all outworn." Pushkin—he wrote that.'

She turned. There at her shoulder was the chubby figure of Alexei, his eyes glowing with pleasure at seeing her.

'Alexei—they've got Michael,' she said, as they moved off together into the square, beneath the trees. In an urgent voice she told him what had happened.

Within moments the glow of pleasure had gone from his eyes. He looked at her as though he were suffering physical pain. He took her arm and held her close as they walked. She was grateful that he didn't say, 'Why did you let him go?' She had been torturing herself with the same question. She should have known. He only gripped her arm the more tightly and said nothing.

Having walked round the square, they sat for a few

minutes on the huge half-circle of seat to the side of the statue, but got up as more people joined them, and strolled, as Pushkin himself must have done, under the shade of the trees on Tver Boulevard. For several minutes Alexei remained silent, and when eventually he did speak, it was only to say, 'So, Carol, we now have another problem.'

A breeze teased her hair. It made her think of the wayward lock that fell across Mike's forehead, and she felt a pricking behind her eyes. After another minute or so, Alexei spoke again.

'We have to see what we can do for Michael,' he said, 'without—'

'Without putting yourself in danger,' she interrupted. 'Alexei, you mustn't risk yourself.'

He shook his head sadly.

'Promise!' she said. 'There are other things . . .' She couldn't bring herself to say, 'that are more important,' because nothing was now more important to her . . . but there was still a job that she had to do. Yet she couldn't bear the thought of having to go back to London and leave Michael in the Lubyanka.

He nodded, and held up a plump hand to deter her interruption. They walked on in silence. When he spoke again it was with fresh decisiveness.

'We will meet on Friday,' he said. 'By the white bridge in Alexander Gardens. You know them?'

'Yes.'

'I have to think about this some more,' he continued. 'By then, perhaps, I shall have a plan.' He relaxed his grip on her arm, and gave it an affectionate pat. 'You are not to worry, Carol.'

Her smile was understandably half-hearted; she struggled to remain detached.

'Nothing from the Politburo?' she asked.

He shook his head. 'But the British announcement about nuclear rearmament—that will cause them to speed up their plans. It is mostly logistics now—how to get ships, aircraft, tanks, weapons, supplies from A to B. When that's sorted out, they will decide the timetable.'

'Robert Cresswell—*New York Times*—do you know him?' she asked.

Alexei shook his head.

'He's found out that icons have come, allegedly and very vaguely from old Russian families, on to the American market. But once they've been bought they've all disappeared. Don't you find that rather strange, Alexei?'

'It might be,' he said enigmatically. 'But then I just might have an explanation.' He gave her arm another pat. She saw an infinite sadness in his eyes. 'I . . . I shall have to see,' he added.

They had almost reached the square at the other end of the boulevard when he turned to her with sudden anxiety.

'You're not still in the apartment?' he said.

'Oh, no. The ferrets will have been through that by now. No, I'm at the Embassy.'

'Then, you go back there, Carol—and stay there until we meet again, eh? You must keep yourself safe. They're capable of anything.'

She didn't need telling. That was what worried her. She watched him disappear across the square, and then made her way on to Herzen Street to pick up a taxi.

Dr Graham North was holding a young tongue down with a wooden spatula, peering into a child's throat and murmuring to the mother, 'A little touch of laryngitis, nothing to worry about,' when his telephone bell rang, and his receptionist informed him that there was a gentleman from the Foreign Office insisting on speaking to him immediately.

The doctor slid back into his chair and pulled a pad towards him, but his intention of scribbling a prescription at the same time was abandoned immediately he heard the urgency in the voice that asked, 'Dr North?'

'Yes . . . yes.'

'Geoffrey Makepeace, East European Section, Foreign Office. I'm afraid I have some unfortunate news. Your son Michael is being held in a Moscow prison. He has not been charged with anything. He has done nothing with which he could be charged. The Embassy, of course, is doing all it can to get him released. His wife is quite safe at the Embassy . . .'

The doctor was startled by the mention of Michael's wife. He hadn't yet got used to the idea. He found himself saying, 'I don't give a damn about his wife. What about him?'

The voice at the other end was factual, unemotional. 'You should be prepared, Dr North, for reports on radio and television. There will be nothing before half-past five this evening . . .'

Before Makepeace could continue, the doctor interrupted, 'What do you mean—prepared, man?'

'Well, Michael was sitting on a seat in a Moscow park. There was another man also sitting there, and he suddenly keeled over, dead. The . . .' There was a pause as Makepeace wondered whether to say KGB or police, and finally settled on the latter. 'The police found Michael there and instantly arrested him. Of course, he had nothing whatsoever to do with it. That's why we are . . .' he searched for the right word, 'optimistic that he will be released before long.'

There was a silence. The doctor was thinking. Optimistic—that didn't sound convincing. Who could be optimistic about anything with those barbarians? Why the hell the boy . . .?

'You mean,' he said, forgetting the woman and child in the surgery, 'they think Michael murdered him?'

Makepeace knew very well that was precisely what the Russians would maintain. Instead, he said in as even a tone as he could manage, 'I don't see how they can, Doctor.'

'Well—what are you doing? What the hell are you doing?'

Dr North did not have any great faith in the Foreign Office. He was convinced that he had frequently read stories in the newspapers about Britons being held in jails overseas, and nothing being done to get them out. The years passed, and no doubt the Foreign Office kept sending courteous, diplomatic notes.

'The Embassy is making representations—'

'Representations! Get the boy out. If he's done nothing—get him out!'

'We shall, Dr North,' replied Makepeace, hoping that he sounded more convincing than he felt.

'Humph!'

The doctor felt angry, impatient and impotent. Angry, because it should never have happened; Michael should never have gone there in the first place . . . and then all this complicated business of getting married at the last moment. Impatient, because something should be done and done quickly, and he had no faith in the Foreign Office's capacity for doing it. And impotent, because he knew there was damn all he could do personally. Even swearing at the Foreign Office wouldn't help.

The conversation continued, with Makepeace promising to keep him fully informed and the doctor getting more and more impatient. At last, he put the phone down, looked into space and drummed his fingers on the desk. This girl Michael had married, what had he said? 'I want you to go along with it,' and 'You're just going to have to trust me.' That had been a mistake—damn it. He should have insisted . . .

An apologetic cough interrupted his thoughts. He turned and saw the woman and child. Automatically, his hand went to the prescription pad, and he began to scribble.

For the first night Michael had been left undisturbed. Tea had been brought into him. That seemed unusually civilised. His evening meal consisted of some bread and a bowl of unpalatable fish soup. Twice he was led out to the wash room and lavatories. The latter were little more than holes in the floor, and stank. The brilliant light on the wall above his bed was left burning all night. The bed was excessively hard. Even with all his clothes on the single blanket was scarcely enough to keep him warm. The contribution of the radiator was minimal. Nevertheless he managed to drift in and out of sleep. He never heard the guards in the corridor, but periodically he heard the movement of the spy-hole shutter, and saw an eye watching him.

In the morning he was brought some black bread and a very sloppy porridge-like mixture. He was surprised to see the guard was a woman. She was handsome in a stern way, and there was not a flicker of warmth in her eyes. The porridge mixture looked and tasted revolting. He forced it down. He fought against a realistic assessment of his prospects. That would only undermine his morale. He had heard too many stories from dissidents about treatment in the Lubyanka. How was he going to react to brutality, to torture? No, he mustn't even ask the quesion. He must accept each moment for what it was, maintain his own self-confidence, his assurance, his air of casual disinterestedness. Bloody hell—what was he thinking? Too much self-analysis wasn't going to do any good. They would release him. In the end, they would release him. They would have to. He wasn't convinced. There was no reason why they should. They didn't need reasons for anything. They would do whatever they wanted to do.

It was ten o'clock when the steel door of his cell swung open, and a guard bundled him out into the hall. He was hurried towards the lift. Inside, he was separated from the guard by another steel door, but he could see the man through a spy-hole. When the lift stopped, he came out on to a flat roof. Above him was the sky—a pale blue. The air was warm. There was a momentary illusion of freedom. Then he saw the wooden platform with its guards, guns at their hips. To his left was a large exercise area, but he was poked in the direction of a smaller pen with high walls and a scroll of barbed wire. He didn't have more than twelve or thirteen feet to walk in any direction, but above him was the pale blue sky. God, what would it be like in winter? He shook the thought away, as he tried jogging round his open-air room. After almost an hour he was taken back to his cell. The guard was formal, his face impassive. He was only doing his job.

A few minutes later the man was back and taking Michael to the interrogation room. There, sitting at the table in the middle, was the major—the farmer-major as Michael had already begun to think of him, because of his florid complexion. On the opposite side, by an empty chair, stood two immaculately uniformed thugs.

Michael said, as brightly as he could, 'Good morning, Major.'

'Now, Mr North,' said the major affably, as he opened a folder in front of him, 'we don't want to detain you longer than is necessary. Not that I can promise you an immediate release, but we have done our best to make things easy for you. I hope you have no complaints, so far.'

'The food is hardly up to gourmet standards.'

'Good cooks are so difficult to get.' The major smiled, except for his eyes, which remained hard and expressionless. 'But you've got some money, Mr North. You can buy some additional food. More bread, butter—well, to be honest, it's margarine. If you are lucky there might even be some chocolate—for you, you understand.'

'The Lubyanka Hilton. I never realised.'

This time the major didn't smile. He consulted the papers in his folder. 'I was saying, Mr North, we have done our best to make it easy for you. I'm sure a long interrogation is not necessary. That can be so tedious. Sometimes painful. I'm sure you understand. Anyway, the facts are known, aren't they, Mr North? So, from those facts, I have prepared a statement for you to sign.' He shuffled the papers. 'It's rather long, of course, but then there is a lot to cover . . . to explain, isn't there? If you would sign this, it would save a great deal of trouble for all of us, and especially for you.' He leant forward, his eyes colourless except for the steely pupils, and unblinking. 'No, for such a serious offence your release could not be immediate, but it should not be long delayed. We would be able to come to an arrangement with your Embassy'. He passed the papers over to Michael. 'It's a rather long document. Do please take your time reading it. I'll leave you to give it some thought, Mr North.'

Michael inclined his head. 'That's very considerate, Major,' he said.

The KGB officer left, and Michael bent over the numerous sheets of paper on the table. The two guards remained motionless by the back of his chair.

The document was so detailed that Michael marvelled that it had been assembled so quickly. It began from his first day as BBC correspondent in Moscow. The date was correct. It went on to explain that he had taken the appointment on the instructions of the British Government in order to engage in espionage. It listed a variety of equipment from decoding pads to a miniature radio transmitter which, it maintained, had been supplied to him and since recovered from his apartment. It went on to confess that a number of stories he had broadcast had contained coded information for the British Government. Then it established a long-standing relationship with Konstantin Azhimov, and referred to information regularly supplied by Azhimov which Michael was said to have transmitted to London. Finally, he confessed that Azhimov, eventually concerned about his own safety, had threatened to unmask Michael to the KGB. At a meeting arranged in Sokolniki Park for a final discussion, at which Michael had hoped to dissuade Azhimov from betraying him, there was an argument, and Michael, realising that Azhimov was out to save his own skin, plunged a knife into his back and killed him. The whole confession occupied more than twenty pages.

The major did not return until at least fifteen minutes after Michael had finished reading. He sat down very precisely on the opposite side of the table, spread out his hands and looked up quizzically.

'It's in the tradition of the great Russian novel, Major—a splendid piece of fiction.'

The KGB officer showed no surprise at the casual tone. He said only, 'Have you signed it, Mr North?'

'No.'

'We can discuss it. Of course, there will be a few questions to ask you anyway. You still haven't told us what it was Azhimov gave you to take to London. We shall need to know that in detail.'

Michael was inexplicably amused. He surprised himself by saying, 'Tickets for the Centre Court at Wimbledon.'

The major's expression was a mixture of mystification and anger, but he said punctiliously, 'You have not been very co-operative, Mr North. It was one thing in London, but here—you would be advised to tell us the truth.'

Michael adopted the same correct tone: 'I thank you for your advice, Major. I shall follow it.' He paused and looked directly at his questioner. 'I received nothing from Azhimov to take to London. Had I done so, your very efficient thugs would have found it. Once and for all, Major, I took nothing to London.'

'But you just admitted taking some tickets.' The major was unsmiling, his eyes like metal.

Michael laughed. It was all too ridiculous.

The major said sharply, 'It is not funny, Mr North. You admitted taking tickets to London. What were they? Coded information? What was that information?'

Michael gestured in despair. 'It was a joke.'

'A joke? I don't understand. You admitted Azhimov gave you tickets to take to London. What were they?'

'I've admitted nothing, Major. Azhimov gave me nothing to take to London. Forget it.'

'If you want to do it the hard way, North—that's your fault. It doesn't matter to us. One way or another you are going to tell us in complete detail about the information you took to London.' He paused to allow the threat to sink in. 'In the meantime,' he added, 'you can help yourself by signing that document.'

'I'm not signing this rubbish. You've got the date of my coming to Moscow right—that's about all.'

The florid face peered at him, it even smiled. 'Truth—who is discussing truth? We are talking about your confession—about necessity. Perhaps you don't understand that yet. You will.'

The major gathered up the papers, and returned them carefully to his folder. Then he nodded to the two guards. Michael's arms were seized, and he was taken briskly from the room, and back to his cell.

He sat on his bed to consider the situation. He had heard that the guards in Lubyanka never allowed a prisoner to use his bed except at night, but no attempt was made to stop him, and it was marginally more comfortable than the stool. The joke about Wimbledon tickets had been a mistake. He must avoid that kind of thing in future. Perhaps, in his desire to maintain his own personal morale, he had sounded altogether too light-hearted. But he was not going to show fear. He thought of his father back in his Devon practice. He would be damning this, that, and everything. Michael even smiled faintly at the memory of his father telling him he was a damn fool to go to a place like Moscow anyway. If only he'd gone in for medicine. If only he had. But he had no regrets. Then he thought of Carol, and was determined he must be got out of Lubyanka somehow. There was international publicity, international pressure, and the British Government would be—well, doing all they could. Realistically, he knew the Soviets, in the light of their future plans, were not likely to take any notice of anything the British Government said or did. And he could hardly expect the Americans to worry about him. He wondered what Robert Cresswell was writing. He even began to visualise the stories.

He was interrupted by lunch. It was brought by a woman—a bowl of watery soup with bits of meat in it, and some black bread, and then some additional bread and margarine, and—a bar of chocolate. The guard indicated the additional items, and he paid her from his wallet. Chocolate, he was sure, was an unheard-of luxury. It made him wonder again what his captors were up to.

He had another surprise in the middle of the afternoon. He was taken from his cell, up in the lift to the newer building, and led to a normally furnished office. There, sitting at one side of the desk was Robin Stimson, First Secretary at the British Embassy.

'Robin!' Michael exclaimed, and they shook hands warmly.

The First Secretary was a short, businesslike man, but with features that were permanently pale and drawn, and slightly triangular.

One guard only remained in the room with them. He stood by the door.

Neither Stimson nor Michael remarked on the unusualness of the meeting. They both knew that normally such requests from the British Embassy would be ignored. So why were the Russians playing it correctly?

Stimson spoke quietly and incisively, occasionally hiding his mouth with his hand when he had something of especial importance to say, in case the guard was lip-reading. But everything that passed between them, no matter how quietly they spoke, would almost certainly be recorded. So each chose words carefully. Michael learned that stories would be breaking that afternoon; that, of course, representations had been made demanding his immediate release and, failing that, that he should be properly tried and represented. That, however, was routine. It meant nothing, and the Russians would take no notice. Requests to provide Michael with food had been refused. Stimson advised that he might even have to sign some kind of confession. If it was to avoid torture that would be understood, but he should try to get some undertaking about his release. Surprisingly, if an undertaking were given, it might be honoured, especially if a deal was in the offing. An exchange, said Stimson, was not impossible. Try to keep in good spirits.

Michael looked at the strained face, and smiled. 'You say that with a total lack of conviction, Robin.'

The diplomat nodded. 'Nevertheless, try.'

'And Carol? How's my wife?' he asked.

Stimson smiled. 'She's at the Embassy. She's all right. Just worried.'

The serious interrogation began immediately Stimson left. Michael was taken back to the prison hall, with its three storeys of cells, a steel net at each floor to prevent prisoners from above flinging themselves over the rail to the floor below. From there he was led to the sparsely furnished interrogation room. This time, the major had a companion, and when Michael went to sit at the table he was told sharply to remain standing.

The grey-green guards were uncomfortably close—erect and impassive.

The major began: 'When did you first meet Azhimov?'

'I've never knowingly met him. I don't even know if the man in the park was Azhimov.'

The other officer repeated the question: 'When did you first meet Azhimov?'

'I don't know that I've ever met him.'

The major: 'Azhimov gave you something to take to London. What was it?'

'I took nothing to London.'

The other man repeated, 'What did you take?'

Then the major again; then the other officer. They questioned him alternately, at increasing speed—apparently ignoring his answers, only repeating the same question again and again in slightly different words, the sounds barking out repetitively.

Ultimately, Michael, who had kept coolly repeating that he had taken nothing to London, shouted, 'Stop!'

The two KGB officers looked up, momentarily surprised.

'We can make some progress,' said Michael quietly, 'if you listen to my answers. I have taken nothing to London. Now, what else do you want to know?'

The florid major chortled contemptuously. 'The tickets, North,' he snapped. 'What were the tickets?'

'There were no tickets.'

'You said there were tickets,' said the second officer. 'What were they?'

'There weren't any.'

'What was on the tickets?'

And again the same question was repeated, and the interrogation speeded up.

Michael determined to remain calm. Occasionally he even attempted to smile. They didn't notice. The words shot out like bullets from the barrel of a gun. Then they returned to the beginning again: 'When did you meet Azhimov? What did he give you? What did you take to London? What were the tickets? What was on the tickets?' They reminded him that they knew Azhimov had passed information to him, and that they had found incriminating material in his apartment. No matter how much Michael denied this, the same questions were repeated over and over again. Then ultimately the major's voice choked on a crescendo as he demanded, 'You must tell us what we want to know. You *will* tell us. You will tell us now.' He spluttered into a cough.

Michael said quietly, 'I have already told you. You don't listen.'

The major banged the table with his fist. 'What did you take to London? The details, the details. What?'

Even before he had time to reply, the other officer had barked out the same question.

Michael struggled to remain calm. 'Gentlemen,' he said, 'I am willing to help you. But I can't tell you what I don't know.'

The major, the colour rising in his rubicund cheeks, now slammed both hands, palm downwards, on the table.

'Next time we meet,' he yelled, 'you will feel more like telling us.'

He jerked his head, and the two guards grabbed Michael's arms, and hurried him back to his cell. The steel door slammed.

Ten minutes later it opened again. The severely handsome woman guard stood there. Behind her were two tall, broad men in grey-green boiler suits. For a few seconds all three stood very still, staring at him. Then the two men came into the cell, leaving the woman guard in the doorway.

Michael was yanked to his feet, and told to get his clothes off. One of the men took each garment in turn and tossed it to the woman guard.

When he was naked, they left him standing for a full five minutes, while all three of them silently stared. Then the two men moved in.

# 13

Sir Kenneth Propter had met the American Secretary of State, Carlton Munroe, when he was Opposition spokesman on foreign affairs and was busy attacking the government for ending the historic special relationship between Britain and the United States. The two men had got on well together, both having an academic background. The Foreign Secretary had the advantage not merely of his rowing blue, but commercial experience as well, and an especial aptitude for publicity, which would have seemed more fitting for the American. They were a complete contrast in appearance —Sir Kenneth tall and athletic, eager, and looking a good ten years younger than the American, who was also fifty. Carlton Munroe was short and distinctly podgy, his face a little fleshy with a beak of a nose and an expression that—possibly because of the half-moon glasses—looked permanently surprised.

Sir Kenneth had expected the meeting to take place in Munroe's office, which was more like a vice-chancellor's study, stuffed full of books. Instead, he was whisked to the eighth floor of the State Department building, and taken to the John Q. Adams state drawing-room. This is a panelled salon, discreetly formal, crystal chandeliers and gilt, portraits in oils, eighteenth-century furniture upholstered in wine-red. So presumably, Sir Kenneth thought, it was meant to distance them a little, underline the formality of the occasion. He was being *received*, as a distinguished foreign visitor. So he was agreeably surprised by the contrasting warmth with which he was greeted.

'Sir Kenneth, very good to see you. Much better in government, eh?' The Secretary of State peered over his spectacles.

'It should be,' Sir Kenneth smiled, 'but we've been left an unholy mess.'

'And that's what you want to see me about?' He rolled himself like a sailor into a very upright armchair, and Sir Kenneth chose an uncomfortable end of one of the red settees nearby. The aides settled awkwardly on neighbouring chairs.

In spite of the correct elegance of the setting, the atmosphere, and the whole discussion, were what correspondents would accurately describe afterwards as frank but amicable. It helped that the two men liked each other, but the removal of all American bases from British soil and Britain's withdrawal from NATO had not merely destroyed the special relationship but had finally alienated American opinion from the problems of Europe.

The Secretary of State explained patiently that the United States was very happy to help Britain back into a nuclear role—that was why there had been ready agreement to supply the Trident missiles—but thereafter defence policy was Britain's own affair. In the circumstances Sir Kenneth could hardly expect Americans to feel any differently. The old isolationist instinct had been powerfully reinforced by the actions of the previous British government. Sir Kenneth didn't need telling.

The Foreign Secretary replied authoritatively, hearing in his mind's ear the words like a news release: 'Now there is a new government, determined to accept its proper role in world affairs, determined to right the disastrous wrongs of our predecessors. We have got to get back to the old relationship.'

'No doubt, no doubt,' muttered Munroe, more like an English professor than an American Secretary of State, 'but it is not going to be so easy, Kenneth . . . not at all.'

They reviewed the European scene, the task facing Britain, the programme and policies of the new government, and the American expressed his undoubted satisfaction, and looked forward to improving relations between the two countries. Sir Kenneth then offered immediately to restore to NASA the supply of information regularly gleaned by the GCHQ.

The American nodded his head thoughtfully and peered over the half-moons. He doubted whether U S intelligence was yet ready for that kind of exchange.

'You see,' he said gently, 'when a couple have been divorced, getting married again might be the right decision for them, but a whole lot of other people have their doubts.'

They talked understandingly about the problems facing them and the necessity of carrying American public opinion with them.

It was only then that Sir Kenneth asked directly the one question that was the main reason for his journey to Washington.

'What,' he asked, 'would be the attitude of the United States Government if Britain were attacked by the Soviet Union?'

Munroe looked up like a lecturer who has been asked a pertinent question by one of the better students.

'I take it that's a hypothetical question, Kenneth?'

'I would like to think so, but I doubt it. We have reason to believe the Soviet Union is considering something of the kind.'

The American Secretary of State rolled out of his chair, began a slow pace across the Persian carpet, and turned about when he reached the gold looping drapes that framed the window.

'I hope,' he said, 'we are not faced with the decision.'

'I think you will be. Perhaps quite soon.'

The surprised look changed to one of concern. He pursed and twisted his lips as though in pain. 'I'm rather afraid,' he said, 'it would be a matter for Britain.'

'Carlton, there are Russian warships in the North Sea. Others are in the Baltic. There's a submarine fleet there.'

'I know. We've seen them. You know as well as I do, Kenneth, the Russians do this kind of thing from time to time. They call them exercises. Make themselves a bloody nuisance, show a bit of force, but that's all.'

'And the aircraft in East Germany—have you seen those too?'

The American nodded. 'They've done that before as well.'

'Not on this scale.'

Munroe fiddled with his spectacles, lifted them higher on the beak of his nose. 'Our satellites are keeping a watch,' he said uneasily.

'If all you're going to do is watch, Carlton, you'll get a grandstand view of the Soviet invasion of the UK.'

'We've nothing on that, Kenneth, nothing on that at all.'

'Well, we have. And what are you going to do when it happens?'

Munroe looked uncomfortable. He didn't like what he was going to have to say.

'If there were a threat to the United States, Kenneth, then of course there would be a response. If not, we wouldn't get involved.' He began pacing the room unhappily. 'We could never sell it to the American people,' he continued. 'You know that. So soon after you've kicked us out of Britain, got rid of our weapons and our bases, and then you expect us to come rushing to your aid—it's not on, is it? Americans are disillusioned by the last five years of Britain's anti-Americanism. It's too much to expect. The President couldn't ride it. I mean, if there was really any semblance of the Western Alliance left—well . . . but it's a name, isn't it? Not much more. Without Britain, what's NATO? In any event, wouldn't this be more a matter for Europe?'

'Europe wouldn't think so,' said Sir Kenneth. 'For the same reasons,' he added.

The American sighed. He looked genuinely sorry. 'It's going to take a long time building bridges again. I hope you're wrong, Kenneth. By God, I hope you're wrong.'

Radio and television correspondents waiting at London Airport to interview the Foreign Secretary on his return from Washington waited in vain. All they got was a hurried shot of him scurrying down the aircraft's steps into a waiting car. At 10 Downing Street the Cabinet waited. The Prime Minister had already given them the gist of what Sir Kenneth had told him on the telephone from the British Embassy in Washington. The latest report from GCHQ noted the arrival of even more Soviet aircraft, including troop carriers, in East Germany.

The Foreign Secretary took his seat almost opposite the Prime Minister at the Cabinet table.

'The most we can hope for,' he told his colleagues, 'is some surreptitious help from the Americans—weapons, supplies, and so on, but not enough to be noticed. There'll be no official help at all. Of course, there would be the offer of mediation, help at the United Nations, but none of that is likely to deter the Russians. It never has in the past.'

The Prime Minister stuck out his chin. With his shock of grey hair he looked an impressive as well as an elegant figure. The expected news only fuelled his determination.

'So,' he said, 'we really are on our own.'

The chief of the Defence Staff and the Service chiefs had not been called to the Cabinet; they had desperately urgent work to do. But their assessment was that the Soviets would probably choose the north Norfolk coast for a seaborne and airborne landing. This would be preceded by an attempt to take out the East Anglian airfields by naval shelling, missiles and bombing raids. Until exact information was received about Russian intentions defence planning was going ahead on these assumptions. The nuclear rearming of the British submarines was, inevitably at present, a propaganda device. There was obviously not going to be time to refit them, let alone receive delivery of Trident missiles. It was more important to have the hunter-killer submarines at sea, and that's where they were. They would, of course, be grossly outnumbered. The Service chiefs' detailed plans would be available in the next twenty-four hours. The Prime Minister then announced the formation of a smaller war cabinet which, from now on, would be responsible for the country's defence. He was proposing to delay a statement to the Commons until those preparations were further advanced. Meanwhile the Foreign Secretary and the Defence Secretary were to visit Western European capitals. The Prime Minister, looking defiant, said he had to admit that British intelligence confirmed Russian intelligence—namely that, since Britain had deliberately cut itself off from Europe, her former NATO allies would not wish to get involved. They did not want to risk the possibility of a full-scale war.

'So,' he said, 'it's going to be between the Russians and us. The Americans and the Europeans hope that it will be contained on this island.'

Carol had decided to remain within the British Embassy until her next meeting with Pachenko, and it was there that she received Robert Cresswell. Not even the rooms of the Embassy itself are necessarily free from the electronic surveillance of the KGB; so they went out into the gardens.

The boyish, good-looking features of the *New York Times* man were furrowed with concern as he questioned her about Michael and such information as Robin Stimson had been able to bring back from his visit to the Lubyanka. American papers, he told her, were splashing the story of a Soviet frame-up of the BBC correspondent, and surely this would stimulate international pressure, even if British publicity failed. She looked unconvinced, distracted, preoccupied.

'I guess you're not much interested in icons now,' he said.

She gave him a faint smile. 'Oh, but I am, Bob. Tell me.'

They stopped by the edge of a rose bed. 'There's something mighty funny going on, Carol, and I reckon Mariner has a lot to do with it. I'm sure he's CIA, and you could see him mentally jump when I said to him, "Now, what about these Russian icons that have been selling on the American market?" We had a very funny conversation, Carol. Everything said at one remove, if you know what I mean. I got the feeling there was some other guy involved.'

'Azhimov,' said Carol.

'The dead guy?'

'Yes—and perhaps the other Azhimov, the one the dissident told Mike about—Igor,'

Cresswell looked puzzled, and then suddenly brightened. 'I've got it. It must be like this. Azhimov—the dead one—was the channel for the icons . . . genuine or fake, we don't know. Suppose the painter, Igor, was his brother. He was faking them, passing them to Konstantin, who was the link with Brod. Then supposing something goes wrong between Konstantin and Brod—?'

'It did,' Carol interrupted. 'Azhimov has been spying for your people. Brod told me so, when I went to see his icons.'

'Well, that's it. Azhimov was going to spill the beans to Michael about the trade in icons. He was getting them from brother Igor for Brod. Brod was getting them on to the American market. How? Unless there's a big network using other KGB men in the States—and that's too dangerous, too many people in the know—there's only one way he could do it. Through Mariner.' Cresswell became excited. 'That must be it, Carol—it just has to be. But Mariner is running a hell of a risk if he's only—no, of course not, it's officially sanctioned. I bet you,' he went on, his enthusiasm bubbling over, 'those icons were never sold at all. They were knocked down to mythical buyers; they were bought in. By the CIA. And Brod gets the proceeds, with pay-offs to the two Azhimovs. So, when he wants it, Mariner has complete control over Brod. Brod can be forced to spy for the US. He'd probably have access to useful information himself, but if he had access to someone bigger—then, Jesus, Carol, Mariner has got him by the short and curlies.'

Carol had to chuckle, infected by Cresswell's own excitement.

She said, 'He has—I mean Brod does have access to someone bigger, someone very much bigger.'

'That's it! We've got it—we've broken it.' His face burst into a beaming grin of pleasure and satisfaction. 'Who is it, Carol?'

She took his arm. 'Bob, forgive me. You've been marvellous. But I can't tell you until after tomorrow.'

His disappointment was immediate. She gave his arm a grateful squeeze. 'I'm sorry, Bob, but it's for Michael's sake. I don't know—I only hope—that we may be able to help him. Phone me tomorrow evening . . .'

'Here?' he said incredulously. 'Every word will be monitored.'

'Don't worry, I won't give you the name over the phone,

but we'll be able to arrange something.' She turned to him and smiled. 'I feel so much better, Bob. There's just a chance. But I'm relying on someone else. I have to.' She noticed his quizzical look. 'Don't run any kind of story yet, will you? There's better to come, I'm sure of it.'

The last time Carol had been in the Alexander Gardens it was with Michael. She remembered now, with irony, how he had said, 'Forget the bloody icons. They can't have anything to do with what you want to know.' And all the time she had intuitively felt that they were somehow important. She took a deep breath, inhaling the mixed scent of the flowers and the lime trees.

Alexei was standing beneath one of the arches of the white bridge that linked the Kutafya tower to the Trinity tower, the tallest in the Kremlin.

'I haven't been followed,' she said. 'It's getting more difficult to shake them off, but they're not all that clever.'

The Russian gave her a rewarding smile. 'I think you are well trained, Carol,' he said knowingly, as he embraced her affectionately.

'We believe—' she began, but he interrupted.

'We?' he queried.

'Robert Cresswell,' she answered, and he nodded his understanding, as she whispered, 'We believe that Viktor Brod has been using the American Mariner to smuggle icons—almost certainly fake—on to the American market. And *he's* been getting the money. Bob thinks Mariner was planning to use Brod—probably was already using him.'

Alexei made a brief gesture with his podgy hands. 'I know, I know,' he said quietly. 'Azhimov was getting them—I don't know from where. It's been going on a long time.' He raised his hand to stop her interruption, and the pair walked in silence the length of the garden down to the Borovitskaya tower. Carol sensed that the Russian was facing another personal crisis and weighing up the chances of coming through successfully, or failing.

They turned to retrace their steps, and Alexei said, as though thinking aloud, 'We have to get Michael out.'

'I've thought of little else,' Carol sighed. 'It's frightening —Mike in that place.'

Alexei looked uneasy, directing sharp glances at the people who jostled past on the footpath. 'I have to think of Varinka and Nada,' he said, his dark eyes troubled.

Carol didn't reply. She was thinking of the possibility of having to sacrifice Michael, and it was becoming increasingly difficult to tell herself that the only thing that mattered was to discover the detailed decisions and timetable of the Politburo. But that was what was expected of her. She felt Alexei take her arm.

'Next weekend,' he said, 'you must come to Zavidovo. I'm sorry it's a week away, but . . . things have to be arranged.'

'Will the UPDK let me?'

'I think so. They still have nothing against you. They're convinced Michael is the spy. But come with that *New York Times* man, Cresswell. You'll almost certainly be followed, but—' He shrugged and left the sentence unfinished.

'Shall I bring my rod?' she asked, with something of the old, gently mocking look in her eyes.

Alexei shook his head. 'There won't be time for trout,' he said. They had reached the white bridge again. 'But there will be other fish to catch.' He kissed her cheek, and hurried off to the other end of the gardens.

# 14

Before leaving for Europe with the Secretary of State for Defence, the Foreign Secretary, Sir Kenneth Propter, with the Cabinet's agreement, had decided to see the Russian Ambassador. Ostensibly, the meeting was to enable Sir Kenneth to reiterate the protest the Government had already made about the imprisonment of the BBC correspondent, Michael North, and to rebuke the Ambassador for his government's failure to respond. There was, however, a more important purpose. That was to assess, from the occasional word and the Russian's manner, anything he could of the Soviet Union's intentions. Sir Kennth never imagined it was going to be so easy as it turned out.

His Excellency Anton Markolevsky looked relaxed and irritatingly pleased with himself. His appointment at the Foreign Office had been for nine o'clock, and he arrived on the dot. He shook Sir Kenneth's hand effusively, although the Foreign Secretary had resolved to maintain the formality of the occasion.

'There is only one fault with your summer, Sir Kenneth,' said the Ambassador cheerfully. 'There is no football. Your cricket—I cannot understand.'

Sir Kenneth didn't even smile. He merely said, 'It has infinite shades of subtlety.'

'Ah, like chess,' said the Ambassador, not to be outdone.

'But healthier,' said Sir Kenneth.

The Russian smiled. He seemed determined to be good-humoured. At the Foreign Secretary's invitation he settled himself in an armchair. Sir Kenneth, however, remained standing.

'I have asked you to come here, Ambassador, because

there are certain things outstanding that need clearing up.' He added forcefully, 'Immediately.'

'I hope soon everything will be cleared up, Sir Kenneth, to our mutual satisfaction. I am sure with your co-operation there can be a very happy settlement.'

The man's over-friendly manner and the significance of the words were not lost on the Foreign Secretary, but he maintained his authoritative air and said, 'I think, Ambassador, you could take these matters more seriously.'

Markolevsky's smiling attempt at a rejoinder was dismissed with a sweep of the arm, as Sir Kenneth voiced his exasperation.

'There has been no response from your government to the protest by Her Majesty's Government about the detention of the BBC correspondent, Michael North. What is called for now, Ambassador, is not merely a response, but the man's immediate release. Immediate, Ambassador. He is being held without just cause. What is more,' Sir Kenneth continued, his voice edged with anger, 'no attempt has been made to deliver to the Metropolitan Police the three men responsible for abducting Mr North in this country. We have, in accordance with tradition, respected the diplomatic immunity of your Embassy, but unless this matter is dealt with promptly, Ambassador, we shall have to declare a number of named diplomats *persona non grata*.' The Foreign Secretary turned abruptly and walked to his desk, where he picked up a document, and then spun round to face the Ambassador again. 'I hope,' he said, 'you will convey the contents of this note to your government without delay. And you should be in no doubt, Ambassador, that if we do not have satisfaction, and quickly, I may say, we are determined upon action.'

Markolevsky took the note politely and relaxed back in his chair. He even smiled.

'Murder,' he said smoothly, 'is a very serious crime in the Soviet Union, as it is in this country.'

'You know very well what happened, Ambassador; and you know North to be innocent of any crime. I would remind you that he hasn't even been charged. We must insist on his immediate release. I think that will be all, Mr Markolevsky.'

The Russian Ambassador got slowly to his feet and moved round to the back of the chair. He leant with his hands on the top of the upholstery. 'Not quite all, Foreign Secretary,' he said quietly. Then with exaggerated politeness, he added, 'It is a pity, Sir Kenneth, you spurn the hand of friendship. You see, I don't think you are in a very good position to insist on anything.' His tone changed, he lifted his head aggressively, and from his inner pocket withdrew a document which he held out to the Foreign Secretary. He said formally, 'This is a note for your government, Sir Kenneth, from Mr Boris Konevsky, President of the U S S R and General Secretary of the Communist Party of the Soviet Union.' He bowed his head as Sir Kenneth took the document.

'I hope that this is at any rate some kind of explanation for what has occurred and announces the release of Mr North.'

The Ambassador smiled yet again, and Sir Kenneth knew the advantage had passed to the Russian. The document, he could both feel and see, was long and comprehensive.

'Mr North is not mentioned, but I think you might appreciate a brief *resumé* of what is a very long note.'

'Is it necessary?'

'Helpful.' The Ambassador bowed.

'Well?' Sir Kenneth's tone was sceptical.

'My government, Sir Kenneth, is very disappointed that Britain's new government does not seem to want the very close and friendly relations with the Soviet Union which your predecessors enjoyed. From the outset you have been quite unwilling to pursue the path of friendship.'

Sir Kenneth sighed impatiently. The Ambassador's tone changed.

'I have the honour to present, Sir Kenneth, a series of . . . proposals, from my government. I will summarise a few of them. We must ask for access, immediately, to all British ports for Russian warships. We also require the use of R A F airfields and the bases previously occupied by the United States forces. You see, Sir Kenneth, the Soviet Union, mindful of its responsibilities towards peace throughout the world, is glad to take on the role formerly undertaken by the United States. So the British people can now look to the Soviet Union for their safety and defence. That will cement our friendship. You will also find the note contains proposals that will enable your country to provide the best of British technology, in many fields, to the people of the Soviet Union. We shall naturally require access to North Sea oil, and we have set out quotas for grain production in Britain, and the proportion which it will be necessary to ship to the Soviet Union, together with dairy products and other foodstuffs. The Soviet government has no desire to limit the food consumption of the British people but, in the short term, you may find it necessary, Sir Kenneth, to introduce some form of food rationing. You will find a number of other proposals of benefit to the British people once they are under the protection of their friends in the Soviet Union.'

Sir Kenneth had felt his anger mounting through the whole recital, but he was careful to control himself.

'Is that . . . all?' he asked dismissively.

'The rest is mere detail, Sir Kenneth. I am instructed to request that your government give these proposals their immediate consideration.'

'Of course,' said Sir Kenneth sarcastically. He stroked his chin, largely as a way of maintaining his patience. 'Mr Markolevsky,' his tone was even and firm, 'if the proposals —they sound more like demands to me—are as you have outlined them, I can give you my government's reply now. I don't need to consult. Her Majesty's Government will regard this as the most outrageous and audacious nonsense, and you can tell your government that their demands are rejected. Moreover, they will remain rejected. There is nothing more to say, Mr Markolevsky, except this: *we* demand the immediate release of Mr North. Good day.'

He followed the Ambassador to the door. The Russian shrugged. 'It is a pity,' he said, 'you reject friendship and co-operation. The alternative, Sir Kenneth, will be so much worse for you.'

The Foreign Secretary shut the door behind the departing Russian. He stood in the centre of the room, breathing deeply, composing himself. Then he rang for Geoffrey Makepeace.

When the Head of the East European Section entered, Sir Kenneth handed him the document.

'A note from our would-be Russian masters,' he said. 'It needs translating.'

# 15

Several days had passed since the beating. Michael had been left naked, bruised and sore for the rest of the day and night. He had curled himself as small as possible, so that he could use more than one thickness of the single blanket, and then he had put the pillow on top of him, rather than under his head, for additional warmth. But even if the cold had not kept him awake the pain would.

In the morning when the woman guard had brought in the sticky, sloppy porridge for breakfast, he was standing huddled against the lukewarm radiator, the blanket wrapped round him, the pillow clutched to his stomach. An hour later his clothes were returned. Then he was taken to the interrogation room. The major was sitting at the table, his features ruddy and weathered. He beamed a welcome as Michael sat down. The confession was already on the table. The major pointed to it.

Michael, aching with pain and feeling sick from the porridge, managed to shrug.

'The time has come to sign,' the major said with a smile.

'Am I released if I sign?'

'I can't say that. It will make your release easier. But you still have some questions to answer, Mr North.'

Michael braced himself. It was important not to let them see he was afraid. He shook his head. He scarcely saw the nod from the major before one of the men standing behind him yanked him to his feet. An arm flailed across his face with such force that he was sent staggering back to the wall. As he reached it something struck savagely at his midriff, and he crumpled to the ground, gasping for breath. He waited to feel the boots kick into his ribs and back, but nothing happened. He was left coiled on the floor until he began to breathe more normally. Then the major yelled at him to stand up, and even before he could struggle to his feet, he was lifted bodily upwards and thrust on to his feet with a force that jarred up and down his spine. Then he was taken back to his cell.

That was two days ago. Since then he had even been allowed some additional food. There had been another bar of chocolate, and some better bread. The bruises spread across his body in yellow, green and blue smudges that merged like the washes of a watercolour, but the pain had eased. He realised that they had skilfully ensured that nothing was broken. Now he was taken out again, this time to a different room, still sparsely furnished, but a little less bare than the room used by the major. The one similarity was the cold-eyed portrait of Lenin on the wall facing him as he was told to sit down at one side of a rather commodious table. Two men still stood rigidly behind him. A third Russian came into the room. He was huge, with an enormously broad chest and wide shoulders, a thick frame, and a rugged-hewn face, with eyes that looked as cold as Lenin's and as grey as slate. He was wearing the uniform of a colonel. Michael stood up as the man came to the table. A large hand waved him back to his chair.

In a guttural voice, the figure announced, 'Colonel Viktor Brod.'

Michael had already guessed as much from Carol's description of the man, and he was intrigued at the significance of this new turn of events. He had cultivated interest in even the smallest happenings, because he knew that once he lost interest he would lose hope, and then he would be finished—a kind of physical and mental heap that his captors could mould how they liked. He tried to look alert as he faced the heavy figure of the colonel.

'I have come to help you, Mr North.'

'Ah, a touch more moral re-education, I suppose, delivered by your thugs.' That wouldn't get him anywhere, Michael realised, but he was not going to let Brod believe he was intimidated.

The colonel ignored him. 'If you want to return to your

wife, you will be sensible and co-operate. Otherwise . . .' He left the sentence unfinished.

'I shall be allowed the full benefits of Soviet justice,' Michael supplied.

Brod nodded. He hadn't even recognised Michael's sarcasm.

'I don't know why you killed Azhimov,' Brod said, 'but that is not so important as your work as a spy.'

'You know I didn't kill Azhimov. You know I'm not a spy.'

The colonel made a growling sound, and drummed four large fingers on the table top, as though to emphasise how patient he was being.

'You have admitted taking tickets to London,' he said. 'I want to know what was on them. North!' he suddenly bellowed, 'we know Azhimov has been passing information to you, just as he has to the Americans. We know what most of it is. But we don't know what it was that you took to London.' He paused. 'See, I'm being frank with you, North. I'm trying to help you. We need to know the details of that information you took to London. You will tell us. Don't think you can avoid telling us. No one can. Either you tell us now, or we make you. It's up to you.'

'Ah, *that's* what you call Soviet justice, Colonel, is it—forcing information out of people by torture and brutality?'

'You admit there is information to be obtained.'

'No,' Michael said with feigned weariness. 'And, by the way, Colonel, when am I going to be charged with whatever I'm alleged to have done?'

'When the interrogation is finished.'

'You mean when you have tortured me into saying something that's not true.'

'You can tell the truth now. Why don't you? That's why I'm here. You've admitted taking material to London.'

'I haven't. I didn't take anything to London. Your thugs there would have found it if I had.'

'The tickets?'

'That was a joke—tickets for Wimbledon Centre Court—a joke, Colonel.'

The Russian banged the table with his fist so sharply that Michael jumped. He was surprised the wood hadn't splintered.

'Spying's a joke?' Brod bellowed. 'You'll find it's a joke if you don't tell us. I haven't time to waste with you, North. What did you take to London?'

'I didn't,' Michael said quietly and patiently.

'Don't lie! I won't stand your lies—you mother-fucking bastard. Now, tell me—what was it? What was it, North?'

This was no time for a repeated denial. Michael imagined a great fist lunging across the table and smashing him to the ground. Then the men standing behind his chair would go to work on him again. The colonel was humourless, and this was no moment to be clever.

In as conciliatory a tone as he could manage, Michael said, 'Colonel, I want to be of help. You can't believe I want to stay here in Lubyanka. I will tell you anything I can to get out of here.'

The colonel relaxed back on to his chair. If he had been capable of smiling, the slight movement of his lips might have been interpreted as a faint smile.

'That's better.'

'But, Colonel, I can't tell you what I don't know. I did not take information to London.' He saw Brod glower, the fist about to smash down on the table, and diffidently put up his hand in a gesture of restraint. 'Now you believe that Azhimov passed material to me. If that were true, I would not be likely to know what it was. I would be only a messenger. But it is not true, Colonel. There is nothing I can tell you, because I *have* nothing to tell. I am speaking the truth.'

The colonel took a deep breath. His chest swelled to even greater proportions. Then he leant back on his chair, and Michael marvelled that the wood did not snap. He appeared to be exerting himself to remain patient.

'Very well,' he said at length. 'You're obsessed with truth. You don't yet understand necessity. It's as the Major said. You will have to be interrogated again. The Major has his own methods.'

'No doubt in the end,' said Michael despairingly, 'he will

force me to invent something. Then you'll be satisfied—satisfied with a piece of fiction. Like that confession you wanted me to sign—pure invention. Is it, Colonel, that you have to have something, whether it is true or not doesn't matter? As long as it's there—fiction, nonsense, anything will do.'

The colonel stared, controlling his anger. Michael had in fact diagnosed a characteristically Russian attitude, as traditional as their stubbornness. For a few moments, he even felt his morale rise.

'It may be,' said Brod gruffly, 'that you are incapable of telling us what we want to know. If the Major can't find out, then perhaps the Serbsky Institute would be able to help.'

There was no mistaking the threat. Michael knew about the Serbsky Institute for Forensic Psychiatry—ostensibly a department of the Ministry of Health, but in fact rigidly controlled by the KGB. It was where political prisoners and dissidents were sent for 'treatment', and were often left as gibbering, insane wrecks. At least seven thousand had had 'operations' there, and had been victims of drugs like aminazin, sulfazin and reserpine. Michael knew that he would be lucky to emerge from the Institute with his brain intact.

'Maybe,' he said, making an effort to retain his humour, 'I shall have to write your fiction for you.' He saw that the colonel did not understand.

Viktor Brod towered to his feet, looked contemptuously at his prisoner and then strode out of the room. Michael tensed himself, waiting for the blow from one of the uniformed men standing behind him. It did not come. Instead, they took him firmly, but not roughly, by the arms and led him back to his cell. He sat on his stool, feeling very slightly and incongruously triumphant.

As Robert Cresswell drove out along the Leningrad Highway, Carol briefed him about Alexei Pachenko, emphasising that his relationship with Michael had always and only been one of close personal friendship. He was to be protected in all circumstances. Bob was intrigued and excited as he saw the icon story falling into shape. The only problem would be how much he could tell, and if he would have to go back to the States to do so.

It was early on Friday evening and still light when he manoeuvred the car bumpily up the track between conifers and birch trees to Alexei's *dacha*. The children, Andrei and Novia, were as boisterously welcoming as usual, but Varinka's grip on Carol's arm seemed to express as much anxiety as pleasure. Alexei by contrast looked in better spirits, his dark eyes glowing.

'My brother-in-law, Viktor, is joining us tomorrow morning,' he said, a glint in his eye. 'Let us hope it will be fine.'

The weather had to be fine, because the only place they could talk would be out of doors. The *dacha* of someone as prominently placed as Alexei was sure to be bugged. Carol and Bob exchanged understanding glances. Varinka, however, looked worried, as she busied herself preparing a meal of chicken *zatsivi*, preceded by cold sturgeon.

The whole evening Alexei was in high spirits, keeping them amused with old stories, so that Carol concluded that he had settled the conflicts in his mind, had come to a decision and had a plan. This was confirmed for her when he discussed with Varinka what she and the children and her sister, Nada, would do tomorrow morning before they all met again for a late lunch. Varinka looked apprehensive. Carol, however, felt infected by Alexei's own self-confidence. She longed to know what the next day would bring.

On Saturday morning, Alexei made sure that the colonel and Nada were met outside the *dacha*, and he explained the expedition that had been arranged for the two sisters and the children, because he had some 'official' business to discuss with Viktor. Varinka stood nervously beside her husband. Bob and Carol remained indoors and out of sight. Only after the party had left and Alexei had led his brother-in-law out to a garden seat did Carol and the American correspondent emerge from the house.

The KGB colonel rose stiffly to his feet as they came down the path towards him. For one brief moment his thick eyebrows lifted and his rugged features showed surprise, but then they quickly assumed their normal impassivity. The merest suggestion of a smile twisted his lips, as he bowed his head and muttered, 'Mrs North, I admit I did not expect to see you.'

'I imagine,' said Carol coldly, 'you are now much more acquainted with my husband.'

Before the colonel could reply, a delighted Alexei was saying, 'Robert Cresswell—do you know him, Viktor? Colonel Viktor Brod, KGB.'

The colonel grunted. 'No. I know who he is. *New York Times*.'

Bob nodded. 'A lovely morning, Colonel.'

Indeed it was. The sun was warm, and there was the merest sifting sound of a breeze in the tops of the birches. From where they were the landscape fell gradually through groves of birch trees and conifers towards open fields, a network of streams and, invisible to them, the river beyond.

Carol sat herself at the opposite end of the garden seat from Viktor Brod, Alexei perched like a chubby elf on an upturned tree stump, and Bob pulled nearer a single garden chair.

Alexei did nothing to disguise his pleasure. Carol was tense, but she affected a cool manner, hoping to conceal her anxiety, while Bob was obviously itching with excitement. Brod was as impassive as ever, but his brother-in-law's self-assured, cheerful manner was disconcerting. For once, Brod's great bulk didn't give him a feeling of overpowering superiority.

'You *said* you might have to deal with Azhimov,' Alexei began. 'So you did, Viktor.'

'You're being unfair to Mrs North, Alexei. You know her husband is being questioned about that.'

Alexei ignored the remark. He went on, 'So what was it? Had Azhimov come to the end of his usefulness to the Americans, or to you?'

'This has got nothing to do with you, Alexei, and even less with Mr Cresswell here.'

'Oh, but it has, Viktor.' Alexei was smiling again. 'It has a lot to do with all of us—and most of all with you.'

'Azhimov was spying for the Americans. He was also spying for the British, passing stuff to Mr North. I don't know why he and North quarrelled, why North did what he did—'

'Time to stop the pretence, brother,' Alexei interrupted.

Brod looked up, furious. Then he controlled his anger and lapsed into silence. There was always the anxiety about how far he could go with Alexei. The man was powerful and Brod was never sure how much he might know about his own activities.

'I think, Viktor, Mr Cresswell might tell you what he has found out—what he will undoubtedly write for the *New York Times*, what will be picked up by every broadcasting station in the world. It's not going to please Kharkov . . . even less Konevsky.'

Bob was nervous but the words bubbled out of him.

'For a long time, Colonel, you have had a working relationship with Stacey Mariner of the CIA. That in itself is not necessarily surprising in the world of espionage, but you have regularly received gifts and substantial sums of money from the Americans. That, however, is comparatively unimportant compared with the rest. Azhimov who, admittedly, has been spying for the Americans, has also been working for you. He has had access to a supply of icons, most of them extremely clever fakes, probably painted by Igor Azhimov. These icons he has passed to you. Stacey Mariner has arranged for them to be shipped to the United States, where they have been auctioned. You have received your substantial share of the money. Your real coup was going to be an "original" Rublev. Mrs North, who knows about icons, can tell you that was going just too far. You had become overconfident. Original Rublevs don't come on to the market. Is it still in the chest in your room, Colonel, waiting for Mariner to make the necessary arrangements?'

Brod jumped to his feet. He stood towering angrily over them all.

'That's all rubbish,' he shouted. 'Rubbish. Not a word of truth in it. You can't prove a thing, Cresswell.'

Alexei said quietly: 'Sit down, brother. We have a lot to discuss.'

Bob was impatient to continue. 'Then, you and Azhimov

fell out. Probably he felt that he and Igor were not getting a big enough cut for the risk they were taking. He knew you wouldn't dare inform on him for passing material to the Americans, because that would bring to light your involvement in icon smuggling and the pay-offs you'd been receiving from Mariner. So really he'd got you at his mercy, hadn't he? Why the hell shouldn't he demand a bigger cut for himself? That's why you had him killed. He'd become a threat.'

Brod stared at Cresswell with pure hate. The American's elation was unbearable. And there was Alexei—a kind of Russian Buddha, looking quietly satisfied. Brod struggled with his violent feelings. He had to control himself, discover how much Alexei knew, decide how he could use it to his own advantage. None of them, he tried to console himself, could prove anything. He sat down again, and tried to sound unperturbed.

'It would all make a very good story,' he said, 'if it were true.'

'Ah, but it is,' said Alexei, unashamedly exultant. 'I've no doubt Mr Cresswell can prove it. After all, he must have his own contacts in the American Embassy. But if he can't—I can, Viktor. I can prove it all . . . and more.'

As Brod seemed about to burst into rage again, Alexei stood up, suddenly became very serious, and put out his hands in a calming movement.

'Viktor,' he said, 'let us all stay calm. You are in trouble. More than that, you're finished. If all this comes out, you'll be on your way to one of those Siberian camps you send your prisoners to. There is, however, a way out of all this mess.' He turned towards Bob. 'If Mr Cresswell, and Carol, will agree. Of course, they may not. They may decide to publish all this anyway.'

Brod considered. He wondered—if they did—whether he could bluff it out as Western lies and propaganda, helped by a forced confession from North.

Alexei returned to his tree stump. He knew exactly what his brother-in-law was thinking. 'It won't work, Viktor. You're not taking account of me. You have to reckon with me.'

Brod stared hard at his brother-in-law. 'Nada,' he said. 'There's Nada.'

'I know,' said Alexei firmly. 'I've thought of that. You still have to reckon with me, brother.'

'You know only what they have told you,' the colonel growled, chancing an idea.

Alexei smiled. 'That's a desperate thing to say, Viktor. They know enough to finish you. I know more. Don't forget that.'

Throughout this whole exchange, Carol had sat at the other end of the garden seat, quietly watching and maintaining as cool an expression as possible. Now as Brod clenched his massive hands in his lap, she said softly, 'The way out for you, Colonel Brod, is to release my husband.'

'That's impossible.' And then remembering what Alexei had said, Brod added, 'If he would confess, if he would admit everything—then, perhaps, it could be made possible.'

'No,' said Bob, 'he has to be released. If not, then this material will be published and broadcast worldwide. More than that, Mrs North and I will see that a full dossier is with Kharkov and Konevsky within twenty-four hours.'

'They wouldn't believe you,' Brod snarled.

Alexei interrupted gently. 'I think they would. Anyway, they would believe me.'

Brod looked at him with pure hate. Alexei smiled.

At length the colonel said, 'I told you Kharkov was furious that North wasn't dealt with in London. I can't let him out—that would finish me, too.'

'Then,' said Alexei practically, 'you had better convince Kharkov that it is necessary to release him. I'm sure you'll think of something.'

Brod banged the seat with his fist so hard that Carol was surprised the slat didn't break, and then he sat there thinking. Ultimately, when he spoke, it was more calmly.

'To tell you the truth,' he said grudgingly, 'I'd begun to think North was innocent.'

'You know damn well he is,' said Carol. 'Your men killed Azhimov. Michael was set up—you know that. The KGB were waiting for him.'

Brod nodded. 'Yes, the KGB were waiting, but you don't know it was my men who killed Azhimov. It might have been the CIA—Mariner afraid that Azhimov was going to tell all about the icons. If the icon story came out, Mariner would lose me, wouldn't he? He'd lose me and, more important, he'd lose my contact with Alexei. It may not have produced anything for him yet. But to save that contact it might be worth killing Azhimov. He'd served his purpose—for both of us.'

Even as Bob burst out laughing, Carol remembered the strange encounter with Wyndham Taylor outside the Sokolniki Metro station. For a moment she wondered if Brod's version could be true. Perhaps his men had gone to the park with the intention of killing Azhimov and had found the job done for them. But Bob was already speaking.

'Colonel, you have been taken for a ride. Mariner is not involved in the icon business at all. Those icons auctioned in the States—nothing has happened to them. The people who bought them don't exist. You've been getting CIA pay-outs, Colonel, that's all—no doubt for services rendered.'

'You're trapped, brother,' Alexei said. 'You'd better start convincing Kharkov that North is innocent, both of murder and of espionage.'

'That won't be enough to get him released, you know that. Kharkov has made up his mind. It doesn't matter what anyone else thinks.'

'Then you must persuade Kharkov that there is a better reason for releasing North than for keeping him in prison.'

Brod looked from one to the other. He felt he needed a drink. They were right. He *was* trapped. And there was too much at stake.

'It'll take time,' he said reluctantly.

Alexei considered. On Thursday the Politburo had discussed their plans for an invasion of the United Kingdom but, after fierce argument instigated by the Foreign Minister and the Defence Minister, had reserved their decision until Tuesday when, if Konevsky had his way, they would also approve the timetable. By Thursday Carol could have the information.

'Wednesday,' said Alexei. 'At three o'clock on Wednesday afternoon Carol will be waiting in a car outside Lubyanka to collect him. If he is not there, then the information goes to the Politburo—'

'And to the world press,' Bob interrupted.

Brod took a deep breath that filled out his huge swimmer's chest. He was already anticipating his argument with Kharkov.

Carol said with sudden incisiveness, 'We're serious, you know. Wednesday at three, Colonel.'

He looked at her, the slate-grey eyes expressionless. Slowly he nodded.

Carol smiled faintly. 'Tell me, Colonel, how many of your own icons are fakes?'

'None of them.'

'I thought not. You're a very lucky man,' she said, deliberately underlining his dilemma. 'That Rublev—it looked original, but it just couldn't be. You were over-stretching, Colonel.'

Brod said nothing. For some moments all four sat in silence, and then Alexei spoke. 'I think we all deserve a drink. Would you like bourbon, brother?' he gazed round happily at the others. 'We've got some delicious river trout for lunch. I caught it myself. You're not the only one who can cast a pretty fly, Carol.'

When Colonel Viktor Brod entered the Chairman's office he was standing by the window—a stocky figure blowing clouds of smoke from a large cigar and staring down at the intermittent traffic circling the statue of Feliks Dzerzhinsky.

The first few minutes were difficult. Kharkov pulled at his moustache irritably and shouted that Brod should know what to do with scum like North. It had all been Semensky's fault for not getting rid of the fool in London.

But Brod persevered. He had to. There was no escape. He even dared to say that Semensky had been right in one thing. Whatever the British may or may not have got they hadn't got it from North.

Kharkov bellowed with derision. 'You're not telling me,

Comrade Viktor Leonidovich, that North is innocent, so we must release him?' He drew at his cigar and banged a stubby fist into the palm of his other hand. 'Deal with him.'

Brod remained standing as though to give authority and purpose to his size.

'Azhimov,' he said, 'was not North's only source.'

'So you think if we let him out he'll lead us to the other one? It's not necessary, comrade. Just break him, that's all you have to do. You know that.'

Brod nodded. 'Oh, that would be easy enough, Comrade Chairman,' he said, 'but I think North can be of very much more use to us. North can be turned, comrade. I'm not thinking of his use here in Moscow. But a man of his ability, and his contacts with leading political figures in Britain —well, he could be invaluable in London.'

'I hope we soon shan't need spies in London,' Kharkov said.

'That would be good, comrade. But surely we shall always need spies. Someone we can rely upon in London. It could be important, couldn't it?'

'How do you know we could trust him in London?'

Brod did a rare thing. He smiled, and it was a smile full of significance. 'Oh, I have ways of doing that,' he said with relish.

Kharkov half grunted and half chuckled, and made for the chair behind his huge desk. The argument continued. Brod had the feeling he was fighting for his life—he was certainly fighting for the style of life he had enjoyed for many years —and he argued with a passion and a conviction that he never realised he possessed. Finally Kharkov agreed. It was a grudging, unconvinced agreement, but at last he said, 'It's your job, Comrade Viktor Leonidovich. You do it how you think best.' He looked at the cigar, stubbed it into the ashtray. 'Make him work for it, eh, comrade?' He stretched his hands, palm downwards, across the desk. 'You do what is best for Russia.'

Brod had no idea what he was going to do once North was released, how he was going to justify his argument, how he was going to provide what Kharkov expected. But that was another problem, another day. The immediate thing was to save himself now. If he had thought of praying, he would have prayed that he had also managed to preserve what was dearest to him.

He paused by the double doors before leaving. 'I'll do what is best, Comrade Chairman,' he said.

# 16

Flight-Lieutenant Gerry Manson, his hands resting lightly on the controls of the RAF Tornado F2, had a sensation of almost complete isolation. Even the auto-pilot seemed to be doing a better job than he could in manual control.

The comparative quiet of the cockpit, the deep blue of the world outside, made him feel remote. That was something which even the crucifying training, which had filled him with a variety of automatic responses to every conceivable situation, had not wholly eliminated. Or perhaps the training had even cultivated it. Perhaps that's why, at the touch of a button, he was able to respond to releasing death and disaster, and . . . It was sod's law, too, he thought, that many millions of pounds could be spent designing and producing a highly sophisticated aircraft that was no longer limited by the intelligence of its pilot, and yet leave him sitting so bloody uncomfortably. In this canopied cocoon he was surrounded by what even now seemed occasionally to be a bewildering array of displays and instruments, buttons and levers, panels and screens. So why did they have to give him a control column designed for a man with six fingers and two thumbs? This time he really would write to Boscombe about it. It wasn't the first occasion Manson had succumbed to such thoughts towards the end of a standing patrol—ambling round a racetrack-shaped course over the North Sea. 'It proves I'm human after all,' he thought.

'We've got an Ivan, Gerry.' It was the voice of his navigator, Flight-Lieutenant Tim Fletcher, from the rear cockpit.

Manson noted that his own Foxhunter radar was showing nothing. So Tim was getting it on the data link from the Nimrod AEW.

'So what?' he replied in acknowledgment. There was

nothing unusual in Russian probes of this kind. They happened almost every day, aircraft on their way to Cuba, fist full of cigars, crate of rum, and hello Charlie on the way back.

A moment later, he heard Tim say, 'Different this one, Gerry. He's turned in. You have it.'

'I have it,' Manson acknowledged.

Instantly he was alert. In the seconds while his navigator was waiting for authorisation to investigate, Manson checked his fuel flow indicator and, using one of those six fingers, summoned up information about his fuel consumption and the flying time he had left. He consulted his head-up display, and heard Tim's voice: 'Tab 34—go.'

'Roger,' he responded.

Cancelling the auto-pilot, his left hand went out automatically to the wing-sweep lever. As the Tornado, its wings now raked back, banked and accelerated, the Soviet aircraft came up on his VDU.

'Initiate weapons selection procedure. Make it two,' he said authoritatively, as he sent the Tornado hurtling towards the intercept point with the Soviet aircraft.

'Roger. Initiate weapons selection for two live firings,' the navigator replied, as they both busied themselves with procedural routines.

After about ten minutes he saw the Tupolev TU95, a big reconnaissance aircraft, flying at 35,000 feet and about 500 feet below him—well into British airspace and heading for the coast.

'Here we go,' he said, and sent the Tornado screaming down across the nose of the Russian Bear, and then round in an arc until he was alongside. Manson held his position, waggled his wings and turned in the direction that he wanted the intruder to go. According to the rules of the game the Russian would follow him and fly out of British airspace.

'The sod's going on,' said Tim.

Manson could see that, both on his head-up display and visually from the cockpit. He checked his fuel state. A couple more passes, and that was it. Then he'd have to head for base.

He banked the Tornado again, and manoeuvred it alongside. The Russian ignored him and kept his course. He could see the chap in the rear turret, manning the cannon. 'He'd better not,' Manson thought to himself as he edged the aircraft forward so that he had a view of the Russian pilot. Manson jerked his closed fist with thumb extended in an unmistakably aggressive get-the-hell-out-of-here gesture. The Russian lifted two gloved fingers above the sill of his cockpit. The Tornado turned away.

Manson heard Tim's voice: 'The guy at the rear's blowing us kisses. Maybe he thinks we Brits are all like Maclean.'

'The hell he is.'

The Bear continued on a straight course. It was now only a few miles from the coast.

'He doesn't want to know the rules,' Tim said gleefully.

Manson pressed buttons and cursed that the VDU designer hadn't thought about the size of a pilot's fingers. The computer calculated the amount of flight time remaining at the present rate of fuel consumption. He considered for a moment, pressed more buttons, studied the result on his head-up display. There was one more chance, and that was it.

'Kisses,' he muttered. 'I'll tickle the bugger's balls for him.'

He raised the nose of the Tornado and positioned the aircraft slightly above and forward of the Tupolev's port wing. Then he pulled up in front of the Russian's nose.

'And I'll burn the bastard's paint. Let's see what sort of an airman he is,' he said, as he flicked in the reheat switch.

With an enormous burst of power, gases snorted from the twin jets of the Tornado in an explosion of flame. The aircraft soared upwards, and Manson killed the reheat before they accelerated away too far. He reckoned he'd just about make it home if he broke away now. There was no fuel left for another go.

The Bear bucked and tumbled crazily in the turbulence. When at last it was on an even keel, it banked away, and Manson and Fletcher watched it on their VDUs head out of British airspace.

'Got yer, yer bastard,' Manson shouted delightedly.

So what had the bugger been up to—breaking the rules

like that? And supposing he hadn't turned back? Manson shrugged.

He had already throttled back, tidying up the aircraft for economical cruise, had returned the wings to the forward position and, trimming the Tornado's nose down, he had soon lost enough height to be able to see the green-corn acres of East Anglia.

An emergency meeting of the Cabinet, unusually early in the morning, decided on a series of statements to the Commons that afternoon. The time had come to tell the nation. Already the media had become curious about military movements in Norfolk, and fortunately now plans were so far advanced that secrecy was no longer necessary. Throughout his political career Lionel Bryce had always been astute in judging the right moment for publicity, and he was confirmed in his judgement now by the Foreign Secretary. The violation of British airspace by the Russian aircraft not only demanded a statement in itself, but provided just the opportunity for—to use his own words to his Cabinet colleagues—'a complete and frank disclosure to the British people'.

The Commons was crowded. Westminster has a mysterious way of generating an atmosphere when something important is about to break. It's not so much that the corridors, the lobbies and the tea-room buzz with rumours —although they frequently do—but that MPs, sensitised over the years to the ambience of crisis, instinctively know when something of overwhelming importance is in the air. Their instinct was well fuelled by the indication in the Members' lobby that there were to be statements from the Prime Minister, the Defence Secretary, and the Home Secretary. That in itself was enough to get speculative tongues wagging.

So by 3.30 MPs were squeezed into every space on the green leather benches; they sat on the steps of the gangways; they crowded between the bar of the house and the oak swing doors leading to the Members' lobby, and they overflowed into the side galleries overlooking the chamber. The press gallery, above the Speaker's canopied chair, was full, and the public packed into the steeply pitched Strangers' Gallery opposite.

The Prime Minister, sitting on the government front bench waiting for other questions to finish, looked forbiddingly serious rather than strained. His chin was thrust out determinedly. The mane of grey hair had been neatly brushed, and when he came to stand at the despatch box he had the authority of a man who bore with confidence an immensity of problems. His voice was steady; he spoke slowly and, even in these circumstances, managed something of an actor's timing to achieve the maximum impact. It was one of the attributes which had endeared him to his party's annual conferences. Now it ensured his command of the House.

He began with factual simplicity—describing in detail the violation of British airspace late the previous afternoon by a Russian Tupolev TU95, and the action taken by the RAF. The House was silent. Even his most vociferous critics on the Opposition benches listened with quiet attention. The only sound came from above, as agency members of the press gallery shuffled from their seats to flash scraps of information to their offices.

The Prime Minister came to the end of the story of the day's events. Then he paused, looked over the crowded benches, gave a glance to the clock set in the carved oak gallery at the far end, gripped the brass-bound sides of the despatch box, and said in strong, measured tones, 'Yesterday's violation, serious though it is, is only a foretaste of much more serious and dangerous developments facing this nation.'

He paused again, letting his words dwell upon the expectant silence. Then, quietly, he outlined the demands listed in the Russian note.

The silence of the chamber broke with muttering from the benches behind him. Opposition MPs sat uneasily quiet until the Prime Minister said, 'The Soviet government has suggested that it may be necessary to impose food rationing in Britain to enable our farmers and other producers to meet quotas for the Soviet people.' Then a murmuring broke from them, while the Conservative benches erupted in anger and derision.

The Prime Minister remained standing, and the Speaker did not even call for order. People in the Strangers' Gallery were exchanging glances and whispering with astonishment among themselves. The attendants, resplendent in their tailed jackets with gold chain and badge, made no attempt to stop them. Correspondents were scurrying from the press gallery and back again. The Prime Minister held up his hands for silence, and in a few moments the noise subsided. Then he said, 'The Russian proposals—for that is what they quaintly call them—have been rejected by Her Majesty's Government.'

The tension broke. For a moment MPs burst into laughter. Then, as if realising that their sudden relief was a symptom of underlying anxiety, they simmered into silence again. The Prime Minister told them that the Secretary of State for Defence would be making a statement to the House on measures that were being taken, but for obvious security reasons much would have to remain secret. The Home Secretary would announce a state of emergency and explain what that implied for the country. Then, looking round the chamber, with his chin held aggressively high, the Prime Minister made his only political point: 'I regret to say,' he began, 'that this great nation may be about to reap the "benefits" '—he imbued the word with terrible irony—'of the previous government's policies.'

There was an immediate burst of ironic cheers from his own benches, and angry shouts from the Opposition. The Speaker, bewigged and gowned, shouted for order. At length, the lean tense figure of Tom Henson, Leader of the Opposition, stood at the despatch box on the opposite side of the table. His face showed the anger he felt, but he was an experienced enough politician to recognise that some of his anger was disappointment—the feeling of having been let down—as well as rage at his political opponents. His knuckles showed white as he gripped the despatch box. He had to be careful.

'The right honourable gentleman,' he began, 'will have

the support of the Opposition in rejecting unreasonable demands from any government.' He was greeted with ironic cheers again from the government benches. 'Some of the demands he has outlined to the House are clearly unreasonable, but that, in itself, is a reason for talking to the Soviet government.' Above the interruptions, his voice shrilled out: 'What discussions is the Prime Minister having with the Soviet Union? What is he doing to see that a friendly solution can be found to these difficult problems? Is he not aware—'

Tom Henson got no further. The House exploded with cheers from his own supporters and jeers and angry denunciations from the Conservative benches. It was more than an hour before the Secretary of State for Defence told anxious MPs about the movement of Soviet warships in the North Sea, the massing of aircraft in East Germany, and that he was providing for the immediate call-up of all reservists.

That night the Prime Minister appeared on British television. He told the people what he had told the Commons, but this time he was careful not to make any political points at all. He sat looking straight at the viewer, and explained the dangers facing the country, and what the Government had decided to do. Although he didn't say so, it was obvious that the nation was being put on a war footing.

Finally, he looked hard into the camera lens, and said soberly, 'We may have to stand alone. We have stood alone before. Together, we shall preserve our way of life.'

# 17

In the bare, cold interrogation room at Lubyanka prison Michael North had suffered one more session with the farmer major, as he had come to think of the rubicund KGB officer. The major, and a colleague, had gone over the same ground, repeating the same questions in staccato bursts. Michael, wearily yet as calmly as possible, provided the same answers. These were ignored, and the same questions, phrased slightly differently, were put again.

Once he was lifted to his feet by the two men standing behind his chair, left a moment dangling in the air and then hurled against the far wall. He had managed to cushion the impact with his hands before he crumpled to the floor. They waited for him to recover. Then one of the green-overalled men pinioned his arms high and painfully behind his back. The other first swiped him across the face and then, clutching his testicles in one hand, slowly squeezed. Michael yelled and involuntarily kicked out at his torturer. The man immediately let go, but followed with a sharp blow to the genitals. Michael lost consciousness. When he came to, aching in the groin and in his arms, he was lying on the floor about four feet from the wall. Slowly he got to his feet. The major nodded him back to the chair. As he sat down, he wondered how long he would be able to tolerate this treatment, and yet he knew that he had experienced nothing yet. He remembered what Stimson had said: it might be necessary to sign some kind of confession. He faced the major with a forced smile.

The KGB man continued as though nothing had happened—the same questions, repeated differently, and repeated again by his colleague. After about another hour, the major said suddenly, 'Are you now ready to sign the statement?'

Michael considered, trying to look indifferent. 'Does it earn my release?' he asked.

The major smiled. 'Oh, I can't say that, Mr North. Murder and espionage are serious crimes. It will get you a shorter sentence. Perhaps no more than five years.'

'Oh, balls.' Only after he'd uttered the words in exasperation did Michael smile at their painful aptness.

The major ignored them. 'In the end you will sign the confession. You will sign anything.' He waved his hand dismissively.

Michael was seized by the arms and hurried back to his cell. There he was stripped, and then taken out naked to the smelly washroom that had a shower with a rusty rose. He was made to stand for ten minutes in a stream of cold water, and then led, dripping and shivering, back to his cell. His clothes had been removed. He had heard of prisoners being wrapped tightly from head to foot in cold soaking wet canvas and then left to dry out, so that when the canvas contracted it squeezed and cut into the body painfully. He wondered if he would be able to bear it. But that was postponed. He was merely left naked and wet. He set to vigorously drying himself with his hands, and exercising in his cell. When at last he was reasonably dry and breathless with exertion, he wrapped himself in the single blanket, and curled up with the pillow on top of him.

Then, on Monday morning, there was an unaccountable change. His clothes were returned to him. He was given three more blankets, another pillow, and some books that included Dickens and Shakespeare. The bread at breakfast was better quality and there was more of it, and later there was additional meat in his soup, and he was given some tea. He even began to feel quite cheerful. But what the hell was it all about?

Colonel Viktor Brod knew where the bugs were in his Kalinin Prospekt apartment. He had swept the premises himself, noting carefully where the higher pitch of the detector indicated a device. It meant that when Stacey Mariner called he could choose the deadest part of the flat. Even so, he still switched on the radio, as the gangling American sank into a chair and crossed his legs. This time Brod did not reach into the ornate cabinet for a bottle of vodka. He sat with his huge fists on his desk, elbows up, giving Mariner a grey piercing stare.

'You bastard,' he snarled. 'You mother-fucking bastard.'

'Jesus, Colonel, who's complaining? Who killed off Azhimov?'

Brod thumped his desk. The radio was burbling some endless speech from one of the leaders of the Politburo. 'Who *did* kill Azhimov? He had to be stopped talking to the Brits about the icons.'

Mariner looked as self-satisfied as a college boy with his first date. He even chuckled.

'All good things come to an end, Colonel. Christ, you've done well enough out of it.'

Brod glared. 'All right,' he growled. 'We stop up Azhimov. You open the bleeding floodgate to fucking Cresswell.'

Mariner fingered his university tie. Brod really was a nasty sight when he was angry. However, the American felt comfortingly superior.

'Cresswell,' he said, 'has all the resources of the *New York Times*. In the States, Colonel, we have a freedom of information act. You should know. Some of your *shavki* have made enough use of it. There wasn't much Cresswell couldn't find out. That Rublev, you know, was going too far. I told you not to get too greedy.'

Brod made a hoarse sound in his throat. He could do with a drink, but he was damned if he was going to offer one to Mariner.

'Cresswell,' he muttered contemptuously, 'I may have to deal with him, Mariner.'

'Oh, I don't think so. You're not in a position to deal with anyone, Brod. Oh, sure, your masters would be very happy,' he said sarcastically, 'if you upset old Uncle Sam right now.'

It was the second time in the last forty-eight hours that Brod had felt trapped. The feeling of impotence made him angry.

Mariner added to the Russian's discomfort: 'While you'd

got that boy Azhimov, you'd got something to bargain, Brod. But you ain't got nothin' now.' He chuckled. 'Now that sure is an unfortunate position to be in.'

Abruptly the speech on the radio came to an end. Brod quickly twiddled the knob until some music burst from the speaker. Even the shelves of books that he hadn't read now made him feel hemmed in. He had an overwhelming desire to put his great hands round Mariner's long neck and strangle the life out of him. He saw the American's eyes shrewdly watching him. There was nothing he could do. The bloody man was right. It was no time to offend the Americans. Konevsky was relying on their neutrality. He banged his fists on the desk in despair.

'They know,' he said. 'Pachenko knows—the lot, icons as well.'

'Oh—it's as bad as that, is it?' Mariner made an infuriating tutting sound. 'You may yet have to get used to the idea of living in the United States, Colonel, with all the horrors of democracy.' He grinned.

'Cresswell says the buyers of those icons don't exist.'

Mariner shrugged and recrossed his legs.

'Why?' grumbled Brod. 'Why go to the trouble?'

'You needed convincing—a justification. Besides, I didn't know when I might want to make use of you, Colonel.'

Brod swore between his teeth.

'For example,' Mariner continued smoothly, 'the information the BBC man took to London.'

'I don't know. I don't know that he did.'

'Come, Colonel, copies please. That's what we need—copies.'

'It's no fucking good, Mariner. I haven't got the stuff. I don't know.'

'Now,' said Mariner teasingly, 'I'm not sure I believe that, but if it's true, comrade, then—by God—you'd better find out. If you want to stay a loyal KGB colonel of Mother Russia—and not a traitorous dealer in icons with the capitalist West—you'd better find out, Colonel Viktor Brod.'

The colonel threw himself back in his chair. The radio jumped and went on blaring out music.

'I tell you,' Brod hissed between his teeth, 'North didn't take anything to London. It was all a mistake.'

'I thought Eagle had confirmed the transaction. I also thought, Colonel, the KGB didn't make mistakes.'

'Fuck your mother.' Brod relinquished himself to common Russian swearing. His hand hovered near the radio as though he were about to hurl it at Mariner's head. Instead he slapped his hand on the desk.

Mariner untwisted himself and grinned. 'Then you'd better let me have whatever it was your people thought he'd taken to London.' Before Brod could interrupt, he added, 'You don't have any alternative, Viktor boy. Remember those icons?'

Brod's great bulk fell back in his chair. He glowered beneath his bushy brows as Mariner watched him. For several seconds the only sound came from the radio. At length Mariner spoke again.

'Checkmate,' he said coldly. 'Perhaps your brother-in-law, Alexei Pachenko, can help you.'

'He won't.' Brod muttered the words as though speaking to himself. 'I told you—he knows. He's fucking trapped me, too.'

Mariner fingered his tie. 'Your language is appalling, Colonel. But don't forget, we need to know.'

Brod was in a turmoil. He'd got nothing to force Pachenko to tell him. They were closing in on him—from all sides. At last he said quietly, 'I'll try,' not knowing how or when.

Mariner bent down to the briefcase he'd put beside his chair. He lifted it up and extracted two bottles of bourbon, and passed them across the desk to the Russian.

'Here,' he said, 'drown your sorrows.' He got up to leave. 'Oh,—and Brod, let me know when you want to defect.'

# 18

One by one the black Zil saloons, curtains drawn and flanked by police motor-cycle escorts, seethed over the wet cobbles of Red Square, and through the Spassky Gate to the Kremlin. The fourteen members of the Politburo were arriving for what each knew was going to be a divisive as well as a crucially decisive meeting. Each had carefully considered his own position, balancing the probability of success or failure, and assessing where either would leave him in the hierarchy. It was going to be an uncomfortable morning.

All of them walked the parquet-floored corridor with its strip of blue carpet, and passed through the green leather double doors of the Politburo's chamber, before the Kremlin Chimes—the ten bells in the Spassky tower—peeled out the hour, a sound as sentimentally significant to Muscovites as the chimes of Big Ben are to Londoners. None, on this day of all days, considered the irony that it was an Englishman who had put them there. Outside, tourists watched the goose-stepping soldiers march off to relieve the guard at Lenin's mausoleum.

Inside the salon, its decorations picked out in gold and white, the General Secretary of the Communist Party of the Soviet Union, Boris Konevsky, virtually the ruler of the USSR, was seated at the head of an oval table. Next to him, on his left, was the Prime Minister. He could be relied upon. Then came the Defence Minister, Nikolai Ogarovich, who, with the Foreign Minister, Yuri Groznov, was his most dangerous opponent. Konevsky knew why. Ogarovich, eight years younger, a professional soldier with, unusually, an academic bent, saw himself as Party Secretary. Konevsky looked up as the last member came in—Maxim Kharkov, the head of the KGB. For that matter, he had ambitions for the leadership, too, but in his case they ensured his loyalty.

Konevsky was a technocrat who, impatient at the inadequacies of Soviet technology, had made his way assiduously through the party machine until his succession as party leader became inevitable. He was a lean man with a sharp face and rimless glasses. He had a habit of polishing them slowly and exactly. He understood the origins of his power. Intrinsically, it was no different from that of the tsars before him. Their power had been sustained by their own secret police, the Okhrana, just as his power was sustained by the KGB. It permeated every aspect of life, and he was at the centre of it—calculating, ruthless. Over the centuries the tsars had always had to bring in foreign experts, from architects to administrators; Russia had always had to buy technology. Konevsky was determined to acquire it.

From Kharkov he knew what had been going on—Ogarovich and Groznov, working through the officials and their allies, beavering away at the 287 members of the Central Committee, in the conviction that there would have to be a special meeting of this ostensibly governing body. Normally, it only came together twice a year to rubber-stamp the decisions of the Politburo. Konevksy didn't underestimate this surreptitious manoeuvring, but for the moment he had only to worry about the Politburo. The Central Committee would be presented with a *fait accompli*. He was confident of his strength. On the wall opposite was an oil painting of Lenin, as stern, as unyielding as the bust in the corridor, and Konevsky recalled that it was Lenin who had advised that the law should not abolish terror, but that it should be substantiated and legalised in principle. Konevsky had always known the advantage of that.

Now he called on Comrade Ogarovich. The Defence Minister gave a factual account of the military preparations, the disposition of forces from the assembly of naval vessels in the Baltic and the North Sea to the movement of troops and aircraft in East Germany. His report was long and dry with facts and figures, even down to the provision of stores. He delivered it in a tedious monotone, as though he were perforce addressing a body of students when he would really rather be somewhere else. There was not a hint of disagreement.

Konevsky listened attentively, his eyes squinting behind his rimless spectacles. When at last Ogarovich had finished, the Party Secretary said sharply, 'Comrades, we have now to decide the timetable for attack and invasion. As we agreed, sporadic air attacks on London to frighten the people, aerial and naval bombardment of Norfolk, followed by a missile shower—' it was a phrase he had invented himself, and he rather enjoyed it—'and then a seaborne invasion along the Norfolk coast. We have to decide the timing of each operation.'

'Comrade Secretary . . .'

Konevsky looked up. It was the Foreign Minister, Yuri Groznov, a quiet but seasoned-looking man, senior in years to Konevsky, and in service too. He had been an ambassador in a number of Western capitals, including both London and Washington, before becoming Foreign Minister, and he was renowned for his skilful diplomacy. Moreover he had survived two previous Party Secretaries, and Konevsky didn't underrate either his ability or his influence. 'Yes?' he said.

'With respect, comrade,' Groznov began gently, 'we have more than the timetable to decide. We still have the principle. All the preparations are made. The Soviet Union is ready. That is as it should be. But we still have to decide whether to go ahead.'

Konevsky looked round at his colleagues, as though confirming his previous tally. Kharkov was pulling irritatedly at his moustache.

'So we have,' said Konevsky, a sharp edge to his voice. 'But I thought our discussion on Thursday made it clear that most of us were in favour. A formality, comrade.'

'A formality upon which the lives of many Russians depend.' Groznov had given the word 'formality' an almost ironic significance. 'Are you sure, comrade, that we have fully assessed the likely world reaction?'

Maxim Kharkov was working one stubby fist into the palm of his other hand like a pestle in a mortar. 'We know the Americans will do nothing,' he said gruffly. 'They're fed up with the British. So are the Europeans. There will be no response from what's left of NATO. You've had the intelligence reports.'

The Foreign Minister nodded patiently. 'I know,' he said, 'how reliable Comrade Kharkov's reports are. But there is a new government, a very different government in Britain—'

'That's why we're having to act,' the Party Secretary interrupted sharply. 'This is old ground, comrade. Long ago—under the last British government—we decided we would occupy the United Kingdom, a more valuable accession than any of the others in Europe. The decision was taken, Comrade Foreign Minister.'

Before Groznov could repeat patiently that it was the very existence of the new government that made reconsideration of their decision necessary, the Minister of Defence broke in.

'Comrade Party Secretary,' he said, 'there will be a big loss of Soviet lives.'

'There's always been a big loss of Soviet lives,' snapped Konevsky. 'The people are used to it.'

'The British aircraft are better than ours,' Ogarovich added.

'But fewer.'

'And their hunter-killer submarines—'

'Are far outnumbered,' Konevsky snapped again. He took off his glasses and polished them methodically, as though daring anyone to speak until he had finished. 'Our forces,' he added in a calmer, insistent tone, 'are infinitely greater.'

The Foreign Minister was doodling with his ball-point, as though he were idling the time away at some international negotiation. It irritated Konevsky.

Groznov looked up, straight into the Party Secretary's eyes.

'We made a mistake over Afghanistan,' he said quietly.

'That was a very long time ago, before my time. And who can compare Afghanistan—?'

'I was thinking of international opinion.'

'What does it matter?' Konevsky asked tartly.

'Militarily,' said Ogarovich with professorial composure,

'it will be a formidable operation. The British haven't had an invasion since 1066,' he added.

Konevsky thumped the table. 'We don't want history lessons, comrade. That's got nothing to do with it.'

'I was trying to indicate,' the Defence Minister continued, 'that the British resistance will be unusually fierce. It could be,' he went on ominously, 'that the Soviet losses will be unacceptably large.'

The Foreign Minister was nodding his support. 'I think there can be no doubt about that,' he said.

Konevsky knew that, if he were to be defeated, it would be because of Groznov's skill. The Foreign Minister was a patient man with practical experience of the Western democracies and a keen appreciation of the limits of the possible. But Konevsky had no intention of being defeated.

'I don't accept that,' he said coldly.

The members looked at each other. Konevsky was staring straight at the portrait of Lenin. What happened next convinced him that Groznov and Ogarovich had planned their strategy for this meeting in detail.

The Defence Minister launched quietly and studiously into a detailed assessment of expected losses. He took each stage of the operation, and each unit employed in that stage, examined its capability, estimated the resources that would be deployed against it, and then produced his figures for Soviet dead and wounded on a day-to-day basis. It was an astonishingly formidable exposition, the more so because it was done in such a factually detached manner.

Konevsky saw that it had achieved its purpose. The waverers were less sure of their commitment. He took off his glasses, polished them thoughtfully, and the Politburo waited in silence. He replaced them carefully on his sharply pointed nose and looked round at the men who shared with him the government of the Soviet Union.

'It need not happen,' he said decisively. 'A few losses during aerial and naval bombardment will be inevitable, and acceptable, I think,' he added sardonically to Ogarovich, 'but the rest can be avoided.'

Konevsky sat up straight in his chair, letting the words

work on the ensuing silence. He waited until all eyes, and especially those of Ogarovich, were turned towards him. Then he said, 'The nuclear weapon.' Instantly he held up two thin hands to prevent interruption. 'First, we will threaten its use. Then, if needs be, we will use it.'

He waited. The Defence Minister shifted uneasily in his chair.

'Comrade Secretary,' he said icily, 'there is little sense in using the nuclear weapon on a country you intend to occupy.'

Konevsky bristled. 'You are right, comrade,' he said, getting up from his chair and walking briskly to a globe of the world placed near one end of the table. He turned it with one finger to the position he wanted. 'That is why,' he said, 'the weapon will be targeted on this place.' He jabbed with his finger. 'Or this.' He jabbed again. 'The Orkneys, or the Shetland islands. Total population of the Orkneys is about 17,000, with six and a half thousand of them on Mainland. That would be the target island. Population of the Shetlands is slightly more than 17,000, with just over 6,000 in Lerwick—the target town. In either case, you will see that the fall-out will not affect mainland Britain. If we choose the Orkneys, the north of Scotland may suffer a bit. It probably won't if we choose the Shetlands. And in that event, any drift from the fall-out is not likely to affect anyone. A few oil rigs perhaps. The Norwegian coast—unlikely if we choose the right weapon.' He resumed his seat at the table. 'The British,' he said, 'have no means of retaliation. They will accept our terms rather than allow a nuclear attack.'

'And the Americans?' muttered the Foreign Minister.

Konevsky peered at him coldly. 'We know the Americans have already told the British that they will not become involved.'

'But if they did,' said Groznov, 'we should have a nuclear war.'

'They won't,' said Konevsky irritably.

'They have a common heritage, common values.'

The Party Secretary smacked his hand on the table.

'They've opted out. They've said so.' His voice was edged

with anger. 'Anyway, the threat will be enough. The threat. The Brits are not going to risk it.'

Groznov thought the party leader was underestimating the effect of a change of government in Britain. The Foreign Minister had the advantage of knowing the British Prime Minister and Foreign Secretary personally. He thought Konevsky was making a mistake, and after a glance at Ogarovich decided that perhaps he should be left to make it.

'I tell you, comrades,' Konevsky shrilled, 'we shall only need to threaten them. They have no alternative.'

He paused, looking from one comrade to the next. Votes were only very rarely taken at meetings of the Politburo, and Konevsky had no intention of taking one now. He calculated the risk and took it. 'Very well,' he said, 'that's agreed. Let us now consider the timing.' He sat erect, a lean but commanding figure, and adjusted his glasses. 'Comrade Ogarovich,' he called.

# 19

Some hours after the Politburo had met that Tuesday, Michael North was taken from his cell in the Lubyanka prison and led, not as he had expected, to the interrogation room, but to the office of Colonel Viktor Brod. The colonel sat behind a large and ornately carved desk with a smaller table alongside holding a battery of telephones and filing trays. The desk itself was empty. The back of the colonel's chair was carved to match the curlicues of the desk. That apart the room was sparsely furnished with odd chairs, and gave the appearance of not being in regular use. Brod indicated a hard wooden chair on the other side of the desk, which meant that Michael could look beyond him through the tall windows. The guard withdrew.

The colonel leant towards him. There was an unconvincing attempt at a smile.

'I hope you have no complaints about the way you are now being treated,' he said.

'Soviet kindness and generosity know no bounds.'

'You haven't been very co-operative.'

'And you seem to have forgotten a piece of paper signed at Helsinki many years ago.'

The colonel glowered. Michael could see that either his manner was irritating the colonel or something else had put him at a disadvantage. He looked uncomfortable.

Michael tried to smile non-commitally.

'In fact, Mr North, you are a very lucky man, luckier than you deserve to be.'

'You surprise me, Colonel.'

Brod continued to stare. Michael thought the look was one of hate, and yet that seemed too simple an explanation. There was something puzzling about the man's expression, or perhaps it was just his natural ugliness.

'You are to be released,' Brod said, drawing air between his teeth and swelling his chest. When he expelled the breath it was like an explosion of despair. 'Yes, tomorrow afternoon.'

'It can't be that truth has triumphed? Or even logic prevailed?'

The colonel clenched his fists on the desk top. 'Comrade Kharkov,' he said, 'was sceptical. To be frank, he thinks we should have dealt with you more effectively in London.'

'And you persuaded him to let me go?' said Michael sarcastically.

The colonel was oblivious. 'You could say that.'

Michael was unable to restrain a chuckle. The colonel was disconcerted. He didn't understand the Englishman. He only resented and hated the man because, inadvertently, he had provided the bait in the trap. Brod now was glad to be rid of him. That would be one danger out of the way. It left only Mariner. Only? Probably the whole bloody CIA. And there was always Igor in some forgotten village in Azerbaijan. But there was no reason why he should squeal. He could still paint his icons and sell them to unsuspecting Russians and the occasional tourist—if tourists ever got to Azerbaijan.

Brod leant even further across the desk. 'There is no reason now,' he said, 'why you shouldn't sign the confession. It . . .' he paused, thinking to himself, 'it would help.'

Michael laughed. 'Oh dear—what an elaborate hoax, just for that. I might have known, Colonel, I might have known.' The colonel scowled uncomprehendingly. 'It is remarkable —it really is—that a system built for such torture and tyranny can sometimes be so pathetic, so naïve.'

Brod banged the desk.

'So when does the torture start?' Michael asked.

'I tell you,' said Brod angrily, 'you're going tomorrow. Three days to leave the country. Now why don't you sign? I don't understand you, North. What's it matter to you? Sign!' he bellowed.

The colonel was an astonishing sight. Michael was puzzled. It was difficult to believe they really were going to release him. He saw no reason why they should, and yet he didn't believe it was his deliberately nonchalant manner, his bravado, which now gave him an inexplicable feeling of advantage. Something had happened. The colonel was put out.

'I don't want to appear ungrateful,' Michael said with mock seriousness, 'but I couldn't do that, Colonel. You know, as well as I do, that it's a pack of lies. I'm sure you understand that, as a simple reporter, I do like to have the facts right.'

With his left hand, the colonel stabbed at a button at the side of the desk. The guard entered almost instantly. Brod couldn't bring himself to speak. He jerked his head angrily, and the guard led Michael back to his cell.

They never saw each other again.

A few minutes before three o'clock on Wednesday afternoon Carol Rogers drove slowly to a halt alongside the entrance to the KGB headquarters in Dzerzhinsky Square. Two militiamen guarded the closed doors that bristled with brass fittings. All the windows were hung with close-drawn curtains of white net. Traffic circled sparsely round the statue of Iron Feliks. The whole area, with eight or nine streets feeding into it, was more like a circle than a square. The wide pavement by the dreaded Lubyanka was still damp from a shower. Not a soul walked there. It was invariably empty. Muscovites seemed to shun it instinctively. In the grey light the building looked more depressing than usual.

Carol suppressed her nervous excitement, determined to remain calm. She had dressed immaculately, her blonde hair crisp and wavy. She wanted to look good. But the thought of seeing Michael, wondering how he would be, did not disturb her alertness. She kept the car engine running, and watched the closed doors and the impassive figures of the guards. There had been no communication with the British Embassy which, normally, would expect to be informed if a British subject was to be released. The Ambassador had consequently been sceptical, but Carol had no real doubts. She had seen Brod at Zavidovo, and was sure that his main interest now would be to save his own skin. So she waited confidently. It was a simple route back to the Embassy—down Karl Marx

Prospekt towards the Moscow River.

At two minutes past three she was aware of something happening behind her. She glanced in the rear-view mirror, inwardly cursing as she did so. Michael was emerging from the entrance of the post-war building that had been bodged on to the nineteenth-century original. She slammed the car into reverse, so that she was alongside the entrance even before he was on to the pavement. She leant over and threw open the door. She saw Michael run headlong across the space between them.

Then the shooting began. Three shots whined and chipped over the paving stones.

Michael yelled, 'Christ!' He hurled himself into the car and flat on the passenger seat, his head below the windows.

Carol, already holding the car in first gear, let out the clutch and thrust the accelerator to the floor. Even as Michael shouted 'Down!' there was another explosion and shattering of glass. She crouched as low as she could over the wheel, and the car careered towards the square. She heard the ping of a bullet off the coachwork as the door slammed shut. Through the mirror she saw the rear screen had gone. Behind, two black Volgas were racing to close the gap. There was never much traffic in Moscow, but she guessed there was enough about her now to put a stop to the shooting.

'Are you all right?' she called.

'Yes. You?'

'Glass cut on hand—that's all.'

'They would have got me,' he breathed. 'Could have done easily. It was your reversing the car—threw them off, I reckon.'

She changed down, and accelerated past a bus and a lorry, making towards Sverdlov Square. As she approached a car drove sharply from a road on the right and headed straight towards her.

'Jesus!' she breathed, swinging the steering wheel violently left to avoid a collision, and then accelerating straight ahead again, across the top of the square and on towards the National Hotel. Then she saw them, parked just beyond the hotel—two black Volgas. Michael who, by now had prised himself into a half sitting position, saw them too.

'The subway,' he said.

Carol lurched the Volvo left just past the hotel and headed towards the west end of Revolution Square. She changed down, accelerated fiercely, and brought the car to an equally fierce stop right by the entrance to the subway.

As they flung open the doors, they heard brakes squealing, engines revving. They ran as fast as they could through the subway towards the Metro station, bumping into swearing Muscovites as they did so. Voices were shouting behind them. Michael saw Carol now far ahead of him at the Metro entrance, pushing her five-kopek piece into the slot. People seemed to close in on him. He pushed them aside, hurrying after her. By the time he thrust his own five kopeks into the machine he had lost sight of her. He ran on until he was in the main corridor with its balustrades and arcades. At this time of the day the crowds were not all that thick, but he couldn't see Carol anywhere. He was about to shout, then realised the folly of doing so. He tried to merge himself with Muscovites hurrying to catch trains, and instantly felt more conspicuous than before.

All down the main corridors were arched alcoves, sheltering the crouching shapes of bronze statues—idealised figures of workers, sportswomen, soldiers, and other citizens. Looking back, he saw a single grey-coated figure staring all round him, searching. Michael shrunk lower among the stream of people and edged himself towards one of the alcoves, flanked by a bearded figure with a rifle slung over his shoulder. He pressed himself into the shadow, and wondered where the hell Carol was. She had been ahead of him, she must have been. But had he gone on, grey-coat would have seen him, caught up with him. He squeezed himself back behind the bronze statue. Then he saw the KGB man hurry past, impatient among the travellers. A few seconds later another followed. He guessed they would assume that he and Carol were making for the platform—the obvious reason for diving into the Metro. He would give them a chance to get well out of sight, and then make his way back to the street. He was worried about Carol, but assumed, once she realised they had been separated, she would take advantage of the situation, probably lead the followers off and eventually make her way back to the British Embassy.

One more grey-coat passed the alcove. Michael waited, hidden from the people hurrying by. At last, he decided it was safe to move. He stepped from behind the bronze and, as he did so, saw the KGB man coming back towards him, moving close to the wall. Michael jumped back into the recess. But the man had seen the sudden movement. He hurried forward to the front of the alcove. Michael stood hard against the wall at the very back. As grey-coat stepped inside, Michael saw the pistol drawn from the pocket. The KGB man moved in closer, out of sight of the passersby. He jerked the gun and his head at the same time. Michael ignored the invitation to move out. He remained quite still. Surely the man wouldn't shoot him there?

For a few seconds they stayed looking at each other. Then the KGB man said, 'All right, I shall shoot you here.' He lifted the gun. The range was point-blank.

Michael opened his mouth to shout. The sound strangled in his throat. But if grey-coat had noticed the sudden surprised expression, it was too late. From behind him came a sharp chop with the edge of a hand to his neck. Even before he crumpled to the ground, he was swung round and a hand of straight fingers with painted nails drove viciously into his throat. The only sound was a reactive choking and the weight of his body as it hit the floor.

Michael stared in astonishment at the self-confident, slightly mocking smile on Carol's face—the same expression that he had seen when first he'd met her, waiting for him in his own flat.

'Come on,' she said, reaching one hand towards him, as she bent down and picked up the fallen pistol with the other. She gave the recumbent figure a glance. 'I hope I haven't killed him.'

Holding Michael's hand firmly she drew him out into the corridor.

'Not the tube,' he said. 'They'll be there.'

'They are,' she smiled, as they mingled with hurrying,

pushing Muscovites. 'Two of them. They're both on the blue-line platform.'

He said nothing, content to let her take charge. He held on to her hand, feeling rather stunned.

Carol hurried him down to the red-line platform, and they stood hard against the wall while she cast professional glances over the other travellers. When the grey and green train slid to a stop at the platform they were among the first in. They sat holding hands, not even attempting to talk above the roar of the train in the tunnel.

At Sverdlov Square and Marx Prospekt stations, Carol looked keenly at every person entering their car. As that was where the chase had started it occurred to her that the KGB might take a look at the Metro. But no one obviously recognisable boarded the train.

'Are you all right?' she asked. She had already noted how drawn he looked.

He nodded. 'Thanks to you,' he said, squeezing her hand.

The train moved off. When they reached Mayakovskaya station, she said, 'I think we might get out here. We'll pick up a taxi.'

As they walked beneath the massive ceilings, with their brilliantly lit mosaic domes depicting Soviet achievements in the air, she said, 'When I saw you weren't with me, I realised you must have stopped back somewhere. So once I'd located the KGB men, I followed one of them back. It was lucky.'

For the first time Michael chuckled, and he enjoyed the relief. 'Very lucky,' he said. 'I didn't know you were so nifty with your hands.'

She smiled. 'Part of the training,' she added laconically.

They came out into fresh air by the Tchaikovsky Concert Hall on the wide Sadovoye Ring. He paused by a flower stall at the entrance. 'I've still got some money,' he said. 'I'll buy you tulips—red ones.'

She clung to his arm. 'I should have known it wouldn't be that easy getting you out. But Brod was taking a risk. He can't afford to have you dead.'

'I don't think it was Brod. More likely Kharkov's doing.'

'Ah, I see,' she said. 'Anyway, you're here.'

'Yes, why *did* they let me out?'

'I'll tell you later,' she smiled. 'You can thank the icons.'

'I'm being given three days to leave the country. I suppose they'll inform the Embassy—officially.'

'That'll do nicely. I'm seeing Alexei tomorrow. The Politburo met yesterday.'

The second taxi showing its green for-hire light deliberately ignored them. It's not unusual if the driver has done his quota for the day.

'Blast,' Carol muttered. 'I don't want us on the streets for too long.'

Michael, standing with her at the kerbside, held his arm aloft, with two fingers raised. 'We'll get a cab "on the left",' he said.

This was virtually an invitation to anyone with a car, plus the indication that twice the normal fare would be paid. Within a few minutes, a black car, almost certainly some official's vehicle that the chauffeur was using for his private purposes, drew alongside them. The irony of it appealed to Michael. He seated himself beside the driver, and Carol got in the back. He asked to be taken to the British Embassy. The driver looked at him curiously, shrugged, and drove off.

# 20

Carol didn't know whether it was sentiment or a sense of the dramatic that had made Alexei choose the Exhibition of Economic Achievement for their final meeting. It was where it had all started at the beginning of spring, when Michael had been given the microfilm to take to London. Now, only a few weeks later, at the height of Moscow's summer, it was ending. Michael had wanted to come with her to see his old friend for the last time. That had been firmly ruled out, not only by Carol, but by the Ambassador. It had been a little more difficult to dissuade the Embassy from providing an experienced operator to tail her. She had even forbidden Michael to write a farewell note.

She left the Embassy on foot and, only after satisfying herself that she was not being followed, rode the Metro to the VDNKh station. She was lightly clad in a long-sleeved summer dress, and carried only a leather shoulder bag. It would have needed a very observant person to note that the strap nearest the bag was fastened by another strap, beneath the cuff of her sleeve, firmly to her wrist. She carried in the bag, unbeknown to the Ambassador, the KGB pistol that she had acquired the previous day. She had checked that it was loaded.

Carol stepped from the Metro station into brilliant sunlight. It flashed off the sides of the space obelisk that swept 300 feet into the air. She was in good time, and so ambled slowly among the scattering of other visitors down the main avenue towards the central pavilion. She noted one or two envious glances, and hoped her dress was not too obviously of Western style. She had been careful to choose the least flattering that she had with her and looked cool and alert. It was impossible not to feel a certain nervous excitement, although she tried to quell it.

Alexei was there, waiting on one of the lower steps. He smiled sadly and hugged her. She saw the question in his eyes.

'Yes,' she said. 'He's at the Embassy.'

The area is so vast, the paths so wide between the tree-lined lawns leading to the fountains, that they were not bothered by other visitors. Even so Alexei led her off along a path to the left towards the parks and lakes. As they drew away, Carol said, 'There was shooting—a chase.'

Alexei turned towards her, his eyes darkly troubled. 'Kharkov's doing,' he said. 'Brod wouldn't risk it. Too much at stake for him.'

By the time they were walking at the lakeside, there was hardly another person to be seen. There was, after all, enough to keep most people occupied in the seventy-eight pavilions devoted to Soviet achievement. The Russian slackened his pace. When each was satisfied that they were out of sight of anyone else, he took from his inner pocket a package, which he handed to her. She put it in her shoulder bag.

'That must be opened in a dark room,' he said. 'It is undeveloped microfilm. It contains the decisions of the Politburo, and the timetable for each stage of military action against the United Kingdom.'

He took her arm and drew her closer to him. He sounded despairing. 'Carol,' he said, 'they are prepared to use a nuclear weapon. If Britain does not agree our terms, the weapon will be used. The day has been decided. You have the date, too.'

There was a scuttering sound as a mallard's webbed feet braked on the water. The ripples scudded towards the bank. For a split second Carol thought they could be in Regent's Park or St James's Park. And yet there were worlds between them.

'The terms will be rejected,' Carol said.

'Of course, of course.' Alexei nodded and grimaced sadly. 'But it will give you a chance to talk to the Americans. Only the Americans can stop them now. You must return to London at once. Don't try transmitting that. It will only be intercepted.'

Carol nodded. 'Tomorrow,' she said.

He dropped her arm, stopped and looked at her, then threw up his chubby hands in despair. 'There is nothing more I can do,' he said.

They walked on slowly. There was scarcely a breeze on the water. The trees were still, the sun warm. Just a middle-aged man and a younger woman—a father and daughter—were walking in the park. It was so natural that it was hard to believe that not only could both of them be in danger but great nations as well. Carol half turned. A man was walking among the trees a long way behind them, and a moment ago she had seen a woman on the other side of the lake. Otherwise the whole landscape was theirs, the quiet and the peace of it.

'Is Varinka well?' Carol asked, feeling a need to reinforce the naturalness of the occasion.

'H'm. We have talked, Carol. It has been very difficult. Varinka is frightened—for Nada, I think, more than for herself.'

'And you?'

He shrugged, tried to laugh, but the sound didn't come.

'I shall be all right,' he said.

'Brod won't try—?'

'He might. But . . .' he sighed, cleared his throat, 'it's like the balance of terror between the Soviets and the United States. Neither dares because of the other. Brod won't dare because of what I know. If he destroys me, he destroys himself.'

'I wish . . .' Carol began.

He patted her arm. 'I know what you wish. It's not possible. Don't worry. I've thought it through. I haven't betrayed anyone. I've done what I've done because—' he threw up his arms—'because I had to. There was no alternative, not for me.'

She took his arm. 'Thank you,' she said. 'Mike wanted to see you, to . . .' she hated uttering the words, 'to say goodbye.'

'H'm. Give him my love, Varinka's, the children's.'

As he turned towards her, she thought she saw tears in his eyes. 'We shall both go back to London tomorrow,' she said.

'Michael has been given three days to leave. The Embassy were told this morning.'

Alexei nodded. 'Be careful,' he said. 'I don't have to tell you, do I?' he added significantly. 'Fountain pens, pencils, lighters, umbrella tips . . .'

'Don't worry about us. Look after yourselves. You have discussed with Varinka the possibility . . .?'

He held up his hand to interrupt her. 'We could never leave Russia,' he said. 'The children. *I* could never leave. It is all I know . . .'

'But you've been to the West . . .'

He smiled. 'But I am Russia; Russia is me.' He made another despairing gesture with his hands. 'I want only peace for Varinka and the children. If there is a tragedy in our situation—I mean those of us who understand the value of personal freedom, and Russians don't understand that because it has never been part of our history, but those of us who do, and those of us who perhaps can see what is wrong, even why it is wrong—for us, the tragedy is that there is no way out of it; no exit. But I don't think really that it is a tragedy, Carol. It is an inheritance. It is for me as it is for all Russians.'

They had walked back to the shelter of the trees. He took both her hands. 'It's time to say goodbye,' he said. 'If you can stop their plan . . .' He left the sentence unfinished.

'We shall hold a "birthday" for you every year,' she said.

He tried to smile, and embraced her warmly. Then they both turned away, in opposite directions.

Carol walked about fifty yards before she looked back. She lifted her arm to wave, but it stopped, half-raised. A man was walking briskly from the trees beside the path. Already he was drawing level with Alexei. Instinctively, Carol sidestepped into the shrubbery. The professional thing to do was get out quickly. She had what she wanted and that was all that mattered. Then she saw the pistol drawn swiftly and thrust into Alexei's side as the two men talked. She was confident that she hadn't been followed. So either this man had been specifically instructed to tail Alexei—in which case, why weren't there two of them?—or he had picked him up by chance. Carol favoured the latter explanation, but either way, if he had seen the package passed, she was not going to be allowed out of the country with it, unless . . .

She dodged back on to the grass, and moved rapidly between the trees to catch them up. At present they were still standing just off the narrow path, and Alexei was gesturing with his hands. They were all in the remoter part of the park and there was no sign of anyone else nearby. As she skipped from tree to tree, she withdrew the KGB pistol from the centre section of her shoulder bag. With that bag tethered to her wrist she wouldn't be able to take aim in the classic two-handed stance. Oh well, it would have to be at very close range.

The last few yards were difficult. There was an open space between two groups of lime trees, and Alexei and the man were on the opposite side from her. She saw the man gesture threateningly with the pistol. She was sufficiently close now to hear their conversation—the man accusing Alexei of passing something to a foreigner, and Alexei denying all knowledge of it, and then even trying to threaten the man with his own position.

Carol judged the distance between them, even tried with her legs well apart to grip the pistol in both hands and take aim, but the bag made it difficult. She had to cross the space and get in close before the KGB man was aware of what was happening. If she was to get the information back to London, and Alexei remain unsuspected, the man had to die. Well, she'd been trained for just such a situation; there was no point in hesitating.

She checked again that there was no one in the immediate neighbourhood. Satisfied that she was unobserved, she moved stealthily a few feet from the shelter of the trees. Then she rushed across the intervening space, the pistol clutched in her right hand. She intended to fire when she was little more than a yard away.

Half-way across the space the man heard her. He spun round. She saw his gun raised. She hurled herself low at his legs. The gun fired. The bullet veered above her into the trees as the man fell to the ground. Her pistol had fallen from her hand. Already Alexei had bent down and grabbed it. The man rolled over to position himself to fire, and Alexei loosed off two rounds. They made a mess of the man's head.

For a moment Alexei looked unbelievingly at the weapon in his hand, as Carol got to her feet. Then he passed it to her. Without a word she replaced it in her shoulder bag. Alexei grabbed her hand.

'Quickly,' he said.

She was surprised how rapidly the Russian could move, as he drew her away beneath the trees. Only when they were well hidden, and nearly a hundred yards farther on, did he stop. Each of them looked back. There was no suggestion that they had been seen or that anyone was following them. But the sounds of the shots would doubtless send people hurrying into the park. Carol brushed herself down as best she could, and they strolled as normally as possible towards the nearest path. At the far end was the old Trinity church. Now there were people all about them. One man asked, 'Did you hear shots? I thought I heard shots.'

'Yes, so did I,' said Alexei. 'Where were they?'

The man shook his head, and hurried on. Alexei led Carol into the church, and they sat down in the half-gloom.

'I made a mess of that,' said Carol matter-of-factly.

He patted her hand. 'You're very brave. You saved me,' he said.

'Unless they know he was following you,' she said.

'I can deal with that. I've covered myself for this afternoon. Providing he was alone,' Alexei added.

'I'm sure he was.'

'Then,' Alexei gestured, 'everything's all right.'

For some minutes they sat silently. He still held her hand. Then he said, 'I've never done that before—killed a man.'

Carol replied grimly, 'It was necessary.'

'Oh, I know, I know.'

'And I meant to do it myself.'

'It became a joint operation,' he said with heavy-hearted irony. 'But we never act alone, do we? Isn't that what your poet, Donne, said?'

'You mean, "Any man's death diminishes me, because I'm involved in mankind"?'

'H'm.'

'And any man's life,' she said, 'and the saving of life—that involves you too.'

'Yes . . . yes, I hope so. You must go now.'

But there was no urgency in his voice. It was as though he didn't want her to go at all. He fumbled in his inner pocket hesitantly.

'I . . . I wanted to give you this,' he said, 'but then decided it was too risky. But now—well, it's still not very sensible, but I want you to have it.'

He handed her a photograph of himself with Varinka and the two children in the garden at the *dacha*. It was a happy family group.

Carol took it and put it in her shoulder bag. It wasn't sensible at all, she knew that. But she wanted the photograph as much as he wanted to give it to her. Quickly she kissed him on both cheeks. He held her as though he were holding on to life itself, then suddenly let her go.

She stood up to leave. He smiled.

'We shall fish for trout again, Carol . . . one day.'

# 21

Getting the microfilm safely back to London presented no problem to the British Embassy. It would go in the diplomatic bag or, more precisely, in a despatch box chained to the left wrist of one of the Queen's Messengers.

The security of material in the diplomatic bag was respected by the Russians. Michael knew that, and the Ambassador had long ago reminded him that it was the course he should have adopted on the first occasion. But Pachenko had said so firmly, 'Not to the Embassy, Michael. That could only cause trouble. You must go to London, at once.' His friend's insistence, his anxiety, and his sincerity had persuaded Michael to take the material back himself. He couldn't expect the Ambassador to understand that. But this time it was different.

Nevertheless, the Ambassador took the precaution of having the microfilm developed at the Embassy, so that, in the unlikely event of the Soviet authorities being able to arrange some surreptitious surveillance of the diplomatic despatch box, there would be no danger of unprocessed film being damaged. As a further precaution he retained the negative film.

The normal day for the diplomatic bag was Wednesday but an additional bag on the Friday flight was necessary from time to time. So there was no reason why it should arouse Soviet suspicion on this occasion. For his part, Michael saw no reason either why the Russians, this time, should have the least suspicion that he might be taking any information back to London. Carol was less sure. It assumed, she said, that they believed Azhimov to be the only source. Michael, on the evidence of his treatment in the Lubyanka, was convinced that's what the Russians did believe.

'But what was WT doing talking to Azhimov?' Carol asked. 'We know it was him now.'

Michael admitted being perplexed. It was difficult for him to distrust his American friend. Carol was much more sceptical. She even found it hard to believe that WT's presence at Sokolniki on the day of the Azhimov affair was a coincidence. Twice since his release Michael had tried to get WT on the telephone, and had failed. He was inclined to dismiss that as a coincidence too. Carol was suspicious.

'All right, what are you saying—he's spying? Who for?' Michael questioned.

'I'm saying that he could have killed Azhimov just as well as the KGB.'

'I thought the Americans wanted to keep him alive? He was spying for them.'

'They might have decided he had come to the end of his usefulness, and they wanted to prevent him telling you about the Brod-Mariner icon business. Once that had been published Brod would be no more use to them. He was the bigger fish.'

Michael considered. 'And Brod wanted Azhimov out of the way for the same reason?'

'Of course.'

'I don't care,' Michael sighed. 'But I shan't uncross my fingers until we're out of Russian airspace.'

Carol peered at him under her well-shaped brows with a gently teasing look. She had an enormous sense of relief, and she was happy. But that only meant she had to be even more alert. The mission wasn't over yet and, she reminded herself, they still had to face the possibility of Russian military action against Britain, and that included the use of a nuclear weapon.

The journey from the Embassy to the Sheremetyevo International Airport took about an hour. Carol had warned Michael to say nothing that could be the least incriminating during the drive. Garage staff couldn't be guaranteed, and a radio transmitter no bigger than a matchstick could easily be concealed in the car. They were accompanied only by Robin Stimson, on the argument that the less fuss made about their departure, the least suspicion it was likely to arouse. The Queen's Messenger travelled separately.

So Michael chatted about fishing, and Carol pretended an interest that it had never been easy to cultivate in spite of the expertise she had acquired through the skill of her tutor in Devon. As they drove north-west, they saw Muscovites coarse-fishing from the banks of the river. Others were sunbathing. They sped past heavy lorries thundering their way towards Leningrad until they turned off on to the airport road.

They had very little luggage, and the routine of checking in and having their passports examined and stamped by the green-hatted border police was surprisingly quick and efficient. Carol saw the name Carol Anne North on her passport with a little *frisson* of pleasure.

When they came to the security check all they were carrying was Carol's handbag and Michael's briefcase. Each was passed through the electronic devices, and the handbag was returned to Carol without being opened. A copy of *Pravda*, a couple of Russian books and one or two other papers were, however, taken from Michael's briefcase and spread on the bench. Then the case itself was examined minutely, the experienced fingers of the KGB man feeling round the edges and the lining. Michael stood silently watching. He firmly resisted the inclination to joke. They wouldn't understand him, and it would only arouse suspicion. Ultimately the case was taken away, and a few moments later a senior officer returned and announced brusquely, 'We shall have to keep your case, Mr North. You're free to go.'

Michael hesitated. If he made no protest at all, surely that would look unnatural. He didn't dare glance at Carol, whom the officer was eyeing with undisguised lust.

'But there's nothing there,' Michael protested. 'You've seen that. I only want it to hold these books and papers. It's—'

'I'm sorry,' the officer said. 'You can't have it.'

'But—'

'Unless you would like to be detained until we've cleared

your case, Mr North . . .' He left the sentence unfinished, but added, almost as a command, 'You're free to go.'

Making a grumbling noise, Michael took Carol's arm, and they wandered through to await their flight. The briefcase was not returned. Some distance away from them the austere figure of the Queen's Messenger also waited patiently for the flight to be called, the despatch box chained to his wrist.

The curtains in Colonel Viktor Brod's office in Dzerzhinsky Square remained undrawn until late in the evening. He leant back from his huge carved desk, fingering a small slip of paper bearing a coded message. It had been collected from a dead-letter box and, on his instructions, brought to him immediately. So it was the only copy. He had decoded it himself. Its message was brief: *Unconfirmed, North taking plans London—Eagle.*

On decoding the message Brod had sworn angrily, and then instantly reached for the telephone. Even as his fingers clawed at the handrest, he stopped. A deeper instinct for self-preservation intervened. He looked at his watch. Flight BA 711 would still be in Russian airspace. Military aircraft could intercept it and turn it back. But supposing North had nothing on him? The message was unconfirmed. That was underlined. If he put a couple of military aircraft into the air, grounded the jetliner, all for nothing, Chairman Kharkov would round on him for incompetence. It had been difficult enough engineering North's departure. Even if the message proved true, then Kharkov would want to know why North had so nearly got away. Brod could hear him thundering that he'd known all along that North should never have been released. He should have been broken and forced to confess in the usual way. In either event it would reflect badly on Brod.

The colonel considered an alternative. Take Semensky into his confidence, and get him to tackle North at the London end? As he turned the paper in his hand, Viktor Brod saw the weakness of that idea. If it was proved in London that North had returned with Soviet plans, that, too, would reflect on Brod's competence in letting the journalist out of the country. Hadn't Kharkov had his doubts? Why else had he organised the shooting attempt? Brod recalled that with a chill of apprehension.

The more he thought about it the more he saw that there was nothing he could gain from any action that he might now take. He had enough to do to survive. Mariner and his own brother-in-law each had him checkmated.

Brod reached into his tunic pocket and extracted a German-made gold cigarette lighter. He snapped it into flame. He held the small slip of paper above it, and watched it burn, blacken and fall into the large glass ashtray. He carefully shook the ashes into an envelope, sealed it, and put it in his pocket. Only then did he reach for the telephone. This time, he ordered his car to take him home.

At Heathrow, the Boeing Super 737 came to a stop on the airport apron at seven minutes past seven. Steps were immediately in position by the first-class compartment. A black Rover, driven by a green-uniformed woman, drew up alongside. Passport and customs formalities were dispensed with, and Michael and Carol were led by the senior steward straight to the waiting car. In the front, alongside the driver, was a Special Branch man; in the back, waiting to greet them, was the comfortable figure of Geoffrey Makepeace.

'Welcome home,' he said cheerily, as they squeezed in beside him. 'Your parents have been told of your safe return.'

'You've put on weight,' said Michael.

'Too much good living. It's time you sampled some as well, my old lad. By the way, this is Inspector Andie Mackenzie. Wherever you stay tonight—' Makepeace paused and gave them a quizzical look—'both of you, Andie'll be there as well.'

As the car drew off the apron into the roadways of the airport, two police motor-cyclists wheeled in alongside.

'Why the escort?' exclaimed Michael.

'Taking no chances this time, old boy. Oh, and one other thing, while I think of it, the BBC haven't got you until sometime tomorrow. Annersley is fulminating. He really is very angry. Quite right, of course. But we do need to have you first. I'm sorry, old boy, but that does mean a session at the F O right away—'

'Hey,' interrupted Michael, as the car drew out of the airport complex and on to the M4, 'what about my . . . er, "wife"? She's the spy, I'm not.'

Makepeace chortled softly. 'Both of you,' he said. 'We'll be as quick as we can. Then you can go out and have a meal—with Andie, I'm afraid. And see you both in the morning.' He turned to Carol. 'Does the little package in the diplomatic bag tell us *all* we want to know?'

She nodded. 'And more.'

They were greeted at the Foreign Office by Sir Kenneth Propter himelf, and his expression was more eager than usual. 'Congratulations,' he said, shaking each of them warmly by the hand, once Makepeace had assured him that the film had arrived safely and was already being analysed. 'It might have seemed a crazy idea to you at the beginning, Michael,' he said, 'but it's worked.' He looked pleased with himself.

Then, surrounded by officials, the pair of them gave a full account of all that had happened since their arrival in Moscow. Sir Kenneth listened intently, hardly ever interrupting, leaving any necessary questioning to his aides. But before beginning the narrative, Carol said, 'When that stuff Geoffrey has got has been processed, you will find in it a threat to use a nuclear weapon unless Britain accedes to Soviet demands. The day it will be fired is given.'

Sir Kenneth concealed any surprise. He said curtly, 'As soon as we have the details, I'll tell the Prime Minister.'

After more than an hour of debriefing, Sir Kenneth said, 'I'm afraid we'll have to see you in the morning to continue this, but I reckon you've deserved a meal now.'

Accompanied by Inspector Andie Mackenzie they were taken by car to Beotys in St Martin's Lane. While they were there work on the film was completed. The Prime Minister was told immediately that a bomber raid on London was planned for that night. The intention was to show the British people that the Soviet Government was serious. Immediately the war cabinet was summoned to Downing Street.

But first the Prime Minister, his flair for publicity undimmed by the emergency, called in his Press Secretary. 'Tell Fleet Street they'll have to replate—if that's what they still call it in these days of computers—in the early hours. You can't tell them what it is. But it's a big story.'

Then he gave instructions to the defence situation centre—which by now was on full alert—that, assuming the air raid took place, they were to give every possible facility to the press, radio and television. No information was to be withheld. He wanted full coverage. Only then did he say to the controller, 'I want every one of those Russian aircraft shot out of the sky before they reach the coast. And no British losses,' he added. 'No, they're not to be given any warning. No chance to turn back. That'll only put our own planes at risk. Just shoot 'em down.'

Back in the cabinet room at No. 10, the Prime Minister reported to his colleagues of the war cabinet the decisions he'd already taken. There was no dissent as he declared, 'We must show the Soviets from the beginning that we will not be intimidated.'

It was half an hour after midnight when the telephone call came from the defence situation centre. The ministers were still in session. The message was brief. Six Soviet backfire bombers were flying very low, in two formations of three, towards the British coast.

As they approached the coast they were no higher than a hundred feet. It was then that they flew into a barrage of Rapier missiles.

A minute or so later, the voice from the D S C reported, 'All enemy aircraft shot down, Prime Minister, over the North Sea.'

The ministers of the war cabinet continued their discussion of the Russian timetable for military action with the uneasy knowledge that future engagements would be much more hazardous.

Just before seven o'clock in the morning, Michael slid his arm from beneath Carol's shoulders, rolled towards the edge of the bed and switched on the radio. Propped against it on the bedside table was the photograph of a smiling Alexei and a contented Varinka, gathering their children into their arms.

Carol and Michael lay quietly listening to the end of the weather forecast, followed by the six pips of the Greenwich time signal. A few seconds later, they were startled by the first sentence of the news: 'Just after midnight six Russian bombers heading for London were shot down over the North Sea by British Rapier missiles. There was no damage to property, and no British losses. Tornado aircraft, scrambled from RAF Honington as a back-up force, were not needed.'

# 22

That morning a lot of important and urgent telephone calls were made. Lionel Bryce spoke to other Commonwealth Prime Ministers. The Soviet Foreign and Defence Ministers, Yuri Groznov and Nikolai Ogarovich, conferred immediately they were told of the loss of all six Russian aircraft, and each of them instantly began phoning colleagues to organise opposition to Konevksy in the Politburo. And at Chilton Court in Baker Street, Michael North telephoned his father at eight o'clock, before morning surgery, while Carol was trying to find something in the kitchen for breakfast.

'I wondered when the hell you were going to ring, my boy. Those fools at the Foreign Office said you were safe, and home, and that's all. Now, what the devil's been happening to you? Are you all right?'

Michael gave the necessary assurances, and said that he would be coming down to Devon as soon as possible to explain everything, but that wouldn't be for several days yet.

'Why in heaven's name not?' the doctor demanded.

Michael took a deep breath. Carol stood in the doorway holding aloft two glasses of orange juice in triumph.

'Father,' said Michael patiently, 'I'm still the BBC's Moscow correspondent. After what happened last night—'

'What did happen last night?'

'You haven't heard the news?'

'I'd probably be listening now if you hadn't phoned.'

Michael laughed, and then explained. 'So you see,' he added, 'I'm likely to be wanted around here for a bit. But immediately I'm free, we'll be coming down to Devon.'

'We? Oh, yes—of course, that wife of yours. She's all right, is she?'

'Father, she's fine. You'll love her.' He added mischievously, 'But not too much, please. Remember, she's *my* wife.'

Carol raised a glass of orange juice and drained it at a gulp. A spluttering chuckle came along the line from Devon. A slightly soothed Dr North presently said, 'Well, come as soon as you can—both of you. Your mother's been worrying.'

Carol had found some cereal, and some crispbread and marmalade, as well as some instant coffee. This they had to drink black, but both agreed afterwards that it still tasted better than what the Foreign Office had to offer an hour later.

Geoffrey Makepeace told them that they would be released in time for Michael to make the late-night television news, and the BBC had been informed. Annersley had been outraged. After being incarcerated by the Russians his correspondent was now being incarcerated by the Foreign Secretary, but eventually he had had to concede that the national emergency took priority. 'Which reminds me,' Makepeace added, 'the Chief of the Defence Staff will be along to see you shortly, and later the Prime Minister wants to have a word.'

Of all that morning's telephone calls undoubtedly the most important was the one the Prime Minister made precisely at noon to the President of the United States. It was the first of several transatlantic telephone conversations to take place that afternoon.

The Prime Minister sat in his familiar chair in the Cabinet room with the other members of the war cabinet around him. He had given a lot of thought to the way he would handle this conversation. Although he knew the American sufficiently well to be on christian name terms, he began deferentially with, 'Mr President,' and then after apologising for disturbing him at such an early hour, said in measured and dramatic tones, 'But we may be facing nuclear war with the Soviet Union.'

The President had already been informed of the abortive air raid and he congratulated the Prime Minister on the RAF's success. And, of course, he knew of the demands which the Soviet government had made and which the British

Government had quite properly rejected. It was clear that the British people were going to be faced with military action, but that didn't imply nuclear war, and the Secretary of State had already explained to the British Foreign Secretary the American attitude.

That, said the Prime Minister patiently, was both understood and appreciated. Moreover, he added with quiet determination, the British Government and the British people were prepared to face war with the Soviet Union rather than capitulate to Russian occupation. He then explained, slowly and carefully, that complete details of the Russian plan had come into British hands. As a result, he was able to tell the President that there would now be a gap of three days. This would be followed by a series of air attacks on East Anglian airfields. While this was taking place an overwhelming force of Soviet naval ships, including a big submarine fleet, would be entering British territorial waters. The British navy were ready, and there would certainly be intensive action at sea. But the Royal Navy was greatly outnumbered, and there was no doubt that a substantial force of Soviet submarines would get through. The East Anglian ports, towns and airfields would then be subjected to missile attack. This would precede a seaborne and airborne invasion. The Prime Minister was able to give the President the dates for each action.

'But,' he said, and paused, 'the Russians will put a limit to their losses. Then they will present me with an ultimatum. Surrender, or suffer a nuclear attack.'

The President was silent. The Prime Minister waited.

At last, the American said, 'It's a threat, Lionel. There's British military action. There's international pressure. I give you an assurance that the United States would use all its influence to end the . . .' the President hesitated to use the obviously apt word, but eventually had to, 'the war,' he said, 'and to initiate negotiations.'

The Prime Minister seized on the brief pause to cut in aggressively. 'Influence?' he said disparagingly. 'Initiate negotiations? Negotiations about what—the surrender of the British Isles to the Soviet Union? Is that what you're prepared to negotiate about, Mr President?'

There was a brief silence, and then a nervous cough from the other side of the Atlantic. 'You're being dramatic, Lionel.'

The Prime Minister was outraged. 'Of course I'm being dramatic. It *is* dramatic to have Soviet missiles raining down on our towns and villages, our airfields and ports; to have most of the British navy sunk in the North Sea. Because that's what it would mean. You know how we are totally outnumbered. NATO itself—what's left of it—is outnumbered. *And* it's dramatic to drop the nuclear bomb.' He breathed heavily. He wanted the American to be aware of his desperate anger.

'It won't come to that. They'll be forced—'

'To negotiate, Mr President. Is that what you were going to say? They're not going to stop a war they can win, to negotiate about nothing. Negotiate means trading away the freedom of the United Kingdom. That's what I'm talking about. The oldest democracy in the Western world falling to the rule of the Soviet Union. Isn't that obvious, Mr President?'

'With American and international pressure,' the President continued, 'the Soviets will be forced to . . . to call it off.'

'What, when they're winning? Because they will. We haven't the resources—you know that. And, Mr President,' he said, playing his trump card, 'it is not merely a threat.'

'What do you mean?'

'The size of Soviet losses will determine when the Soviet Union make their final demand. But when they do, they will announce that, unless we give in, the nuclear weapon will be dropped on Britain on 25 July.'

The Prime Minister deliberately didn't say where it would be dropped.

There was silence at the American end. Then the President said, quietly, soberly, 'How do you know that?'

'We have a complete copy of the Soviet plans, and the timetable for each action. It was obtained from the Politburo itself.'

For the first time Lionel Bryce looked round the cabinet table at his colleagues for approval. There was an understanding nodding of heads. Bryce could almost hear the American thinking.

The President said, 'I am calling a meeting, Prime Minister.'

The two men had talked for almost half an hour. During the next four hours they spoke together on three more occasions, and there were transatlantic exchanges between other senior ministers and defence chiefs.

In the middle of the afternoon all television channels in Britain transmitted a ministerial broadcast live from 10 Downing Street. The recorded version was used in news bulletins throughout the day.

A tired but determined-looking Prime Minister told the British people about Russian plans, and said that, although there had been no declaration, it was only realistic to consider the two nations to be at war. That was the meaning of last night's attempted air raid. The Russians had plans for bombardment and invasion. The evacuation of East Anglian coastal towns had already begun. Regrettably it had to be done, to avoid unnecessary loss of life. He said nothing about the nuclear threat. That would only have caused avoidable alarm. But he ended with a ringing declaration of faith in the British people and British democracy to defeat 'this threat from the cruellest and most savage dictatorship since the rise and fall of Hitler's Nazi Germany'.

The Prime Minister was on his way back to the Cabinet room when, fortunately for him, the Soviet government made a mistake. Angered by their humiliation at the hands of the Royal Air Force, Konevsky departed from the Soviet government's plans and ordered another raid on London immediately. Six more backfire bombers left their East German base for a low-level attack.

By the time the Prime Minister reached the war cabinet, the Controller of the defence situation centre was on the direct-line telephone, reporting that the bombers had been spotted by a patrolling Nimrod AEW, and a squadron of Tornados had been scrambled to intercept them. On the direct line the Prime Minister was given a report of the action as it happened. One Soviet aircraft got through and released its missiles on Margate before being shot down in the Kent countryside. The others were either shot down over the sea or in the estuary. One British aircraft was lost.

The information was instantly fed to the news agencies. Within minutes it was flashed round the world. The American President received it only five minutes after the last Soviet plane had been destroyed. Together with the latest satellite information on the movement of the Soviet surface and submarine fleet in the North Sea, it helped the President in the argument he was having with leading members of his administration. But what clinched it for him was the receipt, at long last, of an intelligence report from Stacey Mariner in Moscow. This confirmed the Soviet intention to use the nuclear weapon.

Five hours after the Prime Minister's first call, the President of the United States made a statement to a crowded news conference at the White House. It was received live by satellite at the BBC's Television Centre, where it was recorded and transmitted a few minutes later in an extended early evening news. Michael and Carol saw it at the Foreign Office.

In those slow and measured tones that all American heads of state reserve for times of international crisis, the President told the American people of the inevitability of war between the Soviet Union and Great Britain, with the Soviet Union, backed by vastly larger forces, determined to occupy the British Isles. He reminded them of the change of government in the United Kingdom, a government set on restoring the country's proper role in international affairs, and breathing new life into that old and valued special relationship with the people of the United States. Could America stand by and see this bulwark of Western democracy fall beneath the heel of Soviet dictatorship? he asked. Gradually and skilfully he built up to the one sentence that was to determine the course of events.

'Let it be understood,' he said, 'especially by the men in the Kremlin, that any attack, of *whatever* kind, on Great Britain, will be regarded as an attack on the United States, and it will be answered in kind.'

There wasn't a correspondent present who did not understand the significance of that sentence. The questions came showering from all directions.

Were the Russians going to stick to conventional attacks? What would the United States do if they didn't? Had the President talked with the British Prime Minister? Had he been on the hot line to Konevsky? Did this mean the United States would be drawn into war? Was this the beginning of the third world war? Did it mean nuclear war?

The President dealt with each one brusquely, saying as little as possible, but leaving his meaning unmistakably clear: America would go to the aid of Britain. Persistently one question came back at him: 'Are we at war with the Soviet Union?'

'That,' said the President, 'depends on the Soviet Union. If it persists in its plan to invade and occupy the British Isles, the United States will do its best to prevent it. USAAF aircraft, equipped with nuclear arms, are on their way back to their old bases in Britain. That, ladies and gentlemen, is in the interests of democratic freedom everywhere; it is in the interests of the American people.'

Many of the correspondents gave him a rough time. Did the American people really want to be thrust into war —perhaps a nuclear war—just to rescue the Brits? The President gave as good as he got, and reminded them that he was talking about defending the values, the way of life, of the free world.

The White House news conference was also seen in the Soviet Union, but it was not transmitted on the television networks. It was viewed privately in the Kremlin by Konevksy and members of the Politburo. It was evidence that Great Britain knew of Soviet plans to use the nuclear threat, which could only mean that Michael North had taken the information back to London.

Sitting behind his ornately carved desk in Dzerzhinsky Square, listening to the BBC's Russian service, Colonel Viktor Brod came inevitably to the same conclusion. That would be the end of him. He recalled his last interview with his KGB chief and Politburo member, Maxim Kharkov, and waited apprehensively for the phone call that surely must come. He stayed in his office until late at night, just waiting. The call never came.

In the gold and white salon in the Kremlin, where the fourteen members of the Politburo were in continuous session, Groznov and Ogarovich were now openly accusing Konevsky and Kharkov of leading the Soviet Union to the brink of nuclear war. They had ignored the warnings, and their judgement had proved disastrously wrong.

The attack by the Defence and Foreign Ministers was the more impressive and effective because of the brisk but calm military precision of the younger Ogarovich, and the patient and persistent tone of the internationally experienced Groznov. Ogarovich didn't even raise his voice when he announced that, in what was now obviously the interests of the Soviet people, he had given orders for the Soviet fleet to halt outside British territorial waters. The two ministers played skilfully upon the impatience and impetuousness of the Russian leader, and Groznov gently ridiculed Kharkov for the failure of security.

Konevsky carefully polished his rimless glasses in an effort to calm himself. Then he struck—with a ruthless and impatient desperation. Speed up the whole operation, abandon the plans for invasion, and give Britain twenty-four hours to meet Soviet demands. Then, if they were not met, fire the nuclear weapon.

By now Ogarovich sensed that he was winning the argument in the Politburo, and he had only to repeat his previous accusation that Konevsky was recklessly throwing the Soviet Union into a nuclear conflict with the United States to see, in the expressions of his colleagues, that he had swung a majority to his view. But the argument, at various levels of acrimony, continued for several days.

During one of the intervals, the KGB chairman, Maxim Kharkov, tired and facing defeat, summoned Vladimir Semensky, the head of the third department of the KGB's First Chief Directorate, and responsible for espionage in the

United Kingdom. Kharkov's ambition was hourly suffering at the hands of Groznov and Ogarovich. He knew that the possibility of succeeding Konevsky as leader had receded irrecoverably, and he felt an inner fury that was the worse for having no constructive outlet. He needed one last act of revenge. That at least would give him some personal satisfaction.

He looked at the weedy figure of Semensky with contempt, and issued what was to prove his last order.

On Monday, the Foreign Secretary, Sir Kenneth Propter, summoned the Russian Ambassador to the Foreign Office and curtly told him he was *persona non grata*, Britain was breaking off diplomatic relations with the Soviet Union, and Anton Markolevsky had a week to close the Embassy in Kensington Palace Gardens and leave the country with his entire diplomatic mission. That included the trade mission at Hampstead, and all other outposts of his Embassy.

Meanwhile, military action against Britain had ceased. The next phase of the plan was not carried out. The Foreign Office having released him, Michael found himself living almost permanently in the news studio at Television Centre in Wood Lane, London, as he interpreted every development in the crisis. By the following weekend he needed a break. On Friday afternoon he set out with Carol to drive to Devon. In a telephone call the night before he had mischievously confused his father by declaring, 'And, Father, I'm bringing with me the woman I'm going to marry.'

Even Inspector Andie Mackenzie was shaken off for this occasion. Both the Special Branch and MI5 reckoned that, facing a Monday deadline, the Russians were now too busy packing up at Kensington Palace Gardens to worry about anything else.

Once London airport had been left behind and they were heading west along the M4, Michael felt a sudden lightening of the spirit. The crisis had diminished. Former American air bases in East Anglia were already reoccupied. The Soviet Union was dithering. There was total silence. He could imagine the power battle going on within the Politburo. And now at last his parents could be told, and his mother, for so long concerned about his bachelorhood, could now look forward to welcoming a daughter-in-law. He chanced a quick glance at Carol. She was relaxed and, he thought with some pride, quite lovely. He was suddenly conscious of all they had shared in the past weeks, and was grateful. It made him feel especially close to her. He saw her carefree smile, and knew she shared his happiness.

Michael redirected his attention to the road ahead. The surface was dry; it was a fine day but dull and cloudy, so that the greens of fields and trees had a heavy look. The speedometer hovered on the seventy mark. A glance in the rear-view mirror confirmed that the pale green car that had been following him for the past ten miles or so was still there. By the time they had passed Reading the traffic had thinned so much that he was prompted to remark that, at this rate, they were going to make very good time, even without exceeding the speed limit.

They talked about how his parents would react to the story they had to tell, and what they might do over the weekend. Michael teased her, 'You'll have a chance to stand up to your pussy in water, and show the old man how you cast.'

'I didn't bring my rod,' she said with mock seriousness.

'Oh, we've got plenty.'

Carol sighed, and they both laughed.

He noticed, as they saw the sprawl of Swindon on their right, that the same green car was behind him. He eased back on the accelerator. The car drew closer. He let his speed fall back to about fifty-five. The green car was now very close. Michael's eyes were fixed on the rear-view mirror almost too long for safety.

'Jesus!' he exclaimed. 'That's Bill.'

'Bill?' Carol looked mystified.

'My God—and Fred!'

Now she remembered. Michael's explanation, 'You know, two of the Russian thugs who met me at the airport,' wasn't necessary.

'Put your foot down,' she said.

He already had, and the car surged forward to 70, then 75

and 80 miles an hour. He pressed a little more on the accelerator and then kept the speed at 85. He had initially drawn away, but now he saw the car was closing the gap. Michael drew into the outer lane. The green car immediately increased its speed and was drawing alongside him in the middle lane. For a moment they were side by side, and the stocky, rolling figure of Bill turned and grinned. Fred was large and humourless beside him. They overtook on the inside, and then slid back in front in the outer lane.

'Unpleasant couple,' Carol remarked. 'Now what do we do?'

But before Michael could answer the decision was made for him. The green car braked viciously. The only way he could avoid crashing into the back of it was to swerve into the centre lane and overtake. This he did, swearing beneath his breath as he wrenched the steering wheel to the left.

He began to accelerate. So did the other car, and within seconds was so close behind him that Michael could not safely draw back into the outer lane. He pressed his foot down, until the speedometer registered 90 and then 95. The green car was edging forward, its radiator now level with the boot of Michael's car. His foot was on the floorboards and the car at its maximum speed of around 100 miles an hour. The green car nosed forward. Just ahead, stationary on the hard shoulder, was a police car, conspicuously white with a day-glow stripe. For once Michael prayed that he would be chased by the police.

He pressed hard on the accelerator, vainly trying to push it lower. The needle still hovered at 100. The other car was gaining. Now it was alongside.

Carol exclaimed: 'Oh no!'

Michael, holding tight to the steering wheel, shot a glance to his right. The side window of the green car was down. For a second Michael stared straight into the cold eyes of Fred. He had raised a gun. He was concentrating all his strength on holding it steady. Michael saw the trigger finger begin to squeeze. Without even checking his mirror, he slammed his footbrake to the floor, and pulled on the handbrake at the same time.

The glass splintered. He felt it slice into his face and blood begin to trickle down his cheek. His foot was still hard on the brake, and the car was now shuddering to a halt. The green car was still speeding in the outside lane.

He turned to Carol anxiously. Splinters of glass covered her lap, but she was all right. His hand went up to his cheek. In the same moment Carol realised that, apart from the sound of the glass, there had not been much of an explosion. It wasn't a bullet that Fred had fired.

She stayed calm, praying to heaven it wasn't what she feared, as she wiped away the blood from Michael's face. 'It's all right,' she said, with sudden relief, 'it's glass.'

By the time the police car drew alongside, the pair of them—oblivious of their stationary position in the centre lane and the hooting of cars passing on either side—were searching the upholstery.

'For Christ's sake get on the hard shoulder!' the policeman shouted and, with all his lights flashing, led the way.

Michael followed, but immediately they were there, and before the police officer, peering through the shattered glass of the side window, could open his mouth, Carol fished her blue card from her handbag, and said, 'We've been shot at by Russians—not a bullet. A poison dart. If it's hit either of us, we may not have felt it. But it's likely to kill us.'

She then turned away from the astounded police officer but, even as she searched her own clothing and Michael's for an entry sign, coolly gave the police the registration number of the green car, and suggested that they used their radio to get it stopped. 'Otherwise,' she said, 'the Prime Minister is not going to be very pleased with the Wiltshire police.'

Then she found it—a tiny dart embedded in the padded cloth of the door panel on her side. It must have missed her by a few inches, and only the viciousness of Michael's braking had prevented it lodging in his flesh.

Carol showed it to the police officers, adding, 'When you prise it out, for God's sake be careful not to touch the point. When it's analysed, I think you will find it contains ricin, the poison that killed Georgi Markov in 1978.'

*

They heard the news on their car radio, as they were following the police car to Chippenham police station. It came as an interruption to the afternoon programmes. The announcer said, 'Here is a news flash. The Russian leader, Boris Konevsky, has resigned. A statement issued by the Soviet news agency, Tass, says Mr Konevsky has been in ill health for some time. His successor has not been announced, but Western correspondents in Moscow report that he is expected to be succeeded either by Mr Yuri Groznov, the Foreign Minister, or by Mr Nikolai Ogarovich, the Minister of Defence.'

Michael shouted with pleasure. 'So the doves have won. Alexei will be pleased.'

He wondered what had happened to Viktor Brod and Maxim Kharkov. Perhaps they would just disappear without trace.

He phoned the BBC from Chippenham police station, and told them that he would make for Bristol, so that he could do an insert from there into the nine o'clock televisions news.

'By the way,' he added, casually teasing before he put down the receiver, 'I've been shot at by Russians.'

Before he made his next telephone call, a police inspector told him, 'We got your Russian friends. They were stopped on the outskirts of Bristol.'

Carol laughed, 'Ah—now,' she said, 'the Prime Minister *will* be pleased.'

The pair of them made their statements, and then Michael dialled a Honiton number.

'Oh, is that you, Father? Sorry, but something has happened. I'll explain later. But I'm afraid we won't be with you tonight—I'm terribly sorry . . . Well, you'd better look at television news—yes, at nine. But I'll tell you all about it later—'

'You're always telling me something later, and never . . . For God's sake, my boy. If only you didn't do that damn fool job of yours. Well, what is it this time?'

'The Russian leader has resigned—Konevsky . . .'

'So?'

'Well, there are other things as well, Father.' He spoke

over the doctor's interruptions. 'So —I'm very sorry, I really am, but I'm afraid you're going to have to wait a bit longer to meet my . . . my "wife".'

There was a half-strangled sound at the other end of the line—a mixture of despair and exasperation.

'Who is this woman? Oh, I know all those newspaper stories. But we've never met her. Looked all right in the photographs. But that's the nearest we've ever got. Damn it, boy, I'm beginning to think this wife of yours doesn't exist.'

Michael paused. He grinned at Carol.

'That's right, Father. You've got it. She doesn't. But she will. Here.' He handed the instrument to Carol.

She said: 'Hello! Dr North?'